THE DAWNING

With best regards
Paul G. Miles

THE DAWNING

Paul A. Miles

Northwest Publishing, Inc.
Salt Lake City, Utah

The Dawning

For information address: Northwest Publishing, Inc.
6906 South 300 West, Salt Lake City, Utah 84047
JAC 6.28.97
SJD

PRINTING HISTORY
First Printing 1995

ISBN: 1-56901-247-4

NPI books are published by Northwest Publishing, Incorporated,
6906 South 300 West, Salt Lake City, Utah 84047.

PRINTED IN THE UNITED STATES OF AMERICA.
10 9 8 7 6 5 4 3 2 1

To my eight children who were my first audience:
Kevin, Pamela Joan, Keith, Kent, Kirk, Kiprian,
Paula Patrice, and Kristen.

ONE

"Gram! Lay flat on the surface. A transitory asteroid will pass three meters above your position in eighty-two seconds."

Gram pulled himself to the surface with his anchor rope at Robert, the robot's, warning. "Have complied...get the ship out of its path."

He watched as the *Lares Compitales* lifted clear of the planetoid's surface. Out of the corner of his eye, Gram could see the approaching asteroid tumbling through space. He flipped over onto his back. Gram wanted a good view of the planetoid as it passed near to him. His face mask's light amplifier made space as bright as noonday in the sun.

The light amplifier was a viewing screen attached to his space suit at eye level. Miniature cameras on either side of his helmet brought the image to a computer that relayed the screen image in natural color. Tiny probes attached to his eyes controlled the camera focus.

The movement of the eye muscles sent electrical impulses through the probes to camera controls to adjust focal distances. A computer combined each camera's image to form a three-dimensional picture on the screen. The screen's image appeared to have height, width, and depth.

Gram had no fear the two planetoids would collide and grind him to dust. Robert said they would pass three meters apart. The robot calculated the gravitational attraction, their irregular shapes as they spun through space, and their orbits. He had never been wrong, so Gram trusted him.

The satellite blotted out the system's sun as it swung slowly and majestically past Gram's position. He felt the weak gravitational pull of his asteroid yield to the superior strength of the other. He gripped the anchor rope beneath him; the mining equipment and their cache of copper ore floated toward the larger planetoid. He saw his feet float upward and a protruding outcrop of rock on the other satellite appeared as though it might smash into his feet. Involuntarily, he pulled his feet back.

His small asteroid gave a lurch toward the other. Gram was willing to bet the two never approached nearer than three meters as Robert predicted. When Gram judged it was safe, he stood up.

"Robert, swing the ship in near me so I can come aboard. The other asteroid swiped our equipment and ore. We've got to get it back."

"I saw the transfer and have the location of the equipment and ore marked," replied the robot.

Gram did not wait for the ship to come to a complete stop as he jetted into the hatch, then to the bridge. Robert stood in a recess next to the outside wall of the ship. A flat cable ran from his waistline and into a cable run connecting to the ship's controls.

He served both as an onboard computer for the ship, *Lares Compitales*, and as a mobile robot. Gram's father, Steve

Ancile, had taken the ship's computer, added a few microchips to the computer circuitry and a metal body with legs, and called it Robert, the robot.

Robert spoke again as Gram strapped himself into the pilot's couch. "Do you want me to match coordinates or would you rather I put the ship on manual and you do it?"

"I suppose I'd better do it. You know what Dad says about me learning to navigate Nashar's system."

"Your father is right. You never know when the enemy may knock me out and you'll have to get this ship out of this system."

"I can rocket this crate around almost as good as you!" Gram gave Robert a defiant glance as he punched in the coordinates on the keyboard.

"There's an ancient saying of Earth which states: 'Almost only counts in horseshoes and hand grenades.' Your reaction time is twice as fast as your father's and you have an uncanny ability to project an asteroid's course without consulting my computations. You are not perfect at the projections; you miss five per cent of them."

"That's only one in twenty tries."

"True," said Robert, "but in this devil's system, there's not time to correct an error manually unless your reaction time is reduced."

Nashar was a pale purple sun that did not have a true planetary system. Like an old maid collecting stray cats, it gathered bits and pieces of space rubble about itself. There was not an orbital plane to the debris; each planetoid and scrap of rock or ice chose its own path about the sun. Often they were on collision course with each other. Each swarmed about Nashar like a hive of angry bees.

It had taken Steve Ancile several months, with Robert's help, to chart a course through to a rocky planetoid deep within the system. To penetrate to the asteroid required a series of hairpin turns and bone-crushing stops and starts.

It was Gram's remark when they first arrived which gave the sun its name. 'It's nasty for sure,' was shortened to Nashar and the name stuck. It explained Robert's calling it a devil system too.

"Aw, you're jealous of my ability to project the proper course," said Gram. He punched in the proper setting, providing the matching spin of the thieving asteroid to place the ship over the tools and ore. He did not consult Robert.

"Robots are never jealous. We do not have human emotions," said Robert. "Although I have to admit you projected the proper coordinates again. My circuitry cannot analyze how you come to your conclusions."

"I get a feeling, Robert. I get a feeling."

The asteroid stopped its spinning on the screens and the heavens appeared to be rotating ever so slowly as the ship matched the asteroid's spin. Gram set the ship's orbit and rocketed to the surface.

Grabbing the handle of the ore container, he rocketed back to the airlock. Afterward, he returned to the planetoid for the mining equipment, then he cycled the airlock closed. Gram waited until the air pressure reached normal and removed his helmet.

"Ah, this is much better. Take us home, Robert, while I anchor down this stuff in the repair-shop/gallery. Dad'll be happy to see how much copper ore we got for him,"

Since his son's eleventh birthday Steve Ancile had allowed Gram to accompany Robert on mining missions for much-needed ores for the home asteroid's forge. Steve used the metals to provide some measure of comfort for them and to devise weapons to protect themselves from the enemy.

At the age of sixteen, Gram acted more like a companion to Robert rather than Robert being his protector. Robert fostered the idea to give Gram a sense of confidence and independence. He let Gram plot his own courses through the heavens and rarely corrected them.

At times, Steve thought his son piloted the *Lares Compitales* with reckless abandon. Whenever Steve questioned Robert as to why he allowed Gram to skim by asteroids with only a hairbreadth clearance, Robert would reply Gram needed to develop his skills and his choice of a course was the most efficient.

Gram would tell Robert his choice of an asteroid for a particular mineral. About sixty-two per cent of the time, Gram was correct. Robert analyzed the asteroids and would confirm or deny the choice to Gram.

After strapping down the equipment and ore bag, Gram walked back into the control room. Robert spoke from his cubicle. “Do you want to plot the course to base?”

“No, you do it. I’m tired. I had to mine all the ore, you know.” Gram flopped into the couch.

“Your father—” Robert started.

“My father and you worry too much. I can handle this ship better than he can and almost as good as you!” Gram leaned over the control panel and punched in the coordinates.

The ship traveled for a minute on the new setting when Robert shut down the engines. Gram protested. “What’d you do that for? The coordinates were good!”

“It’s home base. It’s under attack. Two enemy ships are bombarding the asteroid,” Robert droned. He projected the battle on the viewing screen.

Laser beams from the home base leaped out at attacking ships. Shower after shower of missiles homed in on the asteroid. The beams detonated most of the missiles before they could damage the base. Not all miniature suns were born in space.

At first, just a stray would find its mark and a laser beam would die, no longer lashing out at the bombs. Gradually, as more bombs found their marks, the base glowed with atomic fire.

“Come on, we’ve got to help Dad!” Gram punched the ignition button to the ship’s engines. Nothing happened; Robert bypassed the command.

“No, your father programmed me to protect you in the event the enemy attacked us. I must ignore his peril.”

Gram leaped off the couch and dashed to Robert, attempting to rip the cable plug from his waist. Robert gripped Gram’s arm, preventing him from moving. Gram kicked at the plug with his foot and tears streamed down Gram's face. "Blast your metal case, Robert! Override the program, we've got to help him."

"Sorry, your father's command takes precedence over all other programs. I cannot allow you to endanger yourself," said Robert. He lifted his other arm and pointed at the viewing screen.

"See, it is already too late to help your father. We must flee while there is still time."

Steve Ancile was the only human being Gram had ever known. Now he was dead, too. What was it that caused the enemy to hate Earthmen so violently? According to Steve there had been a whole planet of Earthmen until the enemy destroyed Earth. The planet had erupted in a mind-shattering explosion, wiping out all mankind except a few thousand on different planets in the galaxy.

Now there were only a few hundred, and in a few years there would not be a human left. The enemy pursued relentlessly; they hunted humans down wherever they hid. As far as Gram was concerned, he could be the last human in the universe. He had not seen another human since he was five.

He stared in horror. His father was dead, a part of the bubbling cauldron that had served as home for ten years. Ten happy years—there had been no fear of the enemy, just precautions.

Now they were here, pumping atomic explosives into home base. They had murdered his father. Gram screamed. Robert spoke to Gram.

"We've got to chart our way out of this system. It's too dangerous to you to remain, Gram. Soon they will begin searching for us. We must leave now."

Gram did not answer, but continued to stare at home base. Robert waited until an asteroid slipped between the ship and the enemy ships, then rocketed away. When it became impossible to keep the asteroid between them and the enemy ships, Robert shut down the engines. The *Lares* coasted until another asteroid hid them from the enemy ships.

Slipping free of the asteroid system, Robert placed the ship into hyper space, leaving Nashar light years behind. Nothing followed the *Lares Compitales* as Robert checked all screens. They had shaken enemy pursuit for the time being.

Robert carried Gram to the couch and strapped him down. He gave Gram a sedative, then slipped back into his alcove. He had no orders as to where they should go, so he waited for Gram. No danger existed while in hyper space.

Gram's first question when he awoke was, "Where are we?"

"The ship is approaching the edge of the spiral arm of the galaxy."

"Shut down the drive and check the screens," said Gram.

Robert brought the ship back to normal drive and turned on all the ship's screens, fore, aft and broadside. Gram studied the screens for several minutes.

"There's nothing showing now, but you can bet they're on our trail. I'll punch in a new set of headings. We can finish the enemy ships out there," said Gram.

Robert pointed the ship in the direction of the new heading. "There's nothing out there, Gram. You're taking us out of the spiral arm."

"Trust me, I've got a feeling. Out there we'll destroy the enemy ships following us."

These hunches of Gram's were nothing new. Most of the time, Gram's feeling was the truth. There was nothing in the memory banks to contradict Gram's orders. Steve had ordered Robert to protect Gram. As far as Robert could tell from the ship's sensing devices, no immediate danger existed for Gram.

This being true, Gram's orders could be obeyed.

The ship traveled deep into the space between the spiral arms; after two hours' travel, Gram ordered Robert to drop out of hyper space. Immediately, Robert sounded an alarm.

"There's an asteroid directly ahead."

"Good! Circle to the far side and you'll find a narrow

canyon not much larger than the ship. Land there. The enemy won't be able to spot us unless he passes directly overhead."

Robert did as he was ordered. As he powered down the ship, he spoke. "I've searched my memory banks and this ship has never been in this area of space before."

"There you go wondering again," said Gram.

"Robots never wonder as you mean the word," replied Robert. "I must gather enough data to determine whether I am in compliance with your father's final directive."

"OK, I'll explain my plan," said Gram. "The enemy will come this way. I plan to destroy their ships with this asteroid. I plan to start the ship's engines and switch to hyper space while the asteroid is still in the sphere of influence of the ship. The asteroid will be drawn along with the ship in hyper space at the speed of the ship. We will travel the distance to the enemy ships, then slip back into normal space. We will travel the distance in normal space needed to free ourselves of the asteroid, at which time we'll slip back into hyper space. The enemy ships will crash into the asteroid."

"I'm not certain your plan is feasible, Gram. There is insufficient data."

"If we continue to flee in the same direction, the enemy will overtake us. Their ships are new and faster than ours. If we change directions, it will delay them temporarily. In the end, they'll catch up and destroy us. Check the probabilities, Robert. See if my plan isn't the only one with a chance of success," said Gram.

"Your plan has a probability of less than one per cent."

"Considering their ships are faster than the *Lares*, what chance do we have of escaping them if we don't destroy them?" asked Gram.

"The probability is zero."

"I know you're controlled by my father's final directive," said Gram. "Doesn't my plan have the best probability of success?"

"The time element in your plan is critical. You must start the rocket engines to build up speed and flip over to hyper space while the ship and asteroid are within the sphere of influence. The ship remains in hyper space for approximately ten one-hundred-trillionths of a second, just long enough to transfer the speed of the *Lares Compitales* to the asteroid and not long enough to burn out the helix coils of the hyper space generator," said Robert. "The asteroid will be moving at the speed of the ship as it enters hyper space. You hope the asteroid will be traveling too fast and be too close for the enemy ships to maneuver out of its path."

"That's the plan."

"Including the mass of the asteroid in the sphere of influence of the *Lares Compitales* will burn out the hyper space generator," stated Robert. "I cannot switch the hyper space generator on and off, then on again, within the proper time frames."

"You are a twentieth generation computer—use several circuits for the operation. Circuit one will start the generator. Circuit two will shut down the generator ten trillionths of a second after circuit one turns it on. Circuit three will restart the generator after we are clear of the asteroid as far as the sphere of influence is concerned. You must have three circuits that are within the tolerances of the time frame where you start all three signals at the same time."

"With your father's tinkering, as he called it, I am more like the twenty-second generation computer," stated Robert. "I have three circuits which can be used in this manner. The time differential of the three circuits are ideal for lifting the asteroid at ship's speed."

"Good! As long as you can shut down the hyper space generator before it burns out from the overload, we'll get out of this problem with a whole skin."

"How can you be certain this plan will work?"

"I haven't proof it will," said Gram. "I only have a feeling it's going to work."

TWO

It was so black Gram could not tell if his eyes were open or closed. He squeezed his eyelids shut, then opened them wide. No difference, except there were purple flashes behind his eyes when he closed them. There was nothing to see.

Robert powered down the ship completely. Not a single panel light showed. The ship was quick-chilled to eliminate heat radiation from the hull. Every source of radiation was reduced to zero. This should prevent the enemy from spotting the *Lares Compitales* with their heat sensors. Perhaps they would believe Gram's ship was part of the asteroid.

Suppose they detected the radiation from the stern tubes? A surge of panic rippled up and down Gram's spine. The hair on his arms stood on end. Sweat oozed from the pores of his body. Could the enemy detect the radiation from the stern tubes through the chilled body of the ship?

Sitting in a narrow chasm on an asteroid left no room to run. It was not much safer than sitting dead in open space and hoping they could not detect him.

Suppose his hunch was wrong? His average on being right with hunches was only a little over sixty per cent. This left almost forty per cent of the time being wrong. Forty per cent was nearly half the time; maybe he should run.

Gram shuddered and gripped the edges of the pilot's couch. 'No!' he thought. 'Take deep breaths and relax. Don't think about the enemy catching you. Relax, take another deep breath. This is no time to panic. This idea of using the asteroid to destroy the enemy ships was more than a hunch. It was almost as if you were living a segment of your life again. You knew about this gorge and you were never here before now. You know the plan to use this asteroid will work.'

He wondered how he knew about the chasm. It was almost as if he saw it. No, not exactly saw it...It was more like a vision...

There was no way to describe how he knew about the canyon. Gram shrugged his shoulders; he could not put it into words. Nothing in the language fit how he knew.

Maybe he should check with Robert to make sure those sensors they had placed about the asteroid were functional. It would not hurt to check; maybe they were broken. Gram gritted his teeth; his fear was getting the best of him again. If anything was wrong, Robert would warn him. His problem was he had no idea what was going on. He was like an embryo; his senses were cut off from what was happening.

Like an egg, protected by the shell of the ship. Protected from the outside, no worries. Floating on a sea of warm water, drifting...drifting. "No, can't think like that. You're starting to hallucinate," Gram thought, trying to get a grip on reality. Sweat ran down his cheeks in rivulets; he longed to wipe his eyelids because the salt burned his eyes.

Why was he sweating? His suit was not hot; the oxygen circulated inside the suit. Why was the suit dehumidifier not removing the excess moisture? Was he sweating or was he still hallucinating?

He had to think of something else. His father? No, his father was behind a locked door and would not come out. He did not want to talk to Gram because something bad would happen. There would be fire and explosions if the door was opened.

It was fun to bask in the sun, swimming in the sea whenever he felt like it. There was a rule; Gram did not have to swim unless he felt like it. It was a nice rule because he did not feel like swimming anymore. He wanted to drift with the current, to feel the breeze on his face. There was nothing but endless ocean, warm sun and greenish-blue skies. No clouds, just mild and beautiful sun and skies.

Out of the corner of his eye, he could see dark and ominous clouds blocking out the beautiful sky and heading for the sun. Gram turned and the clouds disappeared below the horizon.

No, out of the corner of his eye he could see the clouds trying to sneak toward the sun again. If the clouds succeeded in blotting out the sun, Gram would be lost forever. He turned again and the clouds receded.

The clouds were trying to destroy him. They were coming from the corners of both eyes now. He turned and turned. They kept coming, higher and higher. They would not disappear anymore. The clouds blotted out the sky now, everything but the sun. Then they touched the sun. If they blotted out the sun, Gram would die. He screamed.

A voice called to him. Was it friend or foe? Maybe he should hide. No…he knew the voice. It was…it was Robert. Good ol' Robert, the robot.

"Gram, answer me."

"What do you want?"

"You were yelling and screaming," said Robert. "It's a good thing I blocked your transmission from the transmitter. The enemy would have heard you without a doubt."

"Are they within range?"

"No, the probes haven't picked up anything," said Robert.

"Why were you screaming?"

"I was hallucinating. I couldn't see any thing, hear anything, feel anything, or smell anything. I became disoriented. Thanks for bringing me out of it," said Gram.

A small panel light winked into being, casting long dark shadows toward the nearest bulkhead. Robert spoke. "I'd better provide you a contact with reality. I don't think one small light will radiate much energy. I doubt if their equipment will detect it through the hull of the ship. I can talk to you, too, if it will help."

Gram felt like a fool, but he was grateful for the light. He could make out the dim outline of his suit. "I don't think it'll be necessary to carry on a running conversation. Just check with me every few minutes. I can't stand being blocked off completely right now. Thanks for the light."

Something new began to bother Gram; he itched in the oddest places. He could swear there was some insect in the suit with him. It crawled along the side of his face, then stopped and shifted back to his earlobe. The insect took off and buzzed around inside the face of his helmet. He shifted the light amplifier above his helmet so he could get a better view through the face of his helmet.

He could see it between him and the light! It was buzzing against the clear face of the helmet. It thumped against the helmet several times, then settled on his other ear lobe.

Gram hunched his shoulders angrily. It was impossible for a bug to be in his suit. He had not been in a planet's atmosphere for more than three years. His nerves were playing tricks on him.

What he needed was to concentrate on something else. He shifted the light amplifier in front of his face shield. He adjusted the brightness to normal. The amplifier did not need more light than a dim star to bring everything to daylight clarity. The panel light was more than enough.

Glancing about the room, everything was normal, solid, and in place. No more bugs flying around inside his helmet. No more dark clouds blocking out the sun.

It seemed like hours since Gram and Robert had sought refuge on this asteroid. Yet, when Gram glanced at the time, less than two hours had passed. Gram began to fret. Was it possible the enemy missed their hiding place? After all, finding a speck of rock light years from the Nashar system was so remote he doubted Robert could calculate the odds.

Maybe he should leave now. They had been extra careful not to let the two enemy ships see them leave the system. More than likely the enemy did not know he and Robert existed.

No, it was better he and Robert waited two or three days before attempting to leave. Should he return to the Nashar system? Oh no, the pesky bug was back again!

It was definitely inside the suit. It buzzed past his nose and landed on his eyelid. Gram blew air up at it by pursing his lower lip over the upper lip and blowing. It buzzed to the front of the face shield. He could see its outline against the shield from the light of the light amplifier.

How did it get in the suit with him? It was not logical. Gram felt and heard a whumping sound through the ship. He stopped worrying about the insect; the enemy had found him.

The ship shuddered as another explosion pummeled the asteroid. Robert powered up the ship. There was no need to worry about their radiating energy. The enemy would not be able to tell it from the atomic explosives raining down on the asteroid.

Gram panicked. They were using atomic rockets and they were not within range to use the asteroid as a weapon. His hunch had been wrong; the thirty-eight per cent was working against him.

How had they found him? What super weapons had they used to find him?

Did they know he was on the asteroid? Did they know he planned to use the chunk of rock as a weapon against them? Is that why they hovered outside his range?

Gram nearly jumped out of his skin when Robert spoke. "The enemy is not in range; the ships are hovering out at fifteen thousand kilometers."

So, the enemy was too shrewd take chances! Gram's hand shifted to the engine's start button. The bombardment stopped. Robert spoke again. "The ships approach slowly. You can see them on the screens now. They will be in range within eighty-five seconds."

The enemy had not suspected anyone was here. They did not take chances; they blasted everything that could be a hiding place. Now they were checking to find out if someone was here.

Gram felt the sta-freeze just as the *Lares Compitales* cleared the canyon rim. Robert switched on the hyper space generator when the ship was less than a hundred meters above the surface of the asteroid. What followed was too fast to register on Gram's mind.

As the *Lares Compitales* cleared the gorge, another explosion splintered the rim, sending several chunks of rock on a collision course with the *Lares Compitales*. Gram's ship built up a tremendous rush of speed, and it, the slivers of stone, and the asteroid winked out of normal space.

Whenever a ship switched to hyper space, it enfolded fifteen kilometers of normal space with it, or anything within the fifteen-kilometer limit. Anything as large as the asteroid would overtax the generator in a matter of seconds.

The generator went from a high-pitched whine to a low-pitched growl as Robert released the ship, stone slivers, and asteroid back to normal space. Gram's ship rocketed away from the asteroid. The enemy ships were not as lucky. They were less than three hundred meters away, traveling toward the asteroid.

The enemy had no time to maneuver. The enemy craft and the planetoid became a miniature sun as Gram's ship disappeared into hyper space a second time.

During the time Gram's ship was in normal space, one of the splinters of rock penetrated the hull, splintered again, and the smaller piece ripped a hole through Robert's chest. The larger chunk slammed into the metal armrest on Gram's couch with such force it broke Gram's arm. It continued through the hull above the control panel.

In the instant the particle slammed a hole through Robert's metal skin, he had already sent out the signal to return to hyper space. By the time the larger rock burst through the hull above the control panel, the ship's hyper space generator and the sta-freeze were functioning without a pilot.

Robert's circuits were broken and Gram was unconscious.

THREE

Wave after wave of pain washed through Gram's mind. He moaned and tried to move his broken arm. The tensing of the muscles was enough to cause him to pass out. The pain was intolerable. After a time Gram awoke again; his arm was a dull ache from his swollen hand to his shoulder. He tried to move, the sta-freeze was still functioning.

"Robert, what happened?"

There was no answer from the robot. It took a full five minutes for Gram to turn his head far enough to see Robert. The entire room was a shambles. Bits of the robot, ship's hull, and the splinter of the rock that penetrated Robert hung suspended in the air about thirty centimeters in front of the robot.

He turned to face the control panel again. The effort to turn back to the control panel had him sweating. Gram stared, fascinated by the sight above the control panel. Suspended about thirty centimeters beyond the hull was the fragment of the asteroid that broke his arm. Hanging directly to the front of the rock were shards of the broken hull.

With the ship in hyper space, everything in the ship and fifteen kilometers beyond the hull was in sta-freeze. Otherwise, everything would be crushed from being turned inside out by the super light speed of the ship. The sta-freeze locked each molecule into a relative position with its neighbors. To move, any object had to have a continuous source of dynamic energy or it came to rest. Sta-freeze caused all kinetic energy without a continuing source of propulsion to lock in place until returned to normal space.

The rock, metal shards, and cabin air remained frozen in place until the ship returned to normal space.

Gram fought to stand up. The sta-freeze made moving next to impossible. He felt as though he walked in thick, liquid glue. It was much worse than trying to run in water chin deep. His movements brought hot needles of agony from his arm. By the time Gram got to his feet, his dehumidifier could not keep his helmet from fogging over.

He stood quietly, letting the sta-freeze hold him upright. He waited until his breathing returned to normal and the suit dehumidifier removed the excess moisture. The suit processed the water and stored it for drinking. Gram rested a half-hour before the ache in his arm receded to a point where he could bear it.

Robert would have to control the ship until his arm was set. Gram did not think he would be able to withstand the throb of his broken limb in normal space. With the sta-freeze turned off, it would flop to his side and more than likely cause him to pass out again.

The three-meter trip to Robert's side seemed like a hundred kilometers. Gram stopped to rest several times before he reach Robert's side. His visor fogged over and he could not see.

Gram inspected the damage to Robert. He placed one of the suit cameras to the hole in Robert's chest. Adjusting the focus, he moaned at the sight. The board of the main computer had a hole with the shredded ends of wires and light fibers exposed in a fluffy cottonlike mass. Several chips were missing.

To rebuild one centimeter of Robert's brain without the special equipment of his father's laboratory would require a board a meter square to handle the parts available on the *Lares Compitales*. Even then he could not replace the missing chips; they were too complex. No one could build a sixty-four-bit chip without very precise equipment.

Robert would have to wait. Somehow Gram would have to pilot the ship. The first order of business would be to set his arm. How could he do it?

The cabin had two holes in it. The air would go whooshing into space the minute the ship returned to normal space and the fragment of rock that damaged Robert would ricochet about the cabin. It might even put a hole in him.

He could not remove his suit without pressurizing the cabin. Gram slowly glanced about the cabin. The airlock—it looked airtight. First he had to work his way back to the couch for the remote control that could operate the ship.

After several rest stops, he got the control, then went to the emergency medical kit. Slipping it under his good arm, he headed to the airlock. It seemed like hours before he moved a portable table and a chair into the small airtight compartment.

He cycled the hatch shut and shut down the hyper space generator. The wrenching change to normal space slammed his broken arm against his side. Black waves of anguish slammed at his consciousness and he fought to hang on. Minutes later, he felt strong enough to shut down the atomic thrusters.

The hyper space generator maintained the surreal world of hyper space. The thrusters supplied the pressure to push the ship through the folds of time and space, much like a needle needs pressure applied to push it through folds of cloth.

He had to set the bone, but the pain had him sweating. He had to inject anesthetic through the injection pad located at the shoulder of his broken arm. Slamming the hypodermic needle through his space suit, he injected a local anesthetic into the muscle. As he removed the needle from the double layered injection pad, a latexlike material oozed into the pinholes in the injection pad and sealed the suit.

Within seconds the limb was numb. Wiggling out of the suit without using both hands was tiring; Gram had to renew the anesthetic twice more. Once the upper half of the suit was off, he grabbed a metal rung on the hull with the fingers of the broken arm. He pulled with his weight. The two ends of the bone clicked into place.

He felt nauseated. Gram could not feel the arm but the grating click of the bones transmitted up the arm to where the nerves were active. Beads of sweat bathed his forehead.

Gram applied a soft plastic material to his arm. Smearing it from the base of the fingers to the mid upper arm, he sprayed a hardener on the plastic. The cast became warm, then hard as rock. He flexed the fingers and the thumb. Yes, he could use them after a fashion.

He slipped into the suit, then noticed the pressure gauge in the helmet. The pressure gauge showed zero pressure in the tanks but the timer indicated five hours of air supply. Gram groaned. There was a hole in his pressure suit. It would be a tough job, repairing the leak while wearing a cast.

A half hour later, Gram had not discovered the leak. He had gone over the entire suit with a magnifier. He put on the suit again and installed new air tanks. He could still hear the high pitched whistle of the escaping air. It was impossible to find the location as he tried to listen with one ear and then the other. He was not sure whether the leak was in the front, back, or on one of the sides.

Gram shrugged; he must wear the leaking suit. There was no air in the control cabin. With the sta-freeze off, the air boiled out the holes in the hull. He cycled the air from the airlock, then stepped through into the control room.

The splinter of rock that destroyed Robert's brain had smashed into the manual control board at the couch. This forced Gram to command the ship from the remote control. Gram was thankful he had not attempted to shut off the sta-freeze from the couch.

Gram stared at the airlock. He wished the designer had placed it next to the inner bulkhead separating the after cabins from the control room. If the airlock and after cabins had a common bulkhead, he could burn through to the after cabins, then install an airtight hatchway there. This way he would be able to use the airlock as a passage between the airless control room and the pressurized after cabins.

The anesthetic and energy pill would wear off in eight hours. He had eight hours to solve the problem of an airlock between the control room and the after cabins. Before he started the project, his curiosity demanded he check to see if the enemy still followed him.

The ship's forward scan cameras showed a faint haze of stars. Gram adjusted the cameras with the remote control to maximum magnification; he was barely able to distinguish individual stars. The side cameras showed no visible stars. The after cameras showed stars slightly brighter than the forward cameras, but no sign of pursuit.

The enemy had lost Gram, Robert, and the *Lares Compitales* for the time being.

Gram checked the timer and pressure gauge of his suit by glancing up above the face shield of the helmet. He was losing too much air because he could not find the leak in the suit. The air in the tanks would not last until his simple airlock to the after cabins was finished. He pulled down the umbilical cord to the ship's main air tanks, then shut off the suit tanks.

He found a ten-centimeter valve and proceeded to weld it to the hatchway to the after cabins. After it was in place he opened the valve full open and burned a hole through the hatchway. The air on the other side blew hot metal back at Gram.

The air whistled around Gram's suit, then it was silent again. With the after compartments closed off, the only air loss was from the companionway. Gram did not wait until pressure zeroed out as he undogged the hatchway. The minute pressure blew the door open.

The hatchway was originally designed to keep pressure in the control cabin and not out of the cabin. Gram wished the door opened into the companionway, but he had to take what was available. He finished burning out metal inside the valve, then welded an identical valve on the other side door. This way he could make the hatchway airtight from either side of the hatch by choosing which valve he closed.

Pain throbbed to his fingertips. The effect of the anesthetic was wearing off. Gram pulled the hatchway shut and closed the valve welded to the after compartment side. Using the remote control, he recycled air into the companionway. This eased the pressure against his compartment hatch and it opened smoothly. He dogged it shut behind him. He did not trust the hatch to the control room to remain airtight with only the hatch-dogs holding the hatch closed.

He could not bend his left arm to take off the helmet of his space suit and it was just as much a problem to get it off as the first time. Finally he pressed the helmet against the mattress of his bunk and used his right hand on the opposite side and twisted. It snapped free and fell to the floor.

The rest of the suit came off much easier, by now the broken arm throbbed continuously. He gave himself another shot of pain killer before he set about heating a meal for himself.

As he ate he studied the viewing screen in his cabin. He was deep between spiral arms of the galaxy and he had two choices: return to the spiral arm he had just left and into the arms of the waiting enemy, or forge ahead into an unexplored spiral arm and leave the enemy behind. This made the choice simple; all he had to do was determine if he had enough air to make the trip.

Exploring the heavens in front of him, he took a sighting on the brightest star, then turned the ship ninety degrees. Punching on the atomic thrusters and the hyper space generator, Gram traveled twenty minutes in hyper space, then returned to normal space. He took another reading on the same bright star.

Since Robert was the computer for the ship, Gram had to work out the problem on a small portable computer. According to Gram, there was sufficient air, food, and water to reach the bright star. He would have an extra month of air to search for an oxygen rich planet.

By the time he attended to all the calculations, his meal was cold. He ate it as he programmed the portable computer to sound an alarm in ten hours. Gram calculated the course for the bright star and pointed the ship in the right direction. He started the atomic thrusters.

While he slept he would travel in hyper space; the rest of the time he would travel at full thrusters in normal space. He had to try repairing some of Robert's circuits. Maybe there were some that were not badly damaged and he could repair them from the limited supplies on board. He crawled into his bunk and made himself comfortable. He flipped on the remote switch for the hyper space generator.

Gram awoke with a start; he tried to move and thought he was in the hands of the enemy. He had forgotten that the sta-freeze was on. It took several minutes to flip the sta-freeze and the hyper space generator off. From now on, he would program the manual controls to automatically shut down after his rest period. It required too much energy to shut down the sta-freeze and the hyper space generator while they were functioning.

Gulping down a quick breakfast, Gram cycled the air out of his homemade airlock and entered the control cabin. He checked the main screens for signs of pursuit. They remained clear of any unknown objects, so he concentrated on the bright star in front of the ship. He had covered over ten light years while he slept; the star still appeared as a bright pinpoint of light on maximum magnification.

Gram spent two hours opening Robert's metal chest to expose the ship's computer, and another hour in disconnecting the computer from its mounting. Working with one hand had its disadvantages.

Gram wished he had bent his elbow when he had applied the cast. Then he could use both hands to work with the wrenches. But if he had bent the elbow, it would have been twice as difficult to take the space suit on or off. Either it would be irksome to work or it would be almost impossible to remove or get into the space suit. By leaving the arm straight Gram believed he had chosen the best of the two alternatives.

The fingers and thumb of the broken arm were swollen and not of much use. He did manage to hold one side of the computer case, or Robert's brain, with his left hand as he took it into the makeshift airlock. He cycled the air back into the companionway and removed his suit. With Robert's brain free of the body he would not need to return to the control room.

One of the after cabins served as Gram's workshop as he set up a portable workbench from the storage lockers. Part of the electronic equipment was a magnifier probe and screen; it projected an enlarged view of the microscopic circuits of Robert's brain. Another screen projected the proper circuits for the damaged sections of the brain.

The mobility circuit for the robot was beyond repair. The rock splinter had destroyed the hundred-thirty-two-bit chip that controlled Robert's walking movements. Another chip, the equivalent of fifty-five thousand transistors, had shattered. His balance circuits were destroyed.

If Gram had about a year's time and enough parts, he could assemble a new ship's control circuit for Robert. As it was, Gram had to be planetside long before he could make the repairs. Gram would have to pilot the ship manually from the remote control.

Of the damaged circuits, the communications circuit had the least damage. A sixteen-bit chip and the circuitry to it would have to be replaced. Most of the other circuits functioned normally. As soon as he patched the damaged communications circuit Robert could tell Gram what course corrections to program as Robert monitored the ship.

Gram cut a meter-square section of plastic card and began rebuilding Robert's communications system. Gram had very few subminiature parts to use in the circuit. He made some of the parts by hand; they were so crude that the tolerances were barely allowable. Gram wished he had some of the laser equipment from home base laboratory.

Work progressed slowly; rest periods came and went. There were times Gram swore he made no progress at all. Many of his workdays were wasted building and rebuilding a vital part to meet tolerances so minute that wiping the terminals changed the values.

After forty rest periods, the communications circuit was ready to test, the new circuit mounted outside Robert's chest. As soon as the last connection made contact, Robert spoke to Gram through his suit communicator.

"Gram, your life is in danger. I've been monitoring the ship's functions but there was no way to warn you until now. The air reserve indicator on the control panel is malfunctioning. There is only five hours' air supply left, plus the air in your portable tanks."

Gram's heart thudded hard deep in his chest. What good did it do him to escape the enemy if he was going to die anyway? "How can you be so sure?"

"Each time you turn on the screens to determine your position, I notice a whisper of a vapor trail leaking from the main air tank through the hull," said Robert. "This is creating a deviation in your course setting too."

"How do you know exactly how much air is left? The indicator is the only instrument monitoring the tank," said Gram.

"You are correct. The indicator is the only instrument monitoring the tank. I computed the exact amount of air required to cause the course changes, then I knew the rate at which you are losing air."

"I'm well past the point of no return. Is there an alternative?"

"There is a star system which I believe we can reach. I have noted from the wobble of the sun, there is a planet circling the sun," said Robert. "It will stretch your air supply to the limit, but you will make it if you follow my instructions. Get the medical kit and bring it back to the control room."

Gram pumped the air out of the air tank as soon as he returned to the control room. He hoped the after compartments and companionway bulkheads would hold against the extra pressure.

"Good thinking, Gram. There is no leak from the after compartments," intoned Robert. "The star system may not contain an E-type planet but we should be able to extract enough oxygen to allow you to repair the ship. Make the following course corrections."

Gram completed the corrections almost as fast as Robert gave them. Robert continued to speak. "Use a relaxant syringe, then switch on the sta-freeze and hyper space generator. As soon as the relaxant takes effect, you will use only forty-eight milliliters of oxygen per minute. With the ship in sta-freeze, the leak from your suit will be minimal. I'll arouse you when it becomes necessary to refill your air tanks."

Gram slept and awoke only to refill his air tanks when Robert called. When the air in the after compartments was exhausted, Robert urged Gram to take an energy pill and an emergency ration tablet. Gram washed them down with water from his suit. Within seconds his head cleared.

"Time to make final approach corrections to the planet's course," said Robert.

Gram wished he could spare the air to remove his cast in the airlock. It was awkward holding the remote control with his arm in the cast and using his good arm fully extended when making the intricate maneuvers of landing. It would be better yet if he could repair Robert's ship control circuit.

He visualized Robert's broken circuit. "If this lead connected to this chip, if this chip was here and made whole like this—" The ship altered direction, then snapped into hyper space. It startled Gram.

"What happened?"

"I am not sure, Gram. My ship's control circuit became operational and I seized the opportunity to make the course alterations."

"Is the circuit functional now?"

"No, it malfunctioned again. I believe some broken circuitry made momentary contact, giving me control of the ship," said Robert. "We'll be planetside in twenty-one minutes."

Gram gave a sigh, then Robert spoke. "Conserve your air. You only have a twenty-minute supply at normal consumption. I suggest you cut back to two hundred milliliters to conserve air until we hit the atmosphere."

Doing as Robert suggested, Gram felt drowsy. Gram knew the danger of his dwindling air supply, but he felt no alarm. It no longer chilled his thoughts. He was too drained to care.

A voice broke through his fog; it was Robert. "Bring your oxygen to normal. It's time to land the ship."

Gram shook his head clear of the cobwebs. He could see the angry planet below him. Storm clouds whipped about in the atmosphere. A giant dust storm lashed the southern hemisphere. Gram did not have the oxygen left to switch landing sites. Robert called out the corrections as the wind buffeted the ship.

The dust and sand were too dense to see through so Gram switched to the infrared, ultraviolet, and gamma radiation sensors. Robert's voice cut through Gram's concentration.

"There is no free oxygen in the atmosphere. Most of the oxygen compounds are too complex to break down readily. I'm sorry, Gram, but I have sealed your fate."

There was nothing to do but continue the landing process. It was like a dream. Gram knew he was dying but he worried about landing in grove of dead trees. He laughed.

Odd. Why should he worry about where he landed? There was not enough oxygen to get him within a mile of the surface. He laughed again.

The red fog enveloped his mind and voices talked to him. His head pounded fiercely. What were those voices saying to him?

It was hard to concentrate.

"Breathe slowly and conserve oxygen" was what the voices were urging. Ah, it was much better. It was all Gram could do to follow directions because of his oxygen-starved lungs. Not much farther, the ship touched down and Gram cut the switch to the engines. He slumped in the couch.

The final exertion of landing exhausted Gram. He could not hang onto consciousness. The voices urged him to fight, to hang on, but he was too tired to care. Why prolong his death with another breath of exhausted air?

He could hear the roaring in his ears as he slipped into unconsciousness. His final vision bothered him. Why was there a limb of a tree growing through the hole above the control panel? What was it doing to his helmet?

The limb removed the helmet and sprayed oxygen across Gram's face. Gram breathed but he never realized help had arrived.

FOUR

A voice spoke within Gram's mind. "Gram! Seek out your enemy."

His body lay on his couch and a branch gently caressed his forehead. The voice spoke within his mind again, and his eyes moved under the lids but he did not open them. He was unconscious. Again the voice commanded, "Gram, seek out your enemy!"

Exhausted from the ordeal of landing, Gram groaned. He had to rest. He refused to respond to the command. It was too pleasant on the grassy knoll where he lay to let some voice order him about.

The breezes blew gently through his dark hair and he dozed. The voice was more persistent and it hurt his head to listen to the voice. Gram took out ear plugs from his pocket and plugged his ears so the voice could not annoy him. It was so pleasant on this grassy knoll.

Now the voice became land crabs with long pincer claws which drove him along a path. Gram raced to the *Lares Compitales* and slammed the hatch behind him. He laughed. There was no way they could bother him in the ship. Gram climbed into his bunk to sleep; nothing could bother him as long as he did not open the hatch. The voice and the land crabs let him sleep.

The ship became unbearably hot. Someone was pouring burning oil on the hull of his ship. As he fled the ship, the burning oil chased him, telling him to seek out his enemy. Gram was no longer as tired as he was when the voice and crabs first asked him to seek out the enemy. He began walking back to where the enemy was waiting.

He glanced back; the burning oil did not chase him as long as he continued along the path to the enemy. It would approach him with its heat when he tarried along the path.

Odd-looking trees lined the path; none had leaves. When Gram tried to look directly at the trees, they would disappear. He could see them from the corners of his eyes when he stared at the path. They were not real trees because they moved along the ground, and they could think.

They were.... The trees knew he was watching them and listening to their thoughts. They erected a brick wall on either side of the path to block his vision of them.

If the trees did not want him to see them, it was OK with Gram. He ignored them and their wall as he walked along the path.

The path became very windy. He knew the windy thoughts of the town because he had been there before. His father had taken him there the last time they bought supplies. The windy thoughts were not unkind. The people there just did not care or worry about human beings. Gram continued on the path; there was not any reason to visit the town.

Rain shrouded the next place on the path. The town made sounds saying they cared what happened to Earthmen. They made the sounds of caring in public. Privately, their thoughts were of dislike for human beings. They secretly hoped the enemy would destroy the last of the Earthmen. Because of these facts, it made the rain bitterly cold. Gram did not leave the path to visit the town.

The path passed by several towns where no sounds came from the towns. Gram visited the first of these towns; he wanted to know why there were no thoughts of Earth beings. Nothing came from the town because the people did not know of Earthmen. No man had ever visited and these towns did not belong to the Federation. Gram could not tell whether these people would be friendly to human beings or not.

He returned to the path and decided not to visit towns that did not have thoughts of Earthmen.

Huge jagged blocks of ice covered the path at one point. Gram knew the town. He had been there once with his father. They detested human beings and they made it next to impossible for men to reach their town. The ice field around the town extended out over the path.

It was nearly impossible to pass the town by until Gram decided to leap over the ice field. Gram discovered he could use the same method to reach one town from another. There was no need to walk along the path from town to town.

He came to a town where the sun was shining and a melodious chiming rose from the town. Gram had never visited the town, but the town's people knew of humans. There were several dozen Earth people living there.

Gram felt the Earth beings' fear of the enemy. The fear swelled like a hard knot, hidden from each other and from the townspeople. One of the human beings attracted Gram's spirit.

The attraction was almost magical. It was as if the human was a missing part of Gram's life. Gram and the other human felt so attracted it was as if they were two interlocking pieces from the same puzzle. Gram sang to the human and it quested for him.

The trees became impatient with Gram and sent their

burning oil, the voice, and the snapping crabs to drive him from the town. Gram fled. The trees erected a brick wall so he could not return to the town.

Gram walked away from the town as he formed a ball of his anger. He hurled the ball at the wall. It exploded in a million pieces. Gram laughed, then leaped to the next town. It pleased him that the trees knew they could not stop him if he chose to return to the friendly town.

A strange ugly thing radiated from this town. There was an individual from which a sick hatred spread. The hatred directed itself at all human beings. Gram recoiled and watched from afar.

The sick fetid thing coiled and twisted about the being from which it fed. This was the enemy. The being had killed many humans and was hunting another to kill. Gram could feel the horror of the Earthman the enemy sought. Her wall of fear pushed at Gram's spirit. She knew she was about to die. Gram fled from the place. The trees tried to coax Gram to return. He refused.

Gram yearned to return to the point where he had begun this journey. This method of searching and traveling was not normal for Gram. An integral part of him had been left behind on this trip and he wanted to be joined with it.

The trees came forward and showed their love for Gram. They talked to him, asking him to continue searching because it was important he find out if there was a whole town that hated mankind. It there was not a town that hated mankind, then it was only a few sick individuals hunting and killing human beings.

It was important if the trees were to help Gram find his enemy. Gram touched the friendly trees. It was strange for Gram to know true friends. Gram glowed with the knowledge. He continued looking for a town of hatred. Gram saw several towns located along the way. None of these towns was the one he was seeking. Gram gathered up the trees and leaped over all these towns. Gram's ability to leap so far amazed the trees.

The path was becoming very distant from where Gram and

the trees had started. As they traveled, echoes of thoughts belonging to billions of Earthlings developed in the path. He stopped and searched for a town, but none existed. It confused Gram and the trees. Gram called out to the area but nothing responded. The echoes continued.

Eventually, the trees determined this was the former location of the destroyed planet, Earth. Gram wept. His tears blinded him and the trees had to lead the way. They were unable to leap as Gram did from town to town. They walked along the pathway.

Gram watched through his tears as the trees tried to check the townspeople of the next town. They were very slow. The townspeople's feelings had very little meaning to the trees. They could not tell whether the townspeople knew Earthmen or not.

He took over when he realized the trees were having difficulty. Most of the towns in this sector of the path knew of human beings. Some liked the Terrans and others did not, but none radiated the blind, coiling wall of hatred Gram had found at the one place.

There were several towns sheltering human beings. Oddly enough, none attracted Gram as the one from the melodious town. Some mildly attracted him, but an important factor was missing. Gram needed to find this being he missed with an ache.

A sensation ahead on the path tickled Gram's senses. He set the trees down on the path and jumped into the center of the town where the aura originated. It was without light; fog surrounded him. The hatred was alive. Its wilting tentacles of rancor beat at Gram.

Gram screamed. It was choking him, filling his being. He ran and found no way out. He wanted to vomit—the vomit could not leave him. The hate filled his nose, his ears, his stomach, and his heart. There was no escape. His psyche shrank. He grew smaller.

If it did not stop, he would disappear into nothing.

He heard the trees trying to contact him. They instructed him on how to build a shell to keep the hatred out. Gram grasped the idea like a drowning man grasps a straw. The thickness of the shell grew and grew as though it were solid steel from the core to the uttermost edge. Nothing could pierce the shell to Gram.

Gram felt secure. His fight with the hatred left him exhausted. He curled up and slept.

The trees reached out for the impenetrable shell in which Gram slept and moved it to a safe place on the path. Here they poured out their love over the shell. It rolled off. They sang of their love for Gram. No sound entered the shell Gram created.

The shell was only three millimeters in diameter; a few seconds ago, the shell would have had to be ten meters across to contain Gram's psyche. Sadly, they picked up the shell and started back for home.

The path back was a long way for the trees. They could not jump as Gram did; they had to walk every step of the way. The trees sang their song of love to Gram, but nothing entered the shell and nothing left. Gram's seal on the shell was complete.

If Gram remained inside the shell with everything shut out when his psyche returned to his body, he would be catatonic. This worried the trees. They made a stop on their way home.

At the town where Gram felt the attraction to the other human being, they stopped and waited until nightfall. The trees approached the other being as it slept and made an appeal. They explained to the being what had happened to Gram and asked the being to call Gram forth from his shell.

The human sang love songs and cooed to the shell. The sounds were so beautiful even the trees grew in stature and felt refreshed after their long journey. A hairline crack appeared in the shell but got no larger.

Gram was too frightened to relax his protection any further. At dawn the trees took Gram's shell from the human and left.

Her strange dream puzzled the human when she awoke in the morning.

Reaching their starting point, the trees replaced the shell containing Gram's psyche back in Gram's body where it belonged. Like a nut about to sprout, thin fibers reached out from the shell and attached itself to the body. It was not a good connection but it was the best they could do for now.

The trees returned to their bodies, and the one that had stayed behind to nurture Gram's body sprouted another limb and sucked in Robert's body. It dissolved Robert's body, then began spewing forth metal spray that took on the shape of Robert. When the body of Robert was finished, Robert unfastened the umbilical cord to the ship's control and strode over to Gram.

He looked at the limb and said. "There is no visible sign of damage."

The limb did not speak aloud but impressed its thoughts directly upon Robert's new brain. "There is no real damage to his body. He created enough oxygen when he was landing to maintain his life. He stopped after we took over for him."

Robert nodded and the limb continued. "The real damage was done when we had him seek out the planet of the enemy with his mind. His spirit nearly disappeared; we taught him how to build a shell to protect himself and now he refuses to come out. We will need your help in developing his mental capabilities. He has a very powerful mind."

FIVE

Gram inhaled deeply. He held his eyes closed at first, wondering how Robert had managed to supply him with oxygen. Then he savored the sensation of breathing clean fresh air, air without the tainted smells of the ship's metal and oil. It was the clean smell of soil and flowers after a refreshing rain.

He frowned. Where was he?

The last he remembered he was dying on a planet containing a carbon dioxide atmosphere. He opened his eyes.

Gram was on board his ship, lying on the control room couch. Robert stood next to him, watching Gram's face. A large branch of a leafless tree filled the hole above the control panel and the ends of the branch were thick and stubby. It reminded Gram of a tentacle with a thousand fingers that moved about.

"Robert, how did this tree limb get in the cabin?"

"Allow me to introduce myself. I am Elfrum, of the Llan. We are a telepathic race but we are unable to converse with you in this manner. We hear your thoughts but you cannot hear ours. So when we repaired Robert for you, we made some minor alterations in Robert's circuits so we could communicate to the robot. Robert relays our thoughts to you."

"Doesn't Robert have any control over what he says anymore?"

Robert spoke. "I still have control of my actions. I am relaying Elfrum's and the others' thoughts to you. I am Robert, your robot."

Elfrum used Robert's voice again. "If you will slip on your space suit and step outside the ship, I will introduce myself and the other Llan to you."

Gram had met so many races it did not surprise him when a tree spoke. It astounded him that they were a telepathic race. He had never heard of any telepathic peoples. He wished he could communicate directly with them.

He eased himself from his couch, thinking he might be a little dizzy from oxygen starvation. He felt fine. He had never felt better. He strolled about the cabin; the hole through the cabin wall next to Robert's recess was repaired.

The hole above the control panel still existed. Elfrum's branch acted as a plug for the hole. The branch began to recede from the room. Finally all that remained was a stubby knob still blocking the hole. The knob sprayed liquid metal until the ship was whole again.

Gram shook his head in wonder and Elfrum spoke again through Robert. "I left this hole in the ship until now so I could nurse you back to health. Now that you are well, I have sealed the ship and it is as strong as it was before the damage."

Elfrum paused for a moment, allowing Gram a chance to ask questions, then continued speaking. "We read Robert's memory circuits and produced the oxygen you needed to exist. We've modified some of the ship's equipment, such as the ship's air conditioning unit. When the air passes through it, it removes the surplus carbon dioxide from the air and it restores the oxygen balance. There is no need for the ship's air storage tank now."

All Gram could say was thanks. Elfrum continued.

"We intruded on your thoughts and found you had a memory of air smelling of flowers after a rain. It was a simple matter to have the air conditioner add this smell."

Gram turned to Robert to speak. "Thank you, it was a pleasant memory I had of a planet my father and I visited one time. How can I repay your kindness?"

"Knowing you are pleased is reward enough for us. We are happy we could help you," replied Elfrum, using Robert's voice. "It is not necessary to speak your words to Robert when you wish to communicate to us. Once you form the words with your mind, we hear your thoughts directly. We only use Robert's voice so you can understand our thoughts."

Gram's mind raced with a thousand questions to ask the Llan. Elfrum laughed over Robert's circuits. "Slow down, we are not used to such an inquisitive creature. Think out your questions one at a time and we'll answer them. If you continue as you are doing, everything comes out a jumbled mass we cannot understand."

"How did you blow metal out of your appendage to seal the ship?" Gram thought slowly.

The voice chuckled as Elfrum answered through Robert's voice. "You'll discover facts about us which are much more strange to you, Gram. We send shoots, or roots, if you like, below the surface of the planet to ore deposits. We suck in the ore, refine it in the roots, then on to a stomach where the ore is liquefied. From there, we spray it out a branch to build whatever we choose."

Gram pulled on his space boots over the legs of the suit and Elfrum continued speaking. "In repairing your ship, we formed the same metal alloy originally used in the hull. We discovered the hydrocarbon used in your space suit would not serve as a pressure suit in our planet's atmosphere so we substituted a tough, flexible metal in its place. Now your suit will serve as both a pressure suit and a space suit for you."

Sealing the helmet, Gram stepped into the ship's airlock. When the ship's air cycled out of the lock and the planet's air cycled in, Gram glanced at the suit's pressure gauge. It read Earth normal inside the suit, yet it showed the outside pressure to be two and a half times more than Earth normal. His suit did not collapse because of the pressure differential. His suit was a true combination pressure and vacuum suit.

Gram threw open the outer hatch to the lock and stepped out onto the platform lift which had extended itself from the hull.

There were about two hundred of the Llan in front of the airlock. They reminded Gram of a small forest. The majority of the Llan were as tall as the hatch or about ninety meters high. Their arms were as flexible as those of a squid. Gram directed his thoughts to the group.

"Thank you for your help. I wouldn't be alive if you hadn't been so helpful. I don't know how I can repay you for repairing the ship and Robert."

"It was our pleasure to be useful," said Elfrum. Gram realized the Llan were communicating through Robert to the radio receiver in his suit. "The repairs to your ship and the robot were nothing. The real damage was done to you in ways you don't understand. These damages may be irrevocable. If you will remain with us, we may be able to help."

"I would like to remain. You've been so kind to me. But if I remain it may be dangerous for you as well. The enemy doesn't care who they destroy to get at Earthmen," thought Gram.

"We understand the problems of mankind much better than you or any other being in the universe may have reason to suspect. We believe we know the explanation why your enemy is systematically killing all Earthmen," said Elfrum. "If you'll stay with us, we'll prove if our assumption is correct."

"It will be dangerous for me to stay," thought Gram.

"When we discover the enemy's identity, we will help you overcome them," said Elfrum. "We almost learned their identity during a visit to their planet, but there was an accident."

"Could you send another agent to the planet?" questioned Gram. "Certainly he could radio back their location and identity."

"We cannot send another agent. Our communicator was our agent; he was damaged," replied Elfrum. "We operate much differently than you. Our agent traveled mentally to the enemy's planet."

Torn between his attraction to the Llan and his fear of the enemy, Gram said, "I would like to stay, but..."

"We know of your fear of your enemy, perhaps as well as you do," stated Elfrum. "We redesigned Robert so he can reason and make value judgments. We added some weapons to Robert's prime directive to protect you. Let me demonstrate what I mean."

Another Llan picked up a boulder capable of crushing the ship and hurled it at Gram. Gram froze. A beam of bluish light radiated from a point on the ship and the stone came to a halt in midair. It hung there for a moment, then vibrated madly until it collapsed in dust. The beam winked out and the wind blew the dust away.

"We altered your sta-freeze so it can be used as a protective weapon. There are other uses, you will discover."

"That's good," replied Gram. "What happens when Robert isn't around and I'm not near the ship?"

"Robert won't leave your side," said Elfrum. "It's a part of his prime directive to remain at your side at all times. He can protect you with the weapons we've installed in him or he can use the ship's new weapons."

"I've never had weapons to protect myself."

"You'll discover you're able to do many strange deeds through Robert's powers. These powers aren't for destruction only. It will be up to you to discover how to use the new tools we have installed in Robert," said Elfrum.

"Why all the mystery?"

"We have our reasons," said Elfrum. "It will be a training

program designed to help you grow. For every one of Robert's abilities you discover, there will be several others you've never thought existed. It'll take time to master Robert's secrets."

Gram shrugged his shoulders and looked out over the Llan. "I don't know what to say..."

"Just say you'll stay for a time, Gram. If you feel at any time we and Robert are unable to prevent an enemy attack upon you, you are free to leave," said Elfrum. "We ask you to stay because there is a symbiotic relationship between Earthmen and Llan."

Gram raised his eyebrows in surprise. "A symbiotic relationship?"

"Yes, a symbiotic-type relationship. Not a simple relationship as with the lichen where the fungus supplies shade and moisture for the algae and the algae provides food for the fungus. Nor is it the same relationship as with the damsel fish and the sea anemones," said Elfrum. "Later we will explain exactly how the relationship benefits both of us. Since we've known you, our knowledge of the universe has increased a millionfold."

"How will this arrangement help me or mankind?" asked Gram.

"We both seek knowledge. We believe we, working with you, will learn the identity of your enemy and put an end to the destruction of the human race."

"How did you learn of the types of lifeforms on the former Earth?" questioned Gram.

"It was easy for us," said Elfrum. "We read all the knowledge your father placed in Robert's circuits."

"OK, I'll stay as long as I think it is safe to remain. It is against the principles my father taught me as a code to stay alive," said Gram. "Now, how do I identify each of you?"

It surprised the Llan to discover Gram could not tell which Llan was speaking. After much limb waving and communicating among themselves, the Llan decided to identify themselves by imprinting their names on their trunks where Gram could see them.

Elfrum's name appeared in bright red letters on her scaly trunk. Each of the Llan chose a different shade or color than any of the others. There were Ihan, Okursis, and Madeah standing closest to Elfrum. Gram smiled at them and called them by name.

"I want to thank you for repairing my space suit too," said Gram. "I noticed the temperature is fifty-four Celsius now and will more than likely get another forty-eight degrees warmer before nightfall. Will the air conditioner protect me?"

"You will never be aware of temperature and pressure differences within your suit." Another tree moved closer to the hatch of the ship. Gram saw the name Ihan imprinted in bright green on the trunk. "The hydrocarbon could not withstand the heat nor did it have the ability to function properly when the interior pressure was less than the exterior. We synthesized a metal compound which was flexible but isn't affected by pressure differentials."

"Was that you speaking, Ihan?" asked Gram.

"Yes."

"Could you please give me some visual signal, like waving one of your limbs when you speak? Robert's voice is tinny sounding and when you talk through him you all sound the same."

"This is Ihan again. We never realized you couldn't tell which of us is speaking. We'll find a method to correct the problem so you'll know which of us is talking."

"Thank you."

"This is Okursis. If you are staying on our planet, you'll need a shelter other than your ship. We will construct a dome of clear material, fill it with air you can breathe, then stock it with a small forest, a swimming pond, grass and flowers. A home will be installed for you too."

Ihan signaled and a dozen of the Llan began forming the base of a dome. Gram could see material squirting from the ends of their tendrils and he strained for a better look. Okursis lifted Gram to a limb with a clear view of the new dome site.

As soon as she touched Gram, he got an impression she was a teacher and a female. He spoke.

"Okursis, are you a teacher and a female?"

The Llan stopped working. They stood with their limbs waving around. Gram suspected they were communicating with each other, although Robert relayed no messages until, "This is Okursis. How did you know I am a female of our species?"

"I don't know, but when you lifted me onto your branch, as soon as you touched me I knew."

"Can you identify the rest of us?"

Ihan reached out and touched Gram with one of his limbs and Elfrum did the same, then a smaller Llan reached over and touched Gram. Gram waited until they finished speaking, then answered Okursis's second question.

"I received the impression all of you who touched me were female except Ihan. He is a male. Okursis, you are a teacher, Elfrum is a nurse, and the last one to touch me is Madeah. Madeah is the youngest of the Llan. Am I right?"

"Yes, you are right," said Okursis. "I'm to be your teacher and mentor. Elfrum is the healer, Madeah is the youngest, and Ihan is male and the sage of our species. Most of our group is female, but not in the same sense as females in your species. Females of the Llan can bear female Llan and the male Llan bear males."

"I got the impression it was this way when you touched me," said Gram.

"We are deeply pleased you know this about us," said Okursis. "It means your mind is on the mend."

Gram did not understand what she meant by her remark, but he let it pass. The progress on his new home caught his interest. The Llan were creating a grove of trees. Gram decided he wanted his house or shelter located in the center of the grove and disguised as one of the trees. He explained to the Llan that the enemy would be deceived by the appearance and it would give Gram a chance to escape if they came to this planet.

The Llan did as he requested.

His tree house was twenty-five feet across at the base and as he approached, a section of the tree base disappeared. He could see the room inside.

The room was simple. There was a couch and chair, a bookcase with genuine books, a music reproducer, and there were paintings on the wall. Gram tried to move one of the small paintings and discovered it was part of the wall. The end tables were a part of the floor. Gram shrugged; it still was the nicest home he had been inside.

The picture window of the living room was modeled after the magnifier in his suit. With the controls he could change the illumination in the room as well as see everything outside the tree home. Lighting was unnecessary in the home. Walking about the room, he located two more openings that opened automatically as he approached.

Stepping into the first room, he discovered his bedroom. The bed felt as comfortable as the one on the ship. Gram noted a closet filled with clothes that were his size. When he stepped to the center of the room, the doorway to the living room became invisible. He had to feel along the wall to locate the opening. It sprang open again as he approached.

The other door from the living room led into a small kitchen. He checked all the cabinets and lockers, noting all the equipment and food stored in them. The house would be a welcome change from the ship.

Outside, Gram stepped away from the doorway and noted its location as it disappeared. Apart from its outrageous size, there was nothing to distinguish it from the other trees of the grove. The enemy would not expect a home to look like an overgrown tree.

Gram crossed over the soft cushion of grass. At a hundred meters, the large tree became invisible among the other trees.

The dome was almost complete. Several Llan were forming the last section. Gram watched as the Llan remained outside the dome and thrust their limbs through bubblelike fittings in the dome. The waterfall began to spill water over the lip of rock into a basin below. When the water reached the depth of ten meters in the basin, the level was established and did not rise any higher.

Okursis spoke through Robert. “Gram, it is safe, you can remove your suit. The atmosphere is as near Earthlike as we could get after analyzing Robert’s knowledge. I think you’ll find it a welcome relief after spending all your time on the ship.”

He slipped off the helmet and sniffed at the air. It smelled of cedar and pine trees. A gentle breeze ruffled his hair. He could hear the rustling of the leaves as the breeze puffed through the branches. It was heaven compared to the suit.

“The dome is great, but why didn’t you build an airlock large enough to accommodate the Llan?” asked Gram.

“Our atmosphere is poisonous to you and yours is toxic to us. We can tolerate putting our limbs in your atmosphere and we can reach any point within the dome from the bubble openings,” said Okursis.

“Sorry, I should have known a being which breathes a carbon dioxide and methane atmosphere couldn’t tolerate an oxygen rich atmosphere,” said Gram. “By the way, can Robert communicate with me or does he echo only your thoughts?”

“I can answer your question for myself,” answered Robert. “I haven’t talked for myself because I didn’t want to interrupt your communications with the Llan. I have only one speaking tone and it would confuse you if I interrupted too.”

“I saw a kitchen in the home the Llan built for us. I’m hungry—how about cooking me something to eat?” asked Gram.

“As you request,” droned Robert.

“This is Okursis speaking. We’ll change Robert’s voice module this evening while you rest and we’ll adapt a voice tone for each of us so you can distinguish which of us is speaking.”

“Thank you. It was a little confusing when you all sounded like Robert,” said Gram.

Okursis continued speaking. “This afternoon we wish you to become acquainted with your new home. We believe you’ll find the pool an excellent place to relax. We'll return tomorrow and show you the rest of our world."

Gram thanked the Llan and he followed Robert to his tree house. Pausing, Gram tried to break off a twig from one of the trees. The branch would not break. Whatever the Llan used to create the trees, they certainly were not real.

He examined the flowers. They had a pleasant fragrance, but Gram could not snap the stems off. They bent easily, but he could not break them or pull them free of the ground. It was impossible to tell the trees and flowers were artificial just by looking at them.

Instead of following Robert inside the tree house, Gram examined the tree from the outside. He searched for traces of the windows but could not see any change in the bark. He used his suit mike to call Robert.

"Hey, Robert, can you see me through the windows?"

"Yes, I can. You are standing almost in front of the kitchen window now," said Robert. "If you move about a meter to your left, you'll be standing directly in front of me."

"I can't see anything that looks like a window. The bark appears to be the same no matter how hard I search," said Gram. "There's nothing to indicate there's a window here."

Gram walked around to the front of his home and as he approached the door, it opened. Gram could smell the lunch Robert had prepared. His stomach growled, and Gram wondered how long it had been since he had eaten. Did the Llan feed him while he was unconscious? Gram did not feel ravenous.

After lunch, Gram put on a pair of shorts and wandered down to the pool. It reminded Gram of the pictures Robert had shown Gram of the Hawaiian Islands. Palm trees and flowering bushes ringed the pool. Yet Gram felt uncomfortable. He had never been out in the open without a space suit more than three times. It made him uneasy, as if he was naked and helpless.

Gram stretched out on the beach next to the pool. He had never learned to swim so he did not go into the water. He could not relax; the open spaces made him nervous.

A chill lay at the back of his mind as though something was waiting to reach out and seize him. Gram fought the sensation as he lay on the beach. Finally, he got up and waded into the water, trying to shake the feeling.

It persisted—like a shadow within a shadow—something that could not be touched or seen. The goose bumps between Gram's shoulder blades were not caused by a chill in the air as Gram hurried back to the house.

Subconsciously, Gram radiated his fear to Robert. Robert sent out detection beams, searching for any unusual movements within a parsec. The Llan sensed Gram's uneasiness and it perplexed them. Gram still had a long way to travel on the road to recovery.

The Llan searched far into the spiral arm in which their sun belonged. There was nothing resembling the dark hatred of Gram's enemy located there. It did not ease Gram's fears when the Llan informed Gram through Robert that the enemy was not in this sector of space. His fear was too deeply instilled.

After his evening meal, Gram lay on his bed trying to read one of the novels the Llan had created from Robert's memory bank. The words blurred as he pictured ships pursuing him through space. No...not pursuing him, but blasting an asteroid out of existence. His father was on the asteroid!

Gram shook himself out of his daze. He paced the room.

During the night, Gram made Robert stand watch at the foot of his bed. He could not stand the darkened sleeping room so he left the window setting at daylight brilliance. Robert set his sensing devices at maximum to give Gram several hours head start should the enemy approach.

Gram's sleep was fitful. He dreamed of a deep pit of no light pulling and tugging at him, trying to devour him. It was like being on a slippery clay slope where he slowly slid into the sucking maw below, a void of total darkness. He awoke, screaming.

He fell asleep again. This time the enemy was a lightless

void with tentacles reaching out faster than Gram's ship could flee. The tendrils squeezed the ship to powder, then pressed against Gram's mind, slowly compressing it to a tiny ball. If the tenebrous thoughts succeeded in withering the size of Gram's psyche to nothing, Gram would cease to exist. Gram's mind sent out bolts of terror reaching out over half the galaxy.

Robert was helpless. There was nothing he could do to quiet the terror in Gram's mind. He called the Llan to help him.

Elfrum plunged one of her arms into the house and into bed with Gram. Gram flung his arm about the rough warm limb. She sang him a melody and almost immediately in his dream Gram floated clear of the enemy. The song shrank the lightless void as it coiled and swirled, slipping into a deep recess within Gram's mind, then disappeared. Elfrum's melody surrounded Gram, preventing him from dreaming again.

It was as if he floated upon a warm sea…

SIX

Gram awoke an hour after dawn. No trace of his nightmare lingered. He felt refreshed by the night's rest. Elfrum's care and help drove the plaguing fear to the deep recesses of his mind. Nothing occupied his mind except an urge to explore this new world.

Going outside, Gram peeked through the branches of the trees to the sky beyond. He could see the blood-red sun through a dust storm raging on the horizon. Near the dome, the air appeared relatively quiet; at least Gram could not see any dust and sand being blown about.

He glanced to the trees and grass within the dome. The grass certainly seemed real, with the dew sparkling on it. He could smell the pine and cedar trees about his house.

The air within the dome was still; somehow the Llan

controlled the movement of the air. Gram could hear bird songs among the trees. He wondered if the Llan created artificial birds or whether they created some type of recordings. The Llan certainly tried to make him feel welcome.

"There's an old Earth saying which states: "A red sky at night, sailors' delight. A red sky in the morning, sailors take warning!" Robert said as he announced breakfast. Gram smelled the warm aroma of cooked food. The fresh morning air whetted his sense of smell and increased his hunger.

"Does the saying hold true on this planet?"

"I doubt it," said Robert. "My sensors reveal these dust storms intensify as the sun rises. Within an hour we'll be in the center of the storm, and we can expect such storms every day. It would be unusual if a storm didn't develop shortly after the sun rises."

Gram finished his breakfast. He felt in the mood to explore the planet. "Hey, Robert, when do you suppose the Llan will be ready to take me exploring? Are they awake yet?"

"Their customs require that you contact them whenever you are ready to begin," said Robert. "The answer to your second question is, they never sleep as do human beings. The night time hours are spent in feeding to renew their energy levels and in reviewing the knowledge gained the previous day. You have given them a whole new universe of knowledge."

"How do I contact them?"

"Think their names and they'll respond," said Robert.

"Elfrum, Ihan and Okursis! I'm ready to explore your world."

"Good morning, Gram. This is Okursis. I'm happy you're so peppy. Slip into your space suit. Ihan, Elfrum and myself will meet you at the airlock."

The voice coming from Robert surprised Gram. It sounded like the voice of a gentle and pleasant-sounding woman. This was the promise the Llan made to Gram yesterday when they said they would alter Robert's voice. The voice pattern chosen by Okursis fit exactly what Gram imagined she would sound like after she had touched him yesterday.

At the airlock, Okursis, Ihan and Elfrum waited for Gram on a giant jet-powered air sled. Ihan reached out with two of his limbs and lifted Gram and Robert into the sled. A shield swung into place, protecting the occupants from the buffeting wind and blowing sand.

"Good morning, Gram. We built this air sled from the knowledge we obtained from Robert's data banks."

Gram knew the voice issuing from Robert's body belonged to Ihan. The voice sounded deep and rich with a quality of kindness and wisdom. The voice reminded Gram of his father. Ihan continued.

"Before you arrived, we traveled a few meters a day by lifting our roots out of the soil and walking on them. We've never been more than a few hundred kilometers beyond our present location. We know what our world looks like through our ability to project our psyche. In spite of this ability, we never have been curious to go exploring."

Okursis spoke through Robert. "We never wondered why a fact was so; we accepted data. We never questioned why anything was true. We never wondered why something didn't act in a totally different manner. Until you came, we had no curiosity. The council of the Llan has studied curiosity and finds it is a good quality. Each of us has adopted your curiosity, and I must confess I'm as eager as you to visit out world first hand."

"You've never explored your world?" asked Gram.

Elfrum answered. Her voice was brisk, like Gram imagined a nurse would sound. Gram suspected she adopted the voice to fit Gram's image of her. "We told you there is a symbiotic relationship between our races. Part of this relationship is curiosity. You teach us how to be curious and we teach you how to control your emotions. We complement each other. There is much for both races to learn."

Ihan raised the sled from the ground and began moving slowly forward to clear Gram's domed home. Ihan handled the sled as through he had been piloting such a craft all his life. Ihan continued the conversation.

"We are growing because of you. We never have known the intensity you feel toward other creatures and beings. Your capacity to love is the most powerful force in the universe and we knew nothing of such a power. Perhaps it is just as well we didn't know. We would have been very lonely here without any other life on the planet."

"You mean nothing grows here on your planet?" asked Gram. "You haven't any birds or animals, trees or grass?"

"Nothing lives here but the Llan," said Ihan. "We are the only life to evolve on the planet. Since we have met you, we realize what we missed. We realize how life evolved on Earth and how many different forms it has taken. Life should have done the same on our planet."

"You keep referring to it as 'the planet'—doesn't it have a name?"

Okursis continued the conversation as Ihan concentrated on piloting. "Ihan is the eldest being of our planet, and I have never heard him refer to the planet by any name. We accept the planet's existence without giving it a personality as humans do. If we designed Robert, we wouldn't give him a name or develop an attachment for a nonbeing as you do. You consider Robert as friend and protector. We would never do it before you arrived among us."

Gram noted there was much limb waving as the Llan communicated telepathically with each other. Finally, Okursis spoke through Robert again.

"It is rude for us to communicate without including you, but all the Llan decided we would be deeply honored if you would name our planet and sun."

He had never known friends before landing on this planet. "I think an appropriate name would be Bonne Amie, for your planet and this system has proven to be a haven for me. How about calling the sun Haven?"

"Your choices please us," said Ihan. "Now Okursis will place you in the specially designed seat for you, and we will begin exploring Bonne Amie together. First we will take you to our birthplace."

Okursis reached down and wrapped one of her limbs around Gram's waist. She lifted him to one of her limbs about thirteen meters above the deck. She placed him on a seat mounted there. Gram had an excellent view as the sled raced above the sand.

Their first stop was a depression stretching from horizon to horizon. The surface was covered with a glasslike material. Millions of spikes of crystalline matter projected up from the surface, catching the sunlight and reflecting it in a billion different hues. The place had a wild primitive beauty no artist's brush could hope to capture. Gram shivered with delight and the Llan noted the sensation. Okursis spoke.

"Millions of years ago, this was a sea of boiling liquid, and as our planet began to cool, a certain chemical reaction occurred. Our first ancestors were born. Unlike your ancestors, ours were crystalline, and they didn't evolve into many different species. When they reached our present stage of development, evolution stopped."

She stopped speaking for a moment, allowing Gram to digest what she said.

"After several hundreds of centuries the sea cooled to the point where we were forced to leave it. We weren't able to communicate telepathically when we left the sea of our birth. Each creature felt it was the only one of its kind, simply because none of us made contact."

Okursis paused again before continuing.

"The magical combination of crystal-producing life didn't happen to all the crystal formation. Most of the crystalline structures are those you see before you—lifeless."

Gram stared out at the sea. Ihan turned on the external microphones and the sound of the wind through the crystal produced an eerie sound. Okursis continued talking.

"Ihan and Elfrum literally bumped into each other, learning everything they could about each other. Their telepathic communication was crude compared to our present standard.

But it was good enough to locate the rest of us two hundred four Llan evolved."

The hot desert wind blew dust and sand across the crystal-decked sea. Each crystal rang with a moaning note as the sand blasted their surfaces. The sad longing sound brought forth a sigh from Gram's lips. The melancholy tone struck a chord in Gram's soul that transmitted directly to the Llan. It became the first direct communication received from Gram since the fear he felt during the night. All other communication Gram formed as thoughts before they received them.

For the first time in their history, the Llan felt sadness. They knew Gram's longing for other human beings.

After flying across a corner of the dead sea, they headed into the desert again. The air sled sped over great dunes of carmine sand. Sometimes the hot raging wind would catch up the sand in great whirlwinds, hurling tons skyward as in anger at the cerulean sun that burned the ground.

Other times the howling banshee would scud sand along the surface in writhing trails—picking up the sand on the windward side of the dune, then dumping it on the leeward side. No matter what the gale did, it screamed and howled its hatred during the daylight hours. At night, it slept exhausted.

Hours passed. Sometimes citron-colored dunes replaced the carmine sand. Gram marveled at Ihan's mastery of the sled. No matter what the wind threw in Ihan's path, the sled rode as smoothly as in a night calm. Gram was about to question Ihan about where he learned to master the sled when he saw craggy mountains soaring in the sky with white mantles that extended more than half their height. The sand thinned as they approached the mountains.

The range stretched as far as Gram could see. Some appeared to thrust their peaks beyond the planet's atmosphere. Among most of the peaks, wind screamed thinly and hurled blinding blankets of frozen carbon dioxide particles at the travelers. The airsled never quivered in its course.

Beyond the first mountain range they came to a large valley. The center formed a shallow sea of water. It was the first moisture Gram had seen on the planet excepting the pool and waterfall the Llan gave him.

Okursis explained that most of the water of the planet collected here between the two mountain ranges. Gram felt thirsty and asked Ihan if he could get a drink from a stream meandering into the shallow sea. Ihan told him to drink from his suit canteen. The stream contained seltzer water charged with carbon dioxide and poisonous chemicals.

"I wonder if grass and other Earth-type seeds could grow here," mused Gram.

"Certainly," replied Ihan. "If we allowed oxygen producing plants to get started on our planet, it wouldn't be too long before the atmosphere became poisonous to the Llan. We cannot tolerate more than a trace amounts of oxygen. Our body chemistry isn't anything like the trees of Earth, although we do resemble them in shape. We are living crystal, not a hydrocarbon cellulose."

"I've always pictured crystal as being brittle and capable of shattering easily," said Gram. "Yet, you are as supple as rubber. Your arms or limbs bend in any direction and they grow or shrink at will. You do resemble a tree in late fall."

"Not exactly, Gram," said Okursis. "I've checked Robert's memory cells too, and where an average tree has untold numbers of limbs, we usually limit our limbs to about twenty. Although we may sprout more for a special purpose temporarily."

"As for crystal being brittle," said Elfrum, "I can make you a silicon ball that will bounce like rubber."

Ihan circled a volcano spewing lava and ash skyward. Ihan dropped to the ground near a river of lava. Gram watched the great cords of cooling lava that darkened and crumbled. It would halt temporarily, then like thick molasses move down a gully. Ihan leaped to the ground directly in front of where the lava approached.

Without warning Ihan sank his roots into the ground. His arms waved wildly about as he communicated telepathically with the other Llan. Okursis spewed metal from one of her arms, creating several metal containers before Ihan. Ihan spewed forth a red powder into the containers. When the last container was full, Okursis and Elfrum placed them on the sled.

When Elfrum and Okursis finished, Gram asked, "What was all the activity about?"

Okursis answered Gram. "Ihan found a deposit of mercuric oxide. We require a minute amount to digest the elements we take into our bodies. On the plain where we live, there is very little mercuric oxide in the soil and sometimes it takes all day and night to find enough for daily consumption."

Elfrum added to the conversation. "This is the reason why we were slowly moving across the plain where we live. We've had to seek out mercuric oxide. It is also the reason our group is so small; we never had enough of the compound to spare for a new member in our group."

"Now we have enough of the oxide to last our entire group for at least a hundred years," said Ihan. "Your curiosity can take credit. Through you, we've made an air sled to explore our planet, and we can use it to mine the minerals we must have for our diet."

The lava pushed closer and the four of them climbed onto the sled. Gram groaned and pointed toward the lava. "It's going to cover the deposit of mercuric oxide!"

Ihan placed the tip of one of his limbs on Gram's shoulder.

"Don't worry about it, Gram. We have a large reserve supply, and even if we didn't, I could come back in a year or so and send a tap root through the lava flow in a matter of seconds. Or we could locate another source if we needed to. Don't worry about it being covered."

"You can bore through solid rock?" asked Gram.

"Though solid metal, if it is required, or through liquid lava," replied Ihan.

"What about the heat? Wouldn't it burn you or tend to melt you down?"

"You're comparing our bodies to your own," said Ihan. "We don't have a low boiling point like your body; there is no free water in our systems to take away the excess heat. When heat becomes intense for us for us we sweat silicon crystals to carry away the unwanted heat. We could stand a temperature in excess of three thousand degrees for short periods of time."

"I suppose I should watch where I touch you," said Gram. "I could burn myself."

"Your protective suit will protect you," said Ihan. "If we touch your bare skin, we'll be sure the hot crystals are located elsewhere on our bodies. We have no wish to harm you."

"Oh, sort of selective sweating?"

"Yes, if we must get rid of a tremendous amounts of heat, the crystals will be nearly white hot. We can concentrate great amounts of heat in one small crystal."

The lava had almost touched the sled when Ihan lifted it clear of the ground. He circled the area, then continued their exploration of the planet. Now that he had found the rare mercuric oxide, Ihan became interested in locating other mineral deposits that were difficult to find in the mineral-poor soil of desert.

Several times Ihan stopped to mine various minerals. Gram would get off the sled and watch in fascination as Ihan spewed ores from a short pseudopod near his base. Okursis and Elfrum supplied the containers and loaded them onto the sled.

As they neared the polar region, it became bitterly cold. Gram wondered if the Llan became sluggish in the cold. Ihan answered the question by landing the sled and mining ore one more time. The wind blew carbon dioxide snow in raging gusts about Ihan as he sank a tap root into the ground. The swiftness of his movements was unaffected by the cold. When Gram asked Okursis about it, she explained they could operate in the cold for hours without discomfort. They learned to retain their body heat when needed.

They passed over the polar cap and headed south again; Gram asked if they could return home. He felt bone weary from all the exploring and investigating. Ihan seemed willing to head for home. He wanted to return with the minerals they mined and share them with the other Llan.

As soon as the Llan anchored the sled so it would not toss about in the wind, Gram and Robert entered the dome. Robert prepared Gram an excellent meal that he barely tasted. He could not keep his eyes open. Gram dragged off to bed and fell asleep almost as quickly as his head touched the pillow. He did not need Elfrum. He slept without dreaming.

The following days sped swiftly into months as Gram explored the Llan's star system with them. The Llan created a larger version of Gram's space launch so they could explore with Gram. The other planets were more hostile than the Llan's home planet, Bonne Amie.

The planet closest to their sun was too hot to visit. The surface exposed to Haven was molten and bulged toward the sun. The thin crust on the night side quaked and trembled as parts of it collapsed into the molten undersurface. There was no way to set down on the planet without danger of breaking through the thin surface shell.

The next planet out from Bonne Amie was an airless sphere cast in Hades. The mountains stood like torturous spires that reached as high as fifteen kilometers from their base. The valleys were frozen obsidian wastes. It was a nightmare planet. If the Llan and Gram chose to land, they would have to blast a landing pad. The Llan decided there was nothing to be learned by the effort so they rocketed out to the next planet.

Gram placed the ship in a parking orbit as Robert analyzed the outermost planet's subzero atmosphere of ammonia. The Llan felt little urge to attempt an exploration of its freezing surface. This ended the Llan's exploratory urge to examine Haven's system. The Llan still lacked the curiosity that drove all Earthmen to seek the next hilltop for what may lie beyond.

The Llan were able to explore with their mind's eye, which mankind never developed. They could picture a distant place without visiting it. They never experienced numbing cold, the fierce wind, or the exhilarating thrill of climbing the unplumbed heights of a lofty mountain. They never experienced the whirlwind speed, the roller-coaster ride, or the ear-shattering roar of catapulting down a canyon of swiftly dropping rapids and managing to cheat death. They did not have the strong feeling of living every minute to its fullest extent.

This attitude of the Llan forced Gram to spend more time inside the dome. He could not bring himself to lie on the beach by his pool because he felt so unprotected. He spent the time reading the books the Llan created from Robert's memory circuits.

One book told of the ancient sport of ice-boating. Gram could feel the biting wind as he imagined himself on one of these type sleds. The urge to handle such a craft led him to design one that could sail before the wind on the sands of Bonne Amie. After all, he was an expert in handling a space launch. He was excelled only by Robert, a computer. It should be a simple task to handle a contrivance such as a sled powered by a sail. Gram requested the Llan to create a sled.

To Gram's surprise, they built two such crafts. Okursis planned to sail with him. Okursis's craft was much larger. Her craft had only one seat on its T-shaped frame and the runners were much longer. Gram's sled was a two-seater. The Llan explained they did this so Robert could take over the controls of the sled should the strong winds tire Gram.

Gram strapped into the seat on one side of the mast and Robert mounted the seat on the other side. While Gram and Robert were doing this, Okursis already had her sled racing with the wind. She was so expert, it appeared she had raced sleds all her life.

Gram released the brake. The wind shook the sled like a puppy dog with a rag toy. He raised the sail; it snapped with a boom as the wind seized it and hurled it like a comet. The sled raced over a small hummock. It became airborne momentarily, then it slammed into the ground on one runner and the mast. Even Robert was unable to make any changes to prevent the accident.

Okursis sailed her sled up to Gram and adroitly brought it to a standstill. "Are you hurt, Gram?"

"No! Just mad!"

"You mean you are angry?"

"Yes! You sail your sled as though you were born on it. The first crosswind that blows I end up bottom over the mast!"

"You will get the idea of operating the sled," said Okursis. "The reason I can operate the sled so well is because of my many arms. My weight acts as ballast. We Llan feel the change in wind direction before it happens. If you develop the ability to feel the wind, you will be proficient."

"Hah! Feel the wind!" growled Gram as he set the sled upright with Robert's help.

"I never realized the ultimate joy of doing something just for the sake of doing it," said Okursis. "Thank you for the idea."

"You're welcome to the sled idea," said Gram. "But don't try to feed me that gruel about you being able to handle a sled better than me because of your many arms or because of your weight. The sleds were made and raced by men first. I'll race this sled yet!"

Okursis waited until Gram mounted his sled; then she sped off in a cloud of dust. Gram groused to himself—no one would beat him on a sand sled, not if he had to practice forever. Several hours and many spills later, Gram turned the battered sled over to Robert. Robert managed to bring the drooping sled limping home with the sail in shreds.

The Llan put down their tap roots and were feeding for the night. Gram noticed Okursis tethered her sled about her waist and her sail appeared as new as when she made it. Gram tied his sled to a ring mounted in the dome. He and Robert went inside. Gram asked Robert to wish the Llan good feeding. They in turn wished Gram pleasant dreams.

After the evening meal, Gram requested Robert to massage his bruised body as he lay on his bed. The gentle kneading of his muscles soothed Gram to sleep. Robert covered Gram, turned down the lights, then stood guard until Gram should awake. This night, Gram's dreams remained peaceful.

In the morning, Gram loaded the food compartments and filled the water tank of his suit. He planned to remain outside until dark if need be, learning how to master the sled. He would sail the sled home himself today.

Outside the dome, Gram noticed none of the Llan were anywhere in sight. "Where are the Llan, Robert?"

"They left a message with me for you," replied Robert. "They manufactured sleds for each of them and they've gone to mine ores they need. They'll be back about dusk, but if you wish, I can contact them for you."

"No! They are busy; I can manage without them."

He did not want anyone who could sail the sleds as well as the Llan watching him bungling along. By evening Gram's skill was fair enough for him to bring the sled to the dome. He wished the Llan good feeding and went inside.

The next day, as before, the Llan worked busily elsewhere. Gram practiced until he saw the Llan return to the dome for the night. He felt envious of the skill they used to bring their sleds to a halt. He managed to stop his sled without ramming full tilt into the dome.

After a month, Gram gained fair control of his sled; the only time he spilled now was when a crosswind would catch him unaware. No matter what he would do, if the wind howled down on him without warning, he would spill over.

Robert was no help when this happened with Gram at the controls. Robert did not spill if he guided the sled when the wind turned crosswise. To Gram, it seemed Robert responded slowly when Gram spilled the sled. Gram wished to prove he could control the sled as easily as Robert.

The crosswind never plagued Okursis. What was it she'd said to him? Oh yes—The Llan feel the change in the wind before it happens. Gram longed for this ability—to reach out, to touch the wind, feel its fury, and to feel its heat...Aha! It blew upward and circled back on itself to charge broadside of the mainstream. A little adjustment of the sail—he did it!

Gram reached out and felt the wind; there would be no more spills! It felt as though he had shed his protective suit, only more so. He could touch the wind in front of him, to the side of him, and to the rear of him. He knew what way the wind would blow before it reached him. He raced the sled to the edge of the sand dune and brought it to a stop. He called to the Llan.

"Whoopee! I can do it! I can control the sled! I feel the wind!"

Ihan replied to his call. "We are happy for you. If you watch, you'll see us as we top a dune about a thousand meters to your left. All of us have taken to the sport of sand-sledding."

As soon as Gram sensed the presence of the Llan on the dune, he raced the sled to where they waited for him. The blinding sand and dust could not block his new found power. He made a reckless swooping curve in front of them, stopping in a swirl of sand. Gram felt breathless with excitement.

"I'll race you back to the dome!"

The Llan answered by taking off at breakneck speed. Gram raced with them. Gradually, they pulled ahead of him. He grimaced. He had challenged them and he resolved to make a good showing. There must be a better way to control the sled speed.

Gram became a part of the sled; he felt the grains of sand as the runners screeched over them. Where the sand packed hard, the sled slowed a fraction as it passed over it. In the liquid moving sand, the sled glided effortlessly. Gram reached out, searching for the moving sand.

He felt the wind as it surged into the billowing sail. Gram felt totally alive. He reached out, testing each shriek of the banshee gale that drove them homeward. He guided the sled into the faster gusts of wind and finally passed the Llan. Gram reached the dome only seconds ahead of Okursis.

Gram could not remember when he had had so much fun. He reached out mentally and touched Okursis. It felt wonderful, having such friends. Okursis cherished Gram as he touched her; she felt proud of his achievement. At last, his illness had slipped away.

Ihan spoke. Gram could feel the rich timber of his thought. It contained the quality of a loving parent. "We haven't been wearing the bright letters and numerals we adopted when you first arrived. You've been identifying us correctly for several weeks. Unfortunately, it was only today you learned some of the powers you control. We've tried everything within our power to awaken these secrets."

"You knew I could do this? Why didn't you tell me?" asked Gram.

Okursis placed a limb on Gram's shoulder as she answered. "Would it help a person to tell him he could swim if he didn't know what water was? We could only guide you toward the technique. There are other powers you possess which we do not have. We cannot explain these powers either, but you will discover them."

"This is why we redesigned Robert's circuits to amplify any thought or gift of talent you develop," said Ihan. "You'll learn how to use him. As you gain control of these new powers, it won't be necessary for him to amplify your thoughts."

SEVEN

The Llan peered into Gram's mind, seeking out the psyche where it had retreated into the subconscious. The shell about the psyche had one hairline crack from which one tenuous tendril stretched from the subconscious to the conscious mind. Elfrum sang a song of love and friendship to Gram.

At first, the tendril shrank and almost disappeared at Elfrum's touch, but as the song progressed and intensified in its call, the crack widened and spread until it partially exposed Gram's psyche. No one could resist Elfrum's beauty as she sang.

Gram reached out and touched Elfrum with his love and friendship for her; she grew in stature at his touch. He then reached out and touched the others, one at a time.

He became one mind with the Llan. They taught him how

to control the shield. The enemy's ugly hatred could never engulf him wholly again. The Llan could not persuade Gram to leave the shell's safety.

The Llan told Gram of the talents he and they both controlled. They hinted at the latent powers he alone possessed. They could sense these powers in Gram but they could not communicate their character because they did not understand.

The Llan felt sad when they withdrew. The crack in the shell around Gram's psyche closed tight to the tendril, leaving only it exposed. The enemy frightened Gram too much to chance exposing himself to their evil thoughts. The tie between the psyche, subconscious, and conscious mind was only slightly stronger than before the visit. Gram dropped into a normal sleep without dreaming.

He awoke as the morning sun peeked over the horizon. Gram loved this time of the morning best because the air was relatively still and free of sand and dust. Gram flashed a greeting to all the Llan. It was easy to communicate telepathically once he had the knack of doing it.

With telepathy, it was impossible to misinterpret the meaning or the feeling of a message. No coloring was added by the sender or the receiver to make it suit what they wanted to hear. The brain centers got the meaning without it being qualified.

Racing through breakfast, Gram queried Ihan if the Llan was ready to brave the weather on the sand sleds. All knew a fierce storm was brewing and it would be a challenge to Gram's newly discovered talent. He would require all his wits to brave the storm and race in its winds.

Most of the Llan chose to remain anchored in their camp and weather the storm there. No Llan had ever remained unanchored by their roots during violent storms and they were afraid to try it. Okursis said she would go because she wanted to sample a thrill like the one racing through Gram's body.

The wind pummeled Gram's suit as he fought his way to his sled. Blast after blast tore at him and he used his powers to brace himself. It was as if he had another hand he used to press against the sand behind him to brace himself against the wind. Robert followed close behind Gram, refusing to yield to the buffeting.

Gram sensed Okursis was alongside him on her sled. The sand blinded his ability to see with his eyes. Gram could not see more than a few centimeters except for an occasional glimpse of his straining sail. Robert complained that the solid wall of moving sand partially blocked his sensors.

The sled raced across the sand as Gram let it go with the wind. He used his new talent to taste the full fury of the gale as it increased in strength. He felt the pounding pressure of the sand and small stones against his suit as the fury scudded him across the landscape. He heard the grinding squeal of the sand under the runners as he sped faster than he dreamed possible. He felt the mast's pressure as the sail strained to be free of its moorings. Gram lived every intoxicating second.

He raced before the wind for almost an hour, covering more than fifty kilometers. Now it was time for the real test of his talent. He planned to head directly into the gale, tacking as little as possible to achieve his homeward flight. Okursis turned with him but her tacking was not achieving the same results as Gram's. After a time she had fallen far behind him as she barely made headway.

"Gram, I have to stop and sink in my roots. Tacking in this storm is draining all my energy. I'm experiencing fear for the first time; I must stop to feed to replace my strength."

"I can't hold my own with the sled if we stop out here in the open," Gram thought back to her. "Can you continue until I can find a shelter of some type? Something to block this wind so I won't be blown away."

"Make it soon," thought Okursis. "I don't have any idea how long I can go on."

Gram reached out with his mind's eye, searching for some kind of protection. There was nothing near them. He reached out farther in every direction looking for anything they could use to hide from the wind. Off to one side about ten kilometers were some rock shards of worn down mountains. Gram pointed them out to Okursis but she did not have the strength to reach them. She would have to stop, but Gram should go on to their shelter.

He thought about it. Okursis would be safe enough in the open with her roots sunk deep, but Gram did not want to leave her if he could avoid it.

"Can you make it if I guide your sled by telling you which way to travel? This way you won't have to expend the energy seeing which way to turn your sled with every gust of wind."

Okursis touched him with a warm smile. "I can try to make it, if you're willing to try guiding two sleds at the same time."

Gram split his probe, using one to see the storm about him and the other to guide Okursis. At first he noticed little effect of the double probe, but after a time he felt a strain, like a muscle bunched up and beginning to ache.

As he fought the wind, Gram began to feel the physical strain as well as the mental strain of battling the storm. His arms ached from fighting the sail of his craft. Gram kicked himself mentally; why was he fighting the sail? Robert could handle the sled as long as Gram directed his movements as he was doing for Okursis.

Robert took control of the sled and Gram tried to relax in the seat. The strain of probing for two crafts in the forever shifting wind kept his body tense. The painful knot in his mind was overpowering him. He ignored the strain, separating the pain from his task before him. It was similar to putting one foot ahead of the other when hiking with painful blisters on each foot. He ignored the pain in his mind and sought out the next sail position for the succeeding gust of wind.

It became more complicated probing for two sleds and maintaining telepathic communications with Okursis and the robot than it would be for placing one foot ahead of the other, but the principle remained the same. Gram concentrated on his task while ignoring everything else.

Time became meaningless as Gram focused on bringing the two sleds to safety. He was still probing wind gusts when the sails of both sleds went slack. They had reached the safety of a protected alcove of rock.

Robert carried Gram over to Okursis as she sank her roots into the soil to regain her strength. Okursis contacted Gram with her mind probe. "Relax, Gram, we are safe from the storm. Relax, and I'll try to ease the blinding pain in your mind."

Gram was hallucinating from his exhaustion. "I can't! I've got to rescue Dad. He's under attack by the enemy!"

Okursis and the other Llan could sense the scene Gram pictured. He was back at Nashar aboard the *Lares Compitales* watching the enemy bombard their home asteroid. Robert tried to stop Gram by uttering the prime directive but Gram drove the *Lares Compitales* into the battle.

When the asteroid exploded, the enemy sent out a dark, impenetrable fog that rolled over Gram. It choked the life from him. Gram screamed and passed out.

When Gram regained consciousness, he was lying in his own bed. Okursis and Elfrum had limbs in his room administering to him. Okursis held his hand with a limb. Gram tried to sit up and Elfrum pushed him back.

"Don't try to sit up, it may cause your headache to return."

"What happened?" Gram asked.

"Supposing you tell me the last thing you remember," said Okursis.

"There was this sand storm and I was guiding your and my sleds toward a rock shelter," said Gram. He rubbed his forehead as though to refresh his memory.

"What happened after you brought our sleds into the alcove?"

"Everything is so hazy, I can't remember. The pain is blocking out everything."

"Don't you remember thinking you were battling the enemy?" asked Okursis.

"All I can remember is the pain."

Okursis squeezed his hand. "Well, if you remember anything, call me. Right now, I believe the best thing for you is rest. You aren't used to prolonged probing with your mind. It's like any exercise. You have to build up your endurance."

They left Gram in Robert's care and Gram sighed. He could not remember being so tired. His eyes closed and he drifted to sleep. Several hours passed before he began dreaming.

Gram was aboard the *Lares Compitales* back in the Nashar system. Two ships were firing upon the home base and Gram wanted to help his father. Wave after wave of bombs crashed upon the asteroid but Gram stood aboard the *Lares Compitales* without doing anything. As the asteroid changed to a molten ball, the enemy sent a snaking tendril of darkness after Gram.

He fled. On the ship's screens Gram's father appeared, pleading with Gram. "Help me, Gram. Help me."

Gram continued to run.

He awoke screaming and wringing wet from sweating. Okursis sent her limb into the room with Gram. "What happened?"

"I had a nightmare."

"Tell me about it."

"I was being attacked by enemy ships."

"Is that all?"

"Well, it's kinda hazy."

Okursis gripped Gram's arm with her tentacle. "Were you responsible for your father's death?"

Silence hung over the room and all the color left Gram's face. "W—why do you say that?"

"You've never talked about your father since you've been here. Do you believe you're responsible for your father's death?"

Tears streamed down Gram's face. "I did nothing…I ran away."

Okursis wrapped her limb about Gram and patted him gently on the back. She let him cry for several minutes before she spoke. "It is time you let this out of your system. It has been choking you for a long time."

"I let him die."

"No, no. There was nothing you could do. You were powerless! It was your father's own doing. He gave Robert the prime directive to protect you at all costs. Robert refused to take the ship into the battle because it violated your father's orders. Your father knew you would be unable to save him."

Gram's sobbing became less violent and gradually faded to nothing. Okursis spoke again. "Your father loved you, Gram. He wanted you to live. He fought the enemy so you could get away. He must have been a very great person."

The tears stopped as Gram thought about his father. "Yes, we had a lot of fun together."

"Why don't you tell me about him. I'd like to know about him."

"Where do I start?"

"Tell me the whole story and start at the beginning."

"My father was born on Nanoon in one of the last large colonies of Earthmen of a thousand or so beings. He got his engineering degree before the enemy wiped out the colony. Dad searched for work.

"Dad got a job working at one of the weather satellites and they were returning to the station after a party for one of the Nanoonian men. Dad's friend was too drunk to pilot his ship back to the station so Dad volunteered to take it back.

"It saved Dad's life. The enemy vaporized the colony city, the weather station, and the shuttle craft Dad was supposed to be aboard. Dad never stopped; he left Nanoon.

"He kept the ship and renamed it the *Lares Compitales*. Dad never trusted any system to protect him after the attack on Nanoon. He wandered down the spiral arm of star systems, hauling freight to replace the supplies he needed, but he kept on the move.

"Eventually, he met my mother. After a day or two they got married and fled the planet where my mother lived. A day later, Dad heard everyone in the city where my mother lived died of radiation poisoning.

"Dad changed his tactics after that. It was safer to mine metals on an unknown asteroid and then sell the ore to some mining company than it was to take cargo from one planet to another. The enemy could not follow him due to his using an unknown course. My parents made out well enough until my mother became pregnant.

"Not trusting himself to deliver a baby, Dad put Mom in a hospital on Staag. The Staagan government set up maximum security at the hospital and they succeeded in blocking one attempt on Mom but they forgot about protecting our ship. Dad was so proud of Mom and me that he was not thinking about the enemy when he opened the *Lares Compitales* airlock.

"Dozens of poisonous flying vipers greeted my Mom when she stepped inside. Dad made a grab for her and me as he leaped off the ramp and onto a cargo hoist still under the ramp. He missed us by a centimeter.

"Poisonous flying vipers don't attack unless they believe there is an immediate danger. They circled about the hatch until the last of them cleared the ship, then they headed back to their mountain habitat. As soon as my Dad was sure the snakes were gone he climbed up to my mother and me.

"Mom had been bitten many times about the face, arms and legs. My blankets protected me; I never woke up until Dad uncovered my face. The cold air set me to crying.

"For the next eleven years, Dad played hide and seek with the enemy. We heard tales there were less than a dozen human beings left in the entire universe. Dad scoffed at the idea. He said Terrans were too tenacious for such a thing to happen.

"Sometimes, I think he said it to bolster my courage because I never saw but one human being besides my Dad. Shortly after the man talked to my Dad and me, we heard he had been killed in a knife fight.

"Dad's wanderings took us to the center of the galaxy, into the Population II stars. We passed Sagittarius A and on beyond the boundaries of the Federation. It was in another spiral arm we found Nashar.

"On one of the asteroids, Dad built a fort that was to be our home for the next six years, until the enemy came... Dad was a lot of fun, he took me everywhere with him. Although the games we played were pointed to increase my speed and reflexes—I think he knew the enemy would find us."

"What makes you think you could have saved him?" asked Okursis.

"I don't know," said Gram. "I should have tried something even if I had to dismantle Robert."

"Robert would never have allowed it to happen. His orders were to get you out of the enemy's path no matter what the cost to your dad or to Robert," said Okursis. "Your father wouldn't have risked everything unless he thought there was a brighter future for you than being chased by the enemy throughout your lifetime."

"Dad believed the enemy was afraid of the human race because we knew something to make us great. He believed if we could hold out until we found out who the enemy was and why they feared us, we would win the final battle over the enemy."

"Did your father ever hint what he thought it was the enemy was afraid of?" asked Okursis.

"Well, he did say we'd come up through the Stone Age, the Bronze and Iron Ages, the Industrial Age, the Atomic and Space Age, and now we stood at the threshold...the dawning of a new age," said Gram. "He said human beings were changing, they were able to do strange things never before possible. He never explained to me what it was people could do.

"He felt it was his duty to find a haven that was safe from the enemy. He thought he'd found it in the Nashar system.

"As soon as he had developed a defense system capable of standing up to the enemy, he planned to bring all the remaining people to the Nashar system for safety. He believed we could start again from there."

Okursis continued to keep her tendril about Gram. "What made your father think he could protect Terrans at Nashar when populated worlds couldn't do the job?"

"The Federation had put us on the endangered species list and it was against Federation law to kill us. They made it the duty of all governments to offer us haven, but like governments of old Earth that allowed the animals of Earth to be slaughtered for whatever purpose, these governments provided only the minimum required by Federation law. It was never enough to stop the enemy.

"Although I must say in fairness to some planetary governments, some took their obligations seriously. Those governments did provide maximum protection to Terrans, and they suffered terrible damage at the enemy's hands.

"The enemy prefer to use messy atomic weapons, which most governments have outlawed. Dad thought they used these weapons to scare planetary governments out of offering sanctuary to Terrans. That was the reason Dad thought it was up to the human race to provide its own protection," said Gram.

"It is the same explanation we discovered on Robert's memory tapes," said Okursis.

"If you knew all this why did you question me about it?"

"The way to get an old wound to heal is to cleanse it," said Okursis. "Your father's death has been festering in your mind since it happened. You blamed yourself for not doing something to save him. It was impossible for you to do anything. The only way to make you see it was to make you talk about it."

Gram blinked away the tears and tried to smile. "Thanks, Okursis."

Okursis gave Gram a squeeze. "Well, what else could a mother do for an adopted son?"

Nearly a week passed and Gram spent the time racing his sand sled while thinking of his father. By now he had come to the conclusion there was not anything he could have done to save his father's life. He could not let it rest there; he had to continue his father's work. He had to help the human race survive. His inactivity wore on his nerves like a sand-burr on a bare foot.

He had to return across the void and rescue Terrans from the enemy. Where would he take them afterward? He paced the living room of his tree home.

Okursis, Elfrum and Ihan signaled Gram; but he was too cloaked in his own thoughts. He never felt the gentle nudge. They waited patiently; it was not polite to interrupt another person's chain of thought. Robert was not chained by niceties.

"Gram—Ihan, Elfrum and Okursis have been trying to contact you for a half-hour."

"Hi, Okursis, Ihan, and Elfrum! I was so busy with my own thoughts I missed your probe. I'm sorry, I didn't mean to ignore you."

"We know you weren't ignoring us, but you radiate a restlessness which is infectious," replied Ihan. "It is similar to an itch that cannot be scratched. Can we help you solve the problem worrying you?"

The statement humbled Gram. "I'm sorry. I didn't mean to radiate my thoughts all over creation. I'll shield them from now on."

"That would eliminate the irritation, but it does distress us you are in this mood," said Okursis. "Can we help?"

"Thanks for the offer, Okursis. What could you do to help?"

"Join us in a common mind and all the Llan will work on your problem together," said Elfrum.

It was a new experience, holding an open-mind session with the Llan. Each one tackled the problem and presented their solutions like a "landscape" which Gram could study from all approaches. He viewed each solution and thanked everyone for their help but he rejected all the answers offered. Each landscape became more complex as he rejected them; finally Elfrum offered her solution. Gram seized it eagerly. All painted it with the bright colors of excitement and anticipation as each of the Llan approved the plan.

The whole time spent on the problem was less than a quarter-hour.

The solution was that Gram would seek out the other Terrans and bring them back to Bonne Amie. The Llan would enlarge the dome to a city where the new arrivals could grow crops and rear children. Between Robert's new protective devices and the Llan's extrasensory powers, Gram believed the human race would be perfectly safe.

Robert provisioned the *Lares Compitales* to accommodate Gram's needs plus enough extra for a dozen passengers. Gram wished the Llan good feeding, then blasted free of Bonne Amie.

The ship circled the planet, picking up momentum, then shot directly toward the sun. Gram used the sun for the slingshot effect to build up speed before he switched the ship to hyper space. Okursis and Ihan remained in contact with Gram until his ship winked out of the third dimension. Their minds could not follow where his ship traveled. It saddened the Llan.

If anyone would have asked Gram why he chose Gallant III of the Population II stars as his first stop, he would not have been able to answer except to say he had a hunch. Gram did not like the Goro of the planet. Their attitude was too superior. Man did not exist on the visible spectrum. If an Earthman attempted a landing, they put red tape on him until he gave up in disgust. So it was when Gram signaled the port authority he wished to land.

At first, they ignored Gram as though they never received his signal. He had to change his orbital pattern abruptly several times because the Goro-in-charge aimed outgoing ships on a collision course with his ship. The Goro were sadistic and did not mind crashing another ship into an earthling ship to rid themselves of a Terran.

Gram would not be delayed. He knew there was a Terran on the planet and he wanted to talk to him. It was not proper to enter another person's mind without the owner's permission but Goro never gave permission to Terrans on any matter. Gram found within the twisted corkscrew mind of the Goro a combination of sounds the Goro found irritating. Gram smiled as he relayed the information to Robert.

The bagpipes of Terra have always been a controversial musical instrument even among Earthmen themselves. It was a matter of opinion whether it was a screeching, ragged noise, or the sound of the human soul singing triumphantly as it expressed its courage for all to hear. Gram enjoyed the pipes which Robert broadcast painfully into the Goro's ear.

"Tellurian, repair your communicator! It emits a blasted static to the point where I can barely make out your voice signal. What do you want?"

"Is there another Earthman on your planet?"

"You'll have to check with Immigration Control."

With a snap he broke contact with Gram. Gram waited an hour, assuming the Goro had communicated with immigration. He wanted to be fair with the Goro. When he probed again, the Goro ignored the fact Gram had called. The Goro thought it was below his dignity to continue his conversation with Gram.

Robert broadcast the pipes on all frequencies. It cut into the commercial frequencies, giving all homeowners who listened to their radios and tri-dee screens a headache.

Gram watched the Goro controller rip his headset off and curse. The Goro screamed into his mike.

"Tellurian! Land your ship and repair your communicator! The Earthman you seek is on the field. His ship needs repairs too! Shut off your communicator and do not broadcast until you repair it. It fuzzes up the entire band of frequencies."

The landing pad assigned to Gram was at the far end of the space port, far from the gate leading to the city and far from transportation. No one would visit off-world freighters. The personnel of these ships used cargo carriers to get about the port, but as luck would have it there were no cargo carriers available.

Gram was angry enough to order Robert to give the Goro another taste of the bagpipes. He decided against it. Why waste the pipes on a tone deaf Goro? He had to make the best of a bad situation. Gram shrugged his shoulders and started walking.

"Why don't you probe him?"

Robert's question startled Gram out of his reverie. He had

momentarily forgotten his talent; old habits were hard to break. He had planned to check physically. He could have checked for the man without landing first but it never occurred to Gram to try. Gram started by probing a pleasure craft at the far end of the field and within a few moments he worked his way back toward the freighters.

Hidden among several large freighters was the other Earthman's ship. Through his vision of the ship, Gram could understand why it was on the planet of the Goro. In its shabby condition, it could not make it to another star system. The pilot had no choice but to land. The Goro had no choice either. They could land him or allow him to make a fiery crash among their population from a decaying orbit. The ship needed major repairs to lift off again.

The human had a gaunt half-starved look; the Goro had refused him supplies as well as a repair crew. Abruptly, Gram halted his probe. Heavy coils of hatred hung about the ship. The sickness floated about the ship. The enemy had been on the ship. The poor starved Terran had been killed.

Gram's subconscious mind recoiled, breaking all contact with the doomed ship. The enemy had mined the ship and the atomic device approached critical; there was a blue glow near the bomb. Gram was terror-stricken. The bomb would wipe out several ships, including Gram's. He had to flee—run…

The stars surrounded Gram's ship; he was half a light year from the Goro planet. Gram blinked. "Robert! What happened?"

"You teleported."

"I what?"

"You teleported. Your psyche gave the order and I amplified its command and the entire ship teleported."

EIGHT

Gram tried to teleport again. He tried for two weeks before he came to the conclusion it had been just a fluke or a secret tightly locked in his psyche. When Gram asked Robert what commands he had received from Gram's psyche, Robert could not answer.

He had received a complicated signal and he had done nothing more than amplify it. Robert tried to reproduce the signal he had received but the best he could do was to reproduce a fractional part. Gram studied the signal on the scanner. It seemed to start at a point, then flow outward in all directions, then reconverge into a point again. Robert admitted there were portions of the signal he could not imitate because he did not understand how to create them.

Robert explained the part he was able to re-create. It was

the transformation of matter to energy then back to matter again. The missing part of the signal contained the information to keep the matter converted to energy from being scattered across the galaxy.

"Do you believe I could teleport again in an emergency, Robert?"

"It is hard to predict. *The Rubaiyat of Omar Khayyam* has two lines which fit the situation: 'There was the Door to which I found no key; There was the Veil through which I might not see.' I am a robot. I don't see the future, I can only predict its possibilities." Robert paused for a moment to let what he had said sink into Gram's mind, then he continued.

"It depends on how strong your will to live is at the time of danger. Your psyche may come to your rescue every time, then again.... My suggestion is you find the key and you learn to penetrate the veil.

"Your psyche rescued you twice which I witnessed. Once when we first reached Bonne Amie. You generated your own oxygen until the Llan sealed the ship and filled it with breathable air. The other time you rescued us on the planet of the Goro. I haven't an idea if your psyche will come to the rescue a third time. I believe it will happen because you have a very strong will to live, but I cannot prove it will happen again."

"What you're saying is I shouldn't depend on it happening when I need it," mused Gram.

"The Christian Bible had the answer in Proverbs 17:21, 'He that begetteth a fool doeth it to his sorrow,'" quoted Robert.

"You can stop the quotations," said Gram. "Steve Ancile raised no fool. I know how important it is I develop all the talents I possess to their fullest capabilities."

"My suggestion is that you practice by attempting to reproduce the signal to teleport. It is a handy weapon of defense. There is no way the enemy can follow you when you teleport."

"I agree," said Gram. "How far must I teleport the ship

before you can detect whether I've done it or not?"

"In normal space, I could detect teleport with as little as two millimeters displacement."

Gram cut the generators of hyper space and relaxed. The subconscious mind yielded secrets poorly; a person had to probe about the edges, searching for a single thread to unravel the mystery. Gram drifted dreamily, his subconscious mind touching lightly on facts, then springing off to seek something new. He found the vinelike tendril that stretched from the conscious mind to the subconscious and its origination at the shell surrounding the psyche. He probed the shell.

When he tried to ram his way into the shell, Gram bounced off. When he applied gentle pressure, he penetrated as through thick tar. He entered until the shell covered him completely, then he could go no farther. He had to fight his way out and felt panicky. If he had been unable to clear his probe of the shell, he would have remained catatonic.

Clear of the shell, Gram contacted Robert. Between the two of them, they devised a program where Robert could withdraw Gram's probe to his conscious mind. Robert was like a safety belt to Gram's sanity.

Gram probed for eight hours before Robert withdrew the probe to Gram's conscious mind by using the ship's power. It had taken Robert a long time to locate Gram's probe. Gram had probed deeper than any other occasion in the search of teleportation. Gram was weak from exhaustion.

He took a pain killer; his head throbbed from his effort. The probing had been a total loss for Gram. He was not any closer to the secret of teleporting than he had been when he first started. There was something he was missing—an important link somewhere within his mind. He would have to go back over every detail on the Goro planet leading to the teleporting after he had rested.

Days passed and his psyche's secret haunted him. He went over every detail time after time but no matter what he tried, the secret remained locked away. He tried to approach it the way he had learned to probe with his mind. He tried to approach it the way he had created the insect in his space suit. He tried to drift into the secret the way he had learned to communicate telepathically. Nothing worked.

The probing was not a total waste of energy; Gram sensed there were human beings on a planet in a system ahead of the *Lares Compitales* and they were in danger. He abandoned the search for the secret. It was more important to reach the Terrans before the enemy.

When Gram signaled the planetary government that he wanted to remove the earth people to another planet, he could almost hear the sigh. The government had spent huge sums of money protecting the family and they were not sure how much longer they could provide protection.

A government agent introduced Gram to the father, George Horvath. The man asked Gram and Robert to step inside as he called to his family. As the mother appeared, Gram probed to Robert. "Is this how all adult females appear?"

"More or less," replied Robert.

The little girl giggled and the father spoke to her. "What on Earth are you giggling about, Helene?"

"He was talking to his robot, Robert," came the reply.

"Don't play games now, Helene. We don't have time for them. This nice man has come to help us." George Horvath shifted his attention to his wife. "Honey, this is Gram Ancile, he will take us to a safer haven."

The woman gripped Gram's hand. "We're so glad to see you. I'm Helen Horvath. Please don't take offense at my daughter's joke, she's only five."

Gram smiled at the woman. "Helene wasn't joking, I was talking to my robot by mental telepathy. As she said, I do call my robot Robert. If you wish, I'll talk to Robert aloud so you can hear what I am saying."

It flustered the woman to discover Gram used powers unknown to her and that her daughter could hear Gram. George covered the awkwardness by introducing his two boys, Steve and Randy. The boys were towheads and both had the same friendly, freckle-faced smile of their father. They took an instant liking to Gram. Robert awed them, along with the fact Gram owned both Robert and a space ship.

Helene was as different from the boys as the mother was from the father. At the age of five, she was as lovely as her mother and had the same jet-black hair. Both of the females puzzled Gram because their reserve shielded their inner thoughts.

George was a large-boned man with a grip of steel. He radiated the relief he felt about Gram's promise. He led all of them to the dining area. "We are about to eat the evening meal. Would you care to join us?"

Gram's meal schedule was different from theirs; he based his on the time at his home on Bonne Amie. He had finished lunch an hour ago. He glanced at Helen and realized she would take offense if he refused. She prided herself on her ability to cook. "I'd be delighted. I've never had a home-cooked meal before. Robert always prepares my meals in the warmer."

"Well then, you're in for a treat," said George. "Helen does wonders with the simplest of foods, but tonight we're having roast skrell. They tell me it's as near to the roast duck of Earth as you can get."

Helene managed to seat herself on one side of Gram while the younger boy argued with the older as to which one of them would sit on the other side. George settled the question by telling the older boy he could sit next to Gram at the next meal. Steve stuck out his lower lip and sat heavily in the uncontested seat.

Gram turned to Steve and said, "My dad was named Steve, and he was the bravest person I've ever known. He taught me to pilot the *Lares Compitales* and he built Robert to help me—how old are you, Steve?"

"Ten," he replied.

"Hey, I was only twelve when my father started teaching me how to pilot the *Lares Compitales* and ten is practically as old as twelve," said Gram. He glanced toward Robert and continued. "How about it, Robert, do you think you can teach Steve to pilot the *Lares Compitales*?"

"Aristotle of ancient Earth once said, 'What we have to learn to do, we learn by doing,'" quoted Robert. "Yes, Steve will make an excellent pilot, if he is willing to obey my instructions and if his father gives his permission."

Steve turned to his father with his eyes aglow and when George nodded his approval, Steve jumped up from the table and did a handspring. "Oh boy, I'm going to be a pilot. I'm going to pilot the *Lares Compitales*! Gosh, thanks, Gram...Robert."

Helene glanced at Gram, then Robert, then blurted out, "How about me?"

Gram probed a message at her. "You are as pretty as your mother."

In response, Helene giggled.

Suddenly little alarm bells began to sound within Gram's mind. A queasy feeling rumbled through his stomach; Gram identified what troubled him. He could feel the fingers of the enemy's hatred. He probed the planet; they were not on the planet yet, but were swiftly approaching.

Gram flashed a message to Robert. "Quick, notify the port control the enemy is approaching and ready the *Lares Compitales* for flight. Erect a shield to protect us until we get aboard the ship."

The alarm on Gram's face frightened the other people. The girl began to cry because she had heard Gram's silent command to Robert. Both parents began to show panic as Gram spoke.

"The enemy is approaching—I've ordered Robert to put up a force shield to protect us until we reach the ship."

"What about our supplies and equipment?" asked George.

"No time, the enemy will be within bombing range in ten minutes," Gram answered as he began herding the children toward the front door. Robert followed behind them.

The mother raced out of the room to the kitchen, rummaged about for several seconds, then returned. In her hands, she held a large crystal punch bowl. "I couldn't leave this behind. It's been in my family for many generations—it came from Earth."

Her attitude was defensive of her actions. The woman's family was in grave danger and she took time to rescue a bowl that the Llan could replace. He was sure he would never understand the females of his race. Their actions were inconsistent with the danger.

On board the *Lares Compitales*, Gram seated the family in the control room as he took his place at the console. Robert lifted the ship at full power. A thousand kilometers out from the planet they saw the enemy on the screens. Atomic warhead after atomic warhead blasted against the shield of the ship as Robert threw the *Lares Compitales* into evasive maneuvers. As soon as they were free of the planet's pull, Robert flipped into hyper space.

"When the enemy is determined to wipe you out, they attack with atomic warheads. Dad often wondered why they didn't use some of the more modern beam weapons or some of the more selective bombs."

The passengers were just beginning to relax when the ship returned to normal space. Gram wanted to take a sighting for Haven and to adjust his course. Within seconds, the enemy ships surrounded them. Robert returned to hyper space. Everyone dozed for hours before Robert tried for a sighting.

An explosion rocked the ship and the force field held. Helene screamed and the boys began to cry. George and Helen paled with the horror. Their fear ate at Gram's mind like a corrosive acid as they broadcasted hysteria. It drove Gram to the brink of madness. It crashed upon him in waves like some thunderous surf, beating him and bruising him to the absolute limit.

The enemy ship winked out of the screen, and the stars did a crazy dance on the scanners, then settled down into steady patterns. No stars showed brightly on the screens.

It had happened; he teleported half the distance between galaxy arms. From here the ship could reach Haven and the Llan within a month in hyper space. A quick scan of the area proved the enemy was nowhere around. They would have been months covering the distance Gram teleported.

The Horvath family's fear receded as they realized the enemy was a long distance behind them and would never catch up to them. George Horvath grabbed Gram's hand and shook it.

"Thanks for saving my family. I'm sorry I had my doubts you could do it. Your ship is the fastest in the galaxy; we must be halfway across the galaxy."

"Well, no, we're not halfway across the galaxy from where we were, but it's far enough that the enemy will never find us. About another month and we'll be safe on Bonne Amie."

Gram felt a tug on his arm; it was Helene with her arms outstretched. He reached down and picked her up. She gave him a big hug and kiss. Gram blushed, not so much because she hugged and kissed him, but at the thoughts he felt surface in her mind.

He was her knight in shining armor. He was the hero who rescued the king, queen, prince, and the princess. She was going to marry him when she grew up.

The boys pretended they were fighting an enemy, shooting imaginary guns while hiding behind their seats. They were space rangers and Gram was their captain. Mrs. Horvath grasped Gram's hand in gratitude. For an instant, Gram felt like flexing his muscles and beating upon his chest while yelling. The feeling was exhilarating.

Robert flashed Gram a warning telling him not to show off. It would detract from his status with the adult Horvaths. As a result, Gram confined his excitement to an infectious grin.

After the excitement wore off and the attitude of the people calmed down, Gram showed the Horvaths to the cabins where they would live. When everyone retired to sleep, Gram tried to contact the Llan. The distance remained too great; his probe could not reach to the nearest star system even with Robert's help. His control of his psi powers was not much greater than a new born baby's control of its arms and legs.

Gram reached out as far as he could with Robert's help for

an indication of the enemy but failed to find any trace of them. The people aboard were safe from discovery.

Before falling asleep, Gram probed the ship. Helene slept soundly; the two boys whispered and giggled to themselves. Gram did not check the two adult Horvaths. They rated their privacy from Gram's probing.

Gram had never met a grown adult female before in his life. From the feeling Helen radiated, Gram knew of her love for her family. Gram knew of her acceptance of him but it radiated no love. She concentrated her love on her family and Gram understood she would be a tigress if something threatened them.

Her cool acceptance of Gram made him shy around her. She was an attractive woman, about thirty years old with jet-black hair. Gram could still feel the soft gentleness of her hands when she had shaken hands with him. He wished he knew a woman who would feel about him as Helen Horvath felt about her husband and children.

Gram's last thoughts were to Robert, to wait until everyone had dropped off to sleep before switching to hyper space. Gram never felt the switchover as he drifted to sleep thinking about how he had teleported again.

NINE

Time aboard the *Lares Compitales* passed pleasantly as Gram became friends with the Horvath family. Steve followed Robert's instructions for piloting. At first, he objected to all the mathematics until Robert explained everything in space moved. The light observed from stars had left years before. Robert drew a vector to determine the true position of the star's location at the present time, then where the star would be located at the ship's arrival. With this information, Robert plotted the ship's course.

Randy wanted to learn how to pilot the ship, until he became lost in the mathematics and became bored. Randy busied himself asking Gram all about his life, his parents, the robot and the Llan. Gram dutifully answered all the questions.

George, his wife and Helene listened to Gram's answers

to Randy. Sometimes, George would interrupt with another question, but Helene and her mother never interrupted. When Gram told of the death of his parents, Helen and Helene radiated something that soothed the loss Gram felt. It seemed to rock and cradle him while cooing to him. He had never experienced such a feeling before, which eased his sense of loss.

It puzzled him too. Why should the females try to comfort him? The males never radiated this aura; they felt a sadness for Gram's loss. It was akin to Gram's own grief, but the females were a whole new experience. He would have to study their reactions more closely.

Helene would wait until Gram was free of Randy's questions and was not helping Steve with a knotty math problem before she would make her presence known to Gram. When he was free, she would slip onto his lap and cuddle without saying anything. If he was standing, she would put out her arms, signaling Gram to pick her up. She would give him a big squeeze. Gram would flash the thought she was his beautiful little princess and she would giggle and kiss him.

Gram practiced using telepathy with Helene. She could pick up the messages easily enough but she could not answer them mentally. Her face would screw up in concentration but nothing would happen. Several times her mother saw her and asked why Helene was making faces. Helene would answer that she thought answers to Gram. Her mother would shake her head in bewilderment and then ignore Helene's contortions.

Two days out from Bonne Amie, Gram contacted the Llan. Helene picked up the messages from the Llan almost as soon as Gram did. When she announced she liked the Llan because they had many arms, her parents doubted her. The boys taunted her until Gram confirmed what Helene had said. Then they wanted to talk to the Llan. When Helene tried to show them how she accomplished it, they would not listen.

"Don't worry, princess," Gram flashed to Helene. "They don't know everything. You've got psi power and they haven't."

As soon as the ship landed, Gram requested the Llan to alter the Horvath space suits for pressure on Bonne Amie. As they all stepped out of the ship, Okursis was the first to greet Gram. She clasped him to her trunk, then challenged him. "Let's see how good you are at racing. I'll bet you can't beat me today. But first introduce us to your new found friends."

Gram saw all the Llan were wearing their letters and numbers again to make it easier for the other humans to identify them. As soon as he completed the introductions, Gram explained the racing challenge Okursis had offered.

"Okursis has challenged me to race her on the sand sleds. Do you want to watch or would you rather go in the dome to rest?"

"I'd like to see the race," George said. "It ought to be interesting to watch a tree handle one of those big sleds in this wind."

The boys started clamoring to go along on the sleds. Gram sent a message to Okursis. "Could you take the two boys with you and still control the sled? If you can, I'll take Helene with me in the extra seat."

"I can hold the boys in my arms and still beat you," Okursis said. "Your sled will be off balance if you put the girl in the other seat; it was designed to carry Robert."

"It wouldn't be off balance if you added some extra weight to her side of the sled," said Gram.

The conversation between Gram and Okursis took so little time, the Horvaths were unaware he was communicating with Okursis. Helene heard both sides of the conversation and waited quietly. Gram addressed his remarks to Helen Horvath because it would be her who decided whether or not the children could go for a ride.

"Can the children come with us? The boys can ride with Okursis and Helene can ride in the extra seat on my sled."

"I don't know, a sled with a sail in this wind doesn't sound like a safe game for children to play," she said. "Suppose the sleds tipped over; everybody would be killed."

Gram protested without avail; Mrs. Horvath would not allow her children near the sleds. Okursis and Gram raced toward the dunes. It was wonderful to be back on Bonne Amie among his friends. Gram probed the wind and reveled in its screaming, untamed fury. It was music to his ears. He glanced over at Okursis's sled; she was racing neck and neck with him.

"I am very happy you're here again, Gram. I missed you," she said. "You'll notice I can keep up with you. I've learned to probe the wind for every favorable current as you do and I've learned to take full advantage of them. You'll never be able to outsmart me with that trick again."

Gram laughed as they swung around in front of the space ship and came to a halt. The children were dancing up and down, pleading to ride on the sleds. "Mom, the sleds didn't tip over. Can't we go for a little ride? Gram and Okursis won't let us get hurt, they'll take very good care of us. Can we go, huh, Mom?"

George Horvath spoke to his wife. "Perhaps one short ride won't hurt them. I know Gram and Okursis can control those sand sleds after watching the race! I'm sure the children will be safe with them."

"Yes, Mrs. Horvath," said Gram. "Okursis and I would be very careful with the children aboard. In fact, we'll stay within sight so you may be sure they are safe."

Mrs. Horvath wavered in her resolve. "Well, I suppose one little ride can't hurt them, if you stay in front of the ship and don't go too fast on the sleds."

The children were wild with excitement as Gram and Okursis guided their sleds back and forth in full view of Mrs. Horvath. After fifteen minutes they brought the children to their parents. They were reluctant to leave the sleds and tried to coax Gram and Okursis into taking them out just for one small ride. Gram laughed and replied maybe another time they could stay out longer when their mother was sure they were safe.

As the boys passed Gram, Steve spoke. "Okursis is super sterling! Did you know she's a girl tree, Gram?"

"How did you know this?" asked Gram.

"I don't know," he shrugged. "When she touched me I knew but I don't know how I knew."

Randy claimed he knew, too, when Okursis touched him. Of course, Helene claimed she knew two days ago when Okursis talked to Gram out in space. Everyone thought she was bragging, but Gram and Okursis knew differently.

When the children touched Ihan they knew immediately he was male. The parents could not tell anything from touching the Llan. Ihan flashed a message to Gram. "The children have latent psi talent but from all present indication the parents don't seem to possess this ability."

Okursis touched Gram with one of her limbs and spoke through Robert so all could hear. "Thank you for bringing these people to us. It will give us much pleasure if we can stimulate their psyches to their full potential—"

"Especially the children!" butted in Madeah, the youngest Llan. "I never dreamed there were such bright inquisitive minds. They want to explore everything at once."

Gram detected a slight freeze in the other Llan's attitude. Madeah broke one of the Llan's cardinal rules: it was unforgivable to interrupt another's thoughts. Almost as quickly as the attitude developed, it melted and faded into nothing. Gram smiled; the Terrans were not the only ones changed by the contact of the two races.

Ihan pointed to the dome Gram called home. "We built a home for the Horvath family when you signaled us you were returning. Do you want to step inside and show it to them?"

The new house was about a hundred meters from Gram's home. The flagstone walk joined Gram's and they walked toward the new home. Gram told them it was safe to remove their helmets. Mrs. Horvath spoke.

"George, smell the grass. Everything smells so wonderful."

She stopped by a flowering bush and picked a sprig of flowers. Gram gave a start. Okursis stole into his mind.

"We're learning, Gram. We're trying to make them feel at home here. Everything is as near to the real thing as we can possibly make it. What do you think of it?"

Gram snapped off his helmet and inhaled deeply. The air

was fresh and clean, containing an odor he had never experienced before. He spoke aloud so the Horvaths could hear too.

"The air's wonderful; it's like I've imagined Earth must have smelled on a warm summer afternoon."

"It's heavenly," murmured Mrs. Horvath. "George, just smell these flowers I've picked."

George smelled the flowers, then turned to Gram. "They're wonderful and so are the Llan. Tell them thanks for us. We sure appreciate this beautiful home they built for us."

"Tell them yourselves, they understand our speech," said Gram. "They can't answer you because they speak telepathically. Perhaps after you've been here a while, you'll be able to pick up their thoughts as does Helene. The Llan taught me to broadcast my thoughts and I've learned to hear their thoughts too."

The next morning Gram awoke early and probed the Horvath house for thoughts. He learned the elder Horvaths were still asleep but the children were not in the building. Probing about the dome, Gram saw they had found the stream. Madeah allowed them to use her lower limbs to jump into the pool.

Gram watched for a while; the children were having a merry time diving and yelling at the tops of their lungs. Gram wanted to join them so he slipped on a pair of trunks and headed for the pool. As soon as he stepped out into the open, he felt naked and unprotected. His impulse was to run back into the house and stay there.

He forced himself to continue until he could see the children. Madeah would lower a limb down next to the water; Helene, Steve and Randy would reach out and grab the limb as Madeah lifted them up and out of the water. When they were clear of the water by a meter they would let loose and drop freely and into the water.

Helene had trouble supporting her weight on her five-year-old arms. Madeah sprouted a small pseudopod under Helene's feet so the girl could stand and not slip loose from the limb she clung to with her arms.

The squeals of excitement and peals of laughter persuaded Gram. He dove into the pool. He had as much fun as the children. Gram would chase the nearest one through the water and as he came almost into reach, Madeah would extend a branch and whip the child clear of Gram's grasp. They would climb through Madeah's branches and when Gram came too close they would jump into the water. Madeah always made sure the branch they were standing on was next to the water when they jumped.

Gram never caught any of them, except Helene. Most of the time she would flee from him as did the boys but occasionally she would jump into his arms when Madeah whipped her clear of the water. Whenever she leaped into his arms, Gram growled and threatened her as though he was about to eat her up. Helene used these occasions to sneak in a hug when she thought Gram was not expecting it. At times, she gave him a kiss, too.

"You knew that I was going to do that, didn't you? You see what I'm thinking."

Helene's frankness startled Gram, and he nodded his answer. Helene turned her dark eyes up at Gram's face she spoke again. "You talk to Madeah in your head and she hears you. Why can't I talk to her that way?"

"Because no one has shown you how to do it."

"Will you show me how?"

"OK, first close your eyes so you see nothing but what I show you with my mind," said Gram. "Deep inside your mind is the home of your psyche, or your subconscious mind. It can control your speech something like your mind does when you are awake. You must train yourself to make your psyche talk in your head. Can you see what I'm showing you?"

"Your psyche looks like a ball with a small root sticking out of it," said Helene.

"You are looking at the physical part of it. Can't you see the essence, the part which looks like me?" asked Gram.

"No." Helene squeezed her eyes tight shut and twisted her face out of shape as she tried to see what Gram spoke about.

"I think…ooooh—I see what you mean. You're beautiful!"

Gram blushed. "Cut the flattery, young lady. And watch what I do. Do you see how I'm making talk in my head to you?"

"Yes, you're talking to me the same way you do with Madeah," said Helene.

"Do you see how I do it?"

"Yes."

"OK, you do it," said Gram.

Helene grunted and squirmed as she tried to talk telepathically to Madeah; nothing happened. Gram could feel the tears in her voice when she spoke. "I tried but nothing came out."

Gram sympathized with Helene as he patted her psyche. He was about to tell her she would learn the secret in time, when he got another idea. "You can listen to me and Madeah talk; let's see how your psyche does it. Maybe you can learn how to talk if you know how you manage to listen."

The two watched as Helene's psyche formed an ear to listen to Madeah speak. Gram grew excited; he glanced at his own psyche. Yes, he formed ears to listen too, although his were not as predominant as the single ear Helene formed. His were a permanent part of his psyche, as was the mouth he spoke through to Madeah. Eventually Helene's mouth would become a part of her psyche. First she would have to learn how to control her psi powers.

"Helene, form a mouth the same way you made an ear, then use it to talk."

The rosebud mouth Helene formed refused to open or to make sounds until after she experimented with it. She managed to make it sound one note mentally. She spoke aloud to Gram. "I'm tired, I can't make it talk."

Gram smiled and helped her onto one of Madeah's branches. Steve protested Gram's chasing Helene more than him or Randy, never realizing anything had happened to Helene. Gram dove after Steve, catching him by the heel. At the same time, Gram flashed a message to Helene.

"You rest; don't try to talk anymore with your mind. Later,

Madeah can practice with you. She saw how humans talk with their minds. She will teach you, Steve and Randy how to talk to the Llan."

Madeah snatched Steve from Gram's grasp by lowering a limb. When Steve had a good hold, she wrapped the branch around Steve, lifting him high above Gram's head. Randy splashed Gram so he could not see to grab the branch Steve had used to escape. Madeah signaled to Gram.

"Their mother is calling for the children; she's worried something has happened to them."

"Why don't you reach out a limb and bring her here?" asked Gram.

"She would be frightened out of her wits if I reached and just grabbed her."

"Not if you talk to her first," said Gram.

"Robert isn't near her," replied Madeah.

"Why don't you grow a voice box similar to Robert's on your limb and talk directly to her," said Gram.

Within two minutes, Mrs. Horvath was standing at the stream's edge. Gram came out of the water and greeted her. "Hi! The kids and I were having fun swimming before breakfast—I should have left a note, I wasn't thinking. You need not have worried though, the kids can't get into any trouble with the Llan watching them."

"That's what Madeah said," said Mrs. Horvath. "I'm glad the Llan appointed her the children's tutor."

"Oh? You know she is female?"

"Humpf! I know a female voice when I hear one!"

Gram laughed. The Llan could imitate any sound they chose, but he did not say so to Mrs. Horvath. Instead he picked up Helene and carried her back to the Horvath house riding on his shoulder.

Mrs. Horvath had set up a table under the trees and George was sitting there waiting for them. "Good morning, Gram! Pull up a seat. The wife's set a place for you."

Gram glanced at Mrs. Horvath and she smiled at him, then beckoned him to a seat. Helene chose a seat next to Gram, leaving the two boys to fight for the other chair next to Gram. Finally, George had to take a hand in the argument and decide who would sit where. This time Randy was unhappy with his father's ruling.

After breakfast, Gram got down on all fours and he let the children take turns riding on his back. George began protesting and Gram stopped him. "Don't make them stop; remember, they're the first kids I've met and I like playing with them."

George grumbled a little about the three of them making a nuisance of themselves, then cautioned them not to climb on Gram's back all at the same time. Gram carried them on his back over near George and his wife. He wished to continue speaking to them.

"You'll be safe here on Bonne Amie with the Llan watching over you. If there's anything you need such as food, clothing or whatever you may want, just ask one of the Llan. They will provide it for you."

"It sounds as if you were planning to leave us here alone," said George.

"Yes, I am," said Gram. "Robert and the Llan restocked my ship while I slept."

"Why?" asked George. "Helen and I thought you were going to remain here with us."

"There are other humans out there who are in danger from the enemy as much as you were," said Gram. "I've got to help them, too."

George stroked his earlobe thoughtfully. "Yes, what you say is true. There aren't many Terrans left; all of them are in danger from the enemy. But it's a large order for one man to carry out alone. I'll go with you."

"Thanks for the offer, George, but your family needs you more than I do," said Gram. "Besides, my ship isn't large. What happens if I locate a dozen people or more? I'd need every centimeter of space for them.... Robert is all the protection I require."

"Well, it was a thought."

Gram felt the relief flood through Mrs. Horvath as George

gave up the argument that he should go. Gram smiled to himself; Mrs. Horvath need not have worried. Gram had probed George to see what arguments would keep him home with his family before Gram spoke a single word to George. It would be pleasant company to have George along on the trip, but Gram did not want Mrs. Horvath or the children worrying while he was gone.

The good-byes to the children were much harder. They knew what waited for him out there—the enemy. There might be a million people out there or maybe only a handful; the children knew none of them. They did know Gram and they did not want to lose their hero.

Nothing seemed to work. Gram could not convince the children it was necessary he should go. Helene hung onto his neck with a ferocity Gram found hard to believe of a small child. He smoothed her dark hair with his hand.

"I must go, Helene. Give me a kiss to remember you and then I've got to go...you would not want me to leave some other small boy or girl out there for the enemy to kill, would you?"

Helene flipped her head forward and then sideways, mussing her hair again. She pouted, then screamed. "I don't care! You don't love me anyhow! I don't care if you do get killed!"

She wiggled out of his arms and slid to the ground. Helene kicked him as hard as she could on the shins, then dashed toward her house as fast as her little legs would carry her. George was about to yell at her when Gram cautioned him not to do it.

The boys hung around as Gram climbed into his protective suit and they walked him to the airlock as they tried to talk him out of going. Gram smiled and told the boys good-bye as he stole a glance toward the Horvath home. Helene was peeking at him from behind a curtain. Gram waved; her face disappeared when she realized Gram had caught her watching him.

Gram climbed into the pilot's lounge, then probed for Helene as the ship blasted off. She sat on the floor, hanging onto the curtain and crying as though her heart would break. A lump came to Gram's throat; there ought to be an easier way to say good-bye to a little girl. Gram reached out with his probe and gave her a kiss on the cheek and said to her, "Good-bye for now, Helene. I'll be back before you know it."

TEN

The ship materialized in normal space and the screens filled with the bright glare of Eta Tauri. Gram's reflexes caused him to shade the scanners before the strong light burned them out. Robert saw the swift response and spoke. "It's not necessary to dim the scanners since the Llan redesigned the *Lares Compitales*. The scanners aren't effected by strong light."

"Reflex action," said Gram. "I acted before I thought."

"Did you know in ancient times on Earth mankind often mistook the seven brightest stars of the Pleiades for the constellation of Ursa Minor which was known as the 'Little Dipper'?" asked Robert.

Gram did not answer Robert immediately. Sometimes he wished the Llan had redesigned Robert a bit more thoroughly.

It annoyed Gram, having Robert give him bits of information at every opportunity. If he wanted, Gram could have named every star in the Pleiad group. He could have told Robert Pleione was a shell star with a ring of rapidly rotating gas about its equator, or that in antiquity the Greeks had created a myth where these stars were the seven daughters of Atlas. When Orion chased them, Zeus changed them into the constellation to help them escape.

Of course, Gram had learned these facts years ago from Robert, so he did not express his annoyance. Instead he said, "I know," and ignored Robert's recital.

Gram's interest in the group focused on one of the three thousand smaller stars of the Pleiads. He had probed the small planet circling the sun and had found Terrans. As soon as Robert had the coordinates he flipped the ship back into hyper space and raced toward the planet. It was only a matter of minutes before they landed on the planet.

It pleased the government to learn that Gram wished to remove the colony of eight humans from their planet. The expense of providing protection was beyond the ability of the government. The enemy had raided the planet twice within the last month. It would be years before the last scars of destruction disappeared.

The news that Gram had removed another family under attack had preceded his arrival. Gram and Robert kept a sensory probe on the enemy, who were racing toward the planet. The *Lares Compitales* made it into hyper space before the enemy was able to attack.

Free of the planetary system, Gram took time to meet his passengers. The first was Jack Rogger, his wife Phyllis and their son Tim. Jack was in his early fifties and bald. The pink top of his head beaded with perspiration. Phyllis appeared about the same age as Jack, but very nervous. She habitually turned her head to see what happened behind her. Tim, a scrawny boy going on thirteen, had a hard time keeping his legs from becoming tangled in every item in sight.

Next, he met Sam and Betty Coulter, newlyweds. They

had lived on Cele II until recently moving to the planet. The enemy had warred on the Terrans on Cele II and the Coulters had heard this new colony was much safer. It seemed to the Coulters the enemy had followed them here. Within months of their arrival the enemy attacked.

Gus and Rose Orosz had left Cele II with Sam and Betty, but since their arrival they had lost two children. They hospitalized their baby son for diarrhea and he escaped death when the enemy bombed their home. The other two were with a baby sitter. Gus and Rose were in the hospital visiting the baby.

The Oroszes blamed themselves for the deaths. They believed that if they had remained on Cele II, the children would be alive. Gram took their minds off their guilt by asking questions about the other colonists on Cele II.

"How many of the colonists were left alive when you and Rose left Cele II?"

"There were twenty when we left, but it's hard to say how many are still alive. The enemy burned or blew up the settlement homes while everyone slept. Of course, there were the daytime accidents too. The vehicles would be faulty and crash, or objects fell from buildings, crushing Terrans, or they would be struck by hit-and-run drivers no one could identify. The enemy had stepped up their campaign against the Terrans."

Gram thanked Gus for the information, then turned to the rest of the group. "I must apologize for placing your lives in danger but I must check on the colonists on Cele II. If they are still alive, they must be rescued. I expect the enemy to attack us when we arrive so I must ask you to remain in the cabins Robert assigns. I will need the bridge free of people so Robert and I can offer you maximum protection."

The passengers murmured as their fears surfaced. Gram continued speaking. "Don't panic. If the enemy attacks the ship, we have weapons to protect you. The ship has a beam which can destroy a space craft and Robert can place a shield about my ship which cannot be penetrated by an atomic blast."

The people complied with Gram's request. Gram promised to allow them to monitor the battles with the enemy from their compartments. It was fear of danger and not knowing what was going on which frightened the passengers. They agreed to remain off the bridge.

An enemy ship began firing upon the *Lares Compitales* almost as soon as it appeared. An atomic blast shook the ship but Robert's shield held. A blue beam lanced out at the enemy, vibrating the ship until the bombs blew in their cradles, destroying the ship. The path to the planet was clear.

Three fighting ships disguised as freighters were positioning themselves for bombing runs on the planet below. Robert radioed the planetary government. Gram did not wait for clearance but went straight in for a landing.

A squad of police surrounded Gram and Robert as they appeared. "What the devil, you are Earthmen. Are you the ones who radioed us about the enemy attack?"

"Yes, I'm sorry I couldn't take the time to identify myself," said Gram. "I am Gram Ancile and this is Robert."

"Gram Ancile," said the officer. "I've heard of you and your robot. If you are here to rescue the Terran colonists, you had better hurry. Their compound was under attack from ground forces before the bombers arrived. Troops are stationed near their homes."

The officer radioed his superiors of Gram's arrival. He spoke to Gram again. "I've been ordered to take you to the compound. I'm sorry my squad can't go with us, but the enemy is trying to rush your ship and they have to remain to set up a blockade."

"Don't worry about my ship. Robert can set up a shield an atomic blast can't penetrate. Tell them to go after the enemy," said Gram.

The officer led Gram and Robert to a nearby hover-craft. As soon as Gram cleared the space port, the enemy ships lashed out. Laser beams tore great holes into the street as the enemy fired on the hover-craft. Buildings disintegrated and crashed as the beams burned down at them. Robert managed to dodge the beams and had the *Lares Compitales* beam at the enemy. One of the attacking ships formed a miniature sun as the blue beam struck it hundreds of kilometers above the city.

Conventional bombs rained down where Gram traveled. Whole buildings leaped skyward as the bombs exploded, then the shock wave knocked over a dozen like dominoes. Debris fell on the craft, and Robert fought the controls as the shock wave battered them about. Gram wondered why the enemy did not use atomic weapons until he contacted Robert.

Hundreds of beams needled spaceward from the *Lares Compitales,* destroying the atomic weapons. Some of the conventional bombs managed to find their way past the ship's defenses. Robert had the enemy ship in the sight of one of the beams and the ship exploded in a ball of fire. The last of the enemy craft withdrew.

As he neared the village, one of the enemy hover-craft began firing. Robert dodged the heat beams and lashed out at the enemy. Their craft puddled into a heap of molten metal. The planetary troops began firing on Gram. The officer radioed them to cease.

The officer in charge of the troops shook Gram's hand and apologized for his trigger-happy boys. Gram smiled and said, "No damage done...can I prevail upon you and your squad to help me round up the Terrans and get them out of here before the enemy attacks?"

"Glad to help. The sooner we get the Terrans out of here the better. It won't be such a job to rid ourselves of the enemy once your people are gone," said the officer.

They hurried the people into the hover-craft. One or two complained that there was not time to gather their belongings, but most had the feeling the departure was taking an exceedingly long time. The trip back to the space port remained free from attack.

The police officer who showed Gram the Terran village reported some news from his superior. "The chief of police would like you to remain here at the space port for several days. The Galactic Federation has a fleet dispatched to our sector of space to capture or destroy the enemy warships. They would like to talk to you."

"I wish I dared to remain," said Gram. "Believe me when I tell you the enemy knows about the Federation fleet. They will disappear before the fleet can arrive but they will blast this planet apart if I remain. Half of your population will die trying to save us."

"How can you be so sure?"

"The same way I know the enemy has just destroyed your last planetary police cruiser," said Gram. "Your planet is helpless against an enemy attack. Check with the port authority, they'll tell you what I've said about your space fleet is true."

"Lightning curse Kala!" said the officer. "What you say is true. The police chief says you should leave before everything is destroyed."

"Thanks," said Gram. "The enemy will follow us when we leave. Your planet should be safe until the Federation ships arrive. Don't worry about us, we can shake the enemy from our tail after we've led them away from here."

Robert sealed the ship and lifted off from the planet. Enemy ships tried to blast him from space before he was free of the planetary pull and could switch to hyper space. Robert exploded the missiles before they reached the ship's shield. The enemy ships followed Gram. He grinned; let them follow him if they could.

Four minutes after Robert slipped into hyper space Gram had him return to normal space to change direction. This would fool the ships following him because they would not know when he would return to normal space. As soon as Robert flipped to normal space, the ship rocked from explosions. Robert flipped back to hyper space.

This shocked Gram—how did the enemy know to appear in normal space at that particular second and place? It should have been impossible for the enemy to know where he was in hyper space. He waited several minutes and ordered Robert to return to normal space and change direction.

Three ships built to look like freighters rushed him, firing lasers. One tried to ram him. Robert winked out of normal space.

Gram was sweating—how did they know his moves

before he did? He ordered Robert to remain in hyper space for an hour before attempting to return to normal space to change direction again.

On Gram's screens, almost out of range, he saw an enemy juggernaut ship when he returned to normal space. It was the most fearsome weapon ever designed for space battle. Bolt after bolt of pure energy ripped at the shield rocking the *Lares Compitales* like a cork in rough sea. Robert funneled more and more energy from the ship's power into the shield.

When Robert tried to switch to hyper drive the generators almost ground to a halt from the overload. The enemy juggernaut held them fast with their powerful tractor beams.

The ship was approaching for the kill with every erg of power they could pour into the drive. Robert was throwing everything at his command at the giant ship. It was like fighting a swordsman with a toothpick. It became an impossible task. They had more fire power and more reach.

The tendrils of hatred preceded the ship and surrounded Gram. He struggled, attempting to retreat until he remembered he could shield himself from the hatred. Once his shield was in place, the peace from the hatred was a blessing.

At first he languished in the peace, then anger began to build deep in Gram. It burned with a heat threatening to consume him. Who was the enemy who dared to attempt the extinction of the entire human race? Who was this enemy who hounded every man and woman to death? How did they dare?

Here was the enemy who had murdered his mother with poisonous vipers. Here was the enemy who killed his father a little over three years ago. Here was the enemy who wanted to harm little children, like Helene Horvath, before they had a chance to live their lives.... Here was the enemy!

Gram's anger grew like a fury; the *Lares Compitales* was much too small to contain it. Gram gathered all the energy the juggernaut could throw at the *Lares Compitales*. It was not enough. He reached and gathered all the energy and matter for light years around and packed it about the enemy ship. When the mass reached that of a star, a new sun was born.

His anger remained hungry; he reached out in space and converted enemy ships to dust that had attacked him as he left the Cele II system. The warships that bombed the planet were next; they novaed to miniature suns. Gram found hundreds of enemy ships scattered among the stars of this sector. He powdered them to nothingness.

Gram shivered. He had never been so angry before. It had been building all his life and now his anger fed itself; it left him exhausted. As weary as he was, he felt happy. He had learned the secret of teleportation and some other secrets he did not fully understand. He needed the council of the Llan, but first he needed rest.

The *Lares Compitales* appeared outside the dome on Bonne Amie. Gram teleported the passengers inside the dome. It was faster and he needed to rest. The Llan were startled but not surprised at how quickly Gram's talents had advanced. When Gram requested that no one disturb his rest, the Llan guarded his house with their limbs, gently removing those who crowded too closely.

Four days later, Gram stepped from his house. The humans and Llan welcomed him. The humans felt relief at seeing him. Rumors had sprung up he was dying. The Llan tried to dispel the rumor but it persisted. Everybody greeted Gram except one person—Helene.

Gram probed the dome for her. He discovered her in one of the trees the Llan had placed in the Horvath yard. Walking over to the tree, Gram glanced about, then spoke aloud. "I wonder where my girlfriend, Helene, is. I've gotten a great big present for her, but I guess she doesn't care. I guess I'll have to give it to some other little girl."

"Am I really your girlfriend? Did you really get something for me?" Helene jumped from the branch into Gram's arms. She hugged him with one arm and gripped the package with the other. After kissing him several times, she squirmed to the ground, tearing paper. There was a large blue-eyed doll almost as tall as Helene.

"It's beautiful! Can I show it to my mama? Don't go away, I'll be back."

Gram grinned to himself; sometimes it did not take much to change an angry child into a happy child. Gram felt Okursis's mind probe and he welcomed her. "Greetings and happy feeding!"

"Greetings, Gram. Welcome back to our planet. I saw you materialize the doll. Does it have permanence or will it disappear?"

"The doll is the genuine article, or at least it conforms with the knowledge contained in Robert's memory banks. Even the paper wrapper is real to the extent it's the same composition as wood pulp. Nothing phony like your trees."

"You sound proud of your new abilities," said Okursis.

"It's so easy once you know how," said Gram. "It makes me wonder why I couldn't do it before. Here, let me show you how it is done."

"Hmm," said Okursis. "It's similar to you learning to walk. When you were a baby, it was months before you were able to stand. You fell many times before you took your first step. Now you can run races without thinking about how you manage to place one foot in front of the other, yet you don't lose your balance. Now I know how it is done, I believe we can teach it to all the Terrans who have latent psi talents."

"I was wondering if you could pass it on to the others," said Gram.

"Certainly, and the Llan will be able to use these powers too," came Okursis's reply.

Helene came running back, still clutching the doll and with her mother in tow. Mrs. Horvath had a worried expression on her face. "I'm sorry, but you mustn't give Helene presents such as this."

Gram looked surprised; then he spoke. "Please let her keep it, Mrs. Horvath. I never had any brothers or sisters and I sort of adopted these three. I have presents for Steve and Randy."

"Oh, you think of them as brothers and a sister," she blurted out. "In that case, I guess it will be OK."

"Thanks, Mrs. Horvath," said Gram. "Next time I want to give them presents, I'll ask you first."

"That won't be necessary," Mrs. Horvath murmured, then left as she said something about checking something on the stove. Okursis probed Gram.

"You know what she thought?"

"Yes, that's why I made it clear I think of Helene as a sister. Be careful what you say because this little ball of energy can hear what we say," said Gram.

"I know you two are talking about me," probed Helene. "I can talk to you this way too."

"Hey!" thought Gram. "You've learned to talk with your mind!"

"Randy and Steve can hear our thoughts, too," said Okursis. "Now we're trying to teach them not to listen indiscriminately, that it is bad manners. They are naturally curious and pick up their latent abilities with amazing quickness once they are introduced to them."

"This is great! I thought for a while I might be the only one with such talents. At least I'm not a freak. It is a natural development of the race," said Gram.

"It confirms what we Llan believe," said Okursis. "All humans have this ability; some will utilize it better than others because they started at an earlier age. I believe the enemy knows you have developed the psi powers. This could be the reason they have stepped up the war to wipe out humans before they develop the psi talents."

"If you are right in your estimation of the enemy and they have stepped up activities, then I ought to set out immediately to round up any other human beings before the enemy kills them off," said Gram.

"Are you planning to leave now?" asked Okursis.

"No, I'll mentally probe the planets about the suns I haven't explored yet. If I sense Terrans, I'll teleport. The ship is too slow traveling and uses too much of my strength to teleport it about. I won't leave here until I actually locate humans."

"Gram, you're impulsive. I suggest you take Robert with

you," said Okursis. "You're not completely in control of your newfound powers yet. You're like a new babe and they may fail you at a crucial moment."

Helen wiggled into Gram's arms and placed her arms around his neck. "I want to go with you and Robert too!"

"No, Helene, your mother wouldn't allow it," said Gram. "It's too dangerous and I don't want to take a chance you might get hurt, because you are my little princess."

"I agree with Gram, it is too dangerous for a little girl," said Okursis. "If you're willing, Gram, to mind share with me, I'll go with you."

"Mind share," said Gram. "What is that?"

"The Llan mind shared with you when we helped you with the problem of where would be a good place to bring the other Terrans," said Okursis. "You relax your mind and let down any barriers you've erected. I must warn you, I'll share everything with you and you with me. I'm not able to probe as far as you nor can I teleport yet, as you do, but I can share your experiences and add my strength to yours in case they are required. Our combined mind will be much more powerful."

Gram was apprehensive at first when he felt the fingers of Okursis's consciousness slide across his mind. It became like having a second personality. It was similar to seeing two perspectives through the same set of eyes.

Okursis's personality reminded him of how he thought his mother must have been—gentle and wise. He knew every thought Okursis had, and he discovered she was old when the first human had built a fire. Age to her had no meaning. Gram-Okursis wondered who controlled Gram's body when two beings occupied one body; before the question formed, the answer became known. Gram was dominant in his own body, but after a little settling in, Gram-Okursis would operate as one mind with two sets of knowledge. Either party could break contact when desired. The Gram part relaxed completely.

Gram-Okursis decided they should explain to the people their thoughts on the enemy and why the enemy was so intense about ridding the universe of all human beings. Jack Rogger was skeptical.

"I've heard and read about human beings having powers to move objects, to hear silent messages and to predict the future, but if it is so, why is it we never see these fabled powers?"

"How did we get here from Cele II so quickly?" asked Gram-Okursis.

"I'm sorry I'm a cynic, but it could be you developed a new wrinkle for a warp drive, or it could be Bonne Amie isn't as far from Cele II as you think. I don't know the answer; but I need something more substantial than our so-called quick trip by space ship," said Rogger.

Gram-Okursis shrugged his shoulders and teleported Rogger to the opposite side of the group of people. Rogger looked about, dumbfounded. "Wha-a-at happened? How did I get over here?"

"I teleported you. It's different from psychokinesis or telekinesis. Because I moved you by teleportation, there is no time or distance crossed. I opened a hole in the fabric of all the dimensions, such as width, depth, height and time and I took you through the fabric where I put you down," said Gram-Okursis. "Now I'll move you back to your original place by telekinesis. It takes time to cross the distance."

When Gram-Okursis returned Rogger to his original position, Rogger continued to talk. "You claim we all can move people about like that?"

"All of you won't learn how to use the psi powers to their fullest extent. If you crawl on your hands and knees for fifty years, you'll develop certain muscles for locomotion. Then you see someone else walking upright; you can't expect to be as proficient at walking as the person who has done it all his life. Most of you will develop some talent," said Gram-Okursis. "The children will develop the power to its fullest extent. Some of you older people will develop it, too, because you're already using the powers. You've been calling them hunches. I believe all of you will develop the ability to receive telepathic thoughts, if you will let the Llan teach you."

A murmur passed through the crowd and Gram-Okursis continued. "Helene Horvath has already developed the ability to listen and speak telepathically. She speaks with the Llan directly."

Randy and Steve piped up in the conversation. "We can hear the Llan talking to Gram and Helene!"

A chuckle passed through the crowd. Jack Rogger continued his protest. "I don't know as though I like the thought of everyone listening to my thoughts. It would get to the point where there is no privacy."

"Not true," said Gram-Okursis. "Your inner thoughts are your own. If you know nothing of psi powers, you still have learned to erect barriers around your most secret thoughts. I can probe but it would take a terrific effort on my part to read thoughts you've screened from me. You'd know what I was up to and you'd be fighting me."

Gram-Okursis searched for a good simile, then continued. "It's like clothes; everyone knows humans are born naked, but no one is afraid to travel among other people. You hide the nakedness with clothes. The same is true of your inner thoughts; you can hide them behind a shield, which you've already developed."

Waiting for Jack Rogger to voice further objections, Gram-Okursis stopped speaking. He seemed to be the spokesperson for the opposition. When he remained silent, Gram-Okursis continued speaking.

"The Llan are the secret of learning the psi-power. Our two races have a symbiotic relationship in which we both benefit. We develop our psi talents and they develop emotions and other horizons with their minds that wouldn't be possible without us. We are each other's catalyst."

Gram-Okursis gave the people a chance to voice any oppositions they might have. When no one voiced an opinion Gram-Okursis continued.

"It is the consensus of the Llan that the enemy suspects I have developed the psi talents. The enemy believes we will use these powers for evil and therefore we must be destroyed."

A ripple of protest traveled through the crowd. Gram-Okursis paused again to give others a chance to speak.

"In my last battle with the enemy I almost lost until I developed a new talent. At the present stage of my development, I don't believe I'll lose any future encounters with the enemy. Still, it won't hurt you to be prepared if I do lose to the enemy. I want you to work actively with the Llan for the purpose of protecting yourselves.

"The danger for Terrans still out there with the enemy has trebled since I rescued you. I must locate them immediately. First, before I leave you, I want to demonstrate an ability called mind sharing. If you will allow this to happen between yourselves and the Llan your ability to learn the talents will be greatly improved."

Gram-Okursis stopped speak directly to the crowd and spoke to Helene, whom he was still holding. "Do you trust me completely, Helene? May Okursis and I enter your mind and reside as we are doing in my body?"

"Yes, Gram-Okursis."

Upon her agreement Gram-Okursis continued to speak to the people. "Helene has just agreed to mind share with me and Okursis. Okursis and I are already mind sharing but just to tell you we are mind sharing proves nothing. Mind sharing with a five-year-old will prove what I say. What you are about to hear isn't the normal speech of a five-year-old."

The settling-in process in Helene's mind proved much easier than it had been for Okursis to settle into Gram's mind. Helene welcomed Gram-Okursis. The affinity of Helene for Gram-Okursis was greater than it had been between Gram and Okursis.

This was due to the fact Gram and Helene's minds were similar. Helene's mind was immature but basically the same as Gram's. Okursis found it easier, too, because now she was used to the different patterns of thought since she shared with Gram. Okursis lacked an id that could be drawn upon as a well of power; she had the superego, but no id. Helene-Gram-Okursis spoke to the group.

"Normally, you wouldn't expect a five-year-old child to be spouting advanced physics so this should be a good demonstration that we, Gram and Okursis, are also present in Helene's mind.

"The term energy level refers to discrete amounts of energy which atoms and molecules can have with respect to their electron or nuclear structure. An atom is stable only when it exists in the state for which the quantum numbers of its electrons give the lowest total energy. The energy of an atom may be increased to a higher level by having an electron excite to another state represented by a different set of allowed quantum numbers.

"The human mind does this when thought is generated. The superego normally is the tap or the control of the id which is the well of psi power. By using quantum light, heat or electrical energy, the ego with training can convert this energy to psi talents, which is the atom's energy increased to a much higher level by the brain.

"Now that I have scientifically explained how I use my ability through the mouth of a five-year-old, do any of you doubt Okursis and I are mind sharing with Helene?"

Helene-Gram-Okursis probed the crowd and found the people believed. Helene-Gram-Okursis continued speaking. "I urge you to cooperate with the Llan. I, Gram, have not developed the talent of precognition yet, but I have a deep rooted feeling I'll need all the extrasensory powers it is possible for you to develop.

"Gram-Okursis is leaving Helene now. Gram-Okursis is going to probe about the galaxy searching for other human beings."

Gram-Okursis watched with his probe as Jack Rogger and the others questioned Helene about extrasensory perception. Her childish answers convinced them it had been Gram and Okursis speaking through Helene's mouth. Gram-Okursis left Bonne Amie. He used their combined will to probe for Earthmen.

ELEVEN

Gram-Okursis noted a hair-thin thread, shining with its own light, rising from Okursis's body, Gram's body and Helene's body and joining the probe that housed Gram's and Okursis's consciousness. The joining to Helene's body puzzled Gram-Okursis for a moment until he realized whenever it involved mind sharing there would always be this hair-thin thread joining them.

Helene was not with Gram-Okursis; he made sure of it. There was no telling what dangers this adventure involved and he did not want her ensnared in it.

Robert, normally, could not mind share because he was a created mind without the breath of life. His mind was cold. It was like walking in a cold, echoing building—it was empty of life. Gram-Okursis had to make an attachment which Robert could use to amplify Gram-Okursis's signal from afar, if it became necessary for Gram-Okursis to tap Robert's power source. As Gram-Okursis rose from the surface of Bonne Amie, he felt more secure to see four threads that tied him to life on the planet.

The teleport brought him back to the Pleiades star group. Gram-Okursis held the probe far out in space so he could survey the entire cluster at once.

Each race had an essence different from the next. The Llan's was a rich, heavy essence, pleasing to the senses. Human beings had a light, almost elusive essence that could be hard to detect at times. No two species had the same essence and it was impossible to mistake an essence once it had been sampled and identified.

He found many essences he could not identify; some the Gram part of the probe had dealt with in the past and he could recognize these essences. On some of the planets the probe found the writhing dark coils of hatred. The Gram part could not stand the choking, vomit-inducing sensation the wiggling coils produced. Yet part of his mind longed to approach and identify the race to which the enemy belonged.

As soon as Gram-Okursis probed a planet and found no trace of human beings, he would move to another planet or star system. The time lapse for exploring each planet was less than twelve minutes, but this was too slow for Gram-Okursis. It would take years to travel to all the known sections of the galaxy.

Gram-Okursis teleported back in space to a point where he saw the entire Pleiades group; here Gram-Okursis tried something different. He allowed the probe to drift in any direction it chose in order to home in on the essence of human beings. There was an instant of hesitation, when the probe merely drifted, then the probe teleported to a small sun in the group.

A grizzled asteroid miner was admiring the street scenes and the sounds of a small town when the Gram-Okursis probe approached. There were several things wrong. The man was relaxing and not fully aware of the dangers lurking about him.

The enemy had laid a trap for him and they were waiting for him to cross the street. Gram-Okursis touched his fear center; the man leaped to an archway with his laser drawn.

Gram-Okursis teleported Gram's body and Robert to the archway where the miner had taken cover. "We're going to need to clear the crowd off the streets so we can pick out the enemy without killing a half-dozen innocent bystanders."

"What the—" growled the miner as he whipped around to face Gram and Robert. "Oh!... Sonny, that's a good way to get killed, sneaking around behind people in dark corners. I didn't see you and the robot back there. In fact, I didn't know there was another human being within a light year of this place.

"Now...what's this about the enemy being over there across the street?"

Gram-Okursis smiled from Gram's body. "I said there's about a dozen of the enemy waiting for you to cross the street. We have to get the innocent bystanders out of the way."

"Son, you'd better be right. I don't relish being locked up in the local hoosegow, or being put in protective custody. Watch this!"

The miner let out a bellow and started shooting at the side of the building, the street lights and anything else except the humanoids in the street. The effect was like magic. The humanoids scrambled for safety and within seconds the street was clear.

A laser beam tore a hole in the stone archway above the miner's head. He snapped off two shots in the direction from which the beam had come. A volley of beams burned holes all around the miner. Gram-Okursis teleported the miner to the back of the archway out of harm's way and he spoke.

"Let my robot attend to the enemy."

A beam lanced out from Robert's forehead and a whole section of the building crumpled into dust. The miner peered over Gram-Okursis's shoulder, touching Gram-Okursis as he did.

"I like that robot of yours, lotta fire power. I could use 'em to open new mine shafts on some of the rocks I mine," said the miner. "How come I saw a tree and your face in your image when I touched you?"

"I am mind sharing with a Llan named Okursis. Her real body looks something like a tree with no leaves," said Gram-Okursis. "I hope it doesn't upset you."

"You don't act as if it was against your will, so I guess it's OK. By the way, my name is Sandy McShane. Who are you?"

"I'm Gram Ancile. I've introduced you to Okursis and my robot's name is Robert."

"Happy to meet 'cha. Let's split," said Sandy.

"Not so fast," said Gram-Okursis "There are more of them. They want you dead."

"Well, how about yourself?"

"They have no idea I'm here yet."

Robert sent another beam crashing into the same building about three stories above the ground. Rubble tumbled to the street below. Gram-Okursis stepped into the open as he heard the sound of a turbine engine roar to life.

He waited; there was another vehicle. As it roared to life, Gram-Okursis hurled a thought at the two vehicles and they winked out of existence.

In the distance, they could hear the wailing sirens of the approaching police.

"Well, sonny, we're in for it now," said Sandy. "By the way, I like the way you and your robot dealt with the enemy. How about you and I teaming up after we settle with John Bull?"

"The law is no problem," said Gram-Okursis. "Certainly, we'd appreciate you joining our group."

"Joining a group?" questioned Sandy. "I don't know about joining a group. Makes too big a target for the enemy."

"Before you say no positively, how about meeting the Earth people first," said Gram-Okursis. "We aren't in any danger from the enemy on Bonne Amie. You saw how I handled the enemy; we'll teach you too."

"Well, I'd like a visit. I haven't seen any Terrans in the last five years," said Sandy.

"OK, follow me through this archway." Gram-Okursis darkened the shadows to shield them from any viewers on the street. He teleported inside the dome on Bonne Amie.

Sandy blinked in the bright sunlight of Haven. "What the devil..."

Gram-Okursis laughed at Sandy's reaction. "I guarantee you this is not part of hell, but a safe haven for Earthmen. They'll explain everything to you. I must leave now because there are other Terrans out there in danger."

Okursis removed her probe from Gram's mind. "I don't have someone, as your Robert, to care for my needs while we're teleporting and probing. I must feed myself. After searching with you, I'm certain you can control your talents well enough to make me as useful as a sixth finger on each hand."

Gram felt a little lonely when Okursis withdrew her probe. It felt like leaving home for the first time, leaving all those you loved behind. Gram watched as Robert administered to his body, then he teleported. He allowed his intuitive nature to seek out the location of human beings.

It was wasn't always on a planet where Gram found Terrans. Often they were aboard star ships fleeing the enemy. The enemy was always nearby since they had intensified their war on the Terrans.

Gram found two girls, one thirteen and the other fourteen, on a star ship fleeing the enemy. Their mother had died on the last planet they were on during an enemy raid. The girls had sold their parents' possessions to buy tickets to the next star system, hoping to evade the enemy assault.

Unknown to them or the star ship crew, the liner contained explosives set to go off an hour before docking at their destination. Gram's sudden appearance on the bridge created havoc among the officers. They rushed him, but stopped short as they smashed into the force field Gram had created around himself.

"If I can appear on your bridge at will, it should prove to you that I can protect myself as well. I'm not a terrorist attempting to take over this ship. Please call the captain to the bridge," said Gram.

It seemed Gram had no more than made his request when a short birdlike humanoid stepped into the room. "Who are you and what do you want on my ship?"

"Captain, I am Gram Ancile, and I'm here to warn you the enemy has planted explosives aboard your ship. They will explode prior to your reaching your destination."

"I've heard of Gram Ancile, but they say he travels with a robot."

Gram pointed his finger and said, "Oh, you mean him."

Robert materialized before the pop-eyed captain. This did not convince him. "How do I know you are who you say you are? Why should I believe a bomb has been planted aboard my ship?"

"You have two Terran passengers aboard," said Gram. "Audette Beaulieu, age thirteen, and Jeanette Beaulieu, age fourteen. Their mother was killed on the planet where they booked passage. They sold everything to pay for the tickets and the enemy has planted explosives aboard the kill the girls."

"No one plants explosives on my ship. I check every item of cargo," said the captain.

"I don't have time to argue with you, Captain," Gram said. He teleported those on the bridge, except the astrogator, to the hold having a common bulkhead with the engine room. "The explosives are in these crates you took aboard at the last minute. Robert, open the crates and show the captain."

Robert ripped the sides out of three crates, exposing hundreds of pounds of detonite, an explosive capable of demolishing all traces of the ship. "The gods have mercy, I've got to get the detonite off my ship before it goes off!" the captain exclaimed.

"Robert and I will take care of the explosives for you if you will loan us one of the emergency life boats and return to normal space. We'll cast the explosive adrift in the life boat."

The captain agreed and ordered the ship to return to normal space. Gram let Robert carry the explosives aboard the emergency life boat. When the life boat drifted from the ship, Gram detonated the explosives.

Gram could have removed the explosives and the girls without the ship's crew ever knowing he had been aboard. If he had, then the enemy would know he had developed his psi powers. This way, the enemy would believe Robert was doing all the miracles rather than Gram.

When the captain introduced Gram to the girls, they refused to leave with Gram and Robert. They trusted no one. Finally, the captain ordered them to leave for the safety of his ship. They became almost hysterical. Gram paused, then spoke aloud to Robert. "Bring Helene to me."

Gram made Robert invisible for a second while he teleported Helene into Robert's arms. Then he caused the two to become visible. Gram had explained the situation to Helene as he teleported her aboard the ship. Helene smiled and held out her hand to Jeanette, the eldest girl.

"Hi, I'm Helene Horvath, and this is my friend Gram Ancile and his robot, Robert. If you will trust us, Robert will take us to a safe place. Come on, they won't let anyone hurt you."

Jeanette hesitated for several moments; then she smiled and grasped Helene's hand. She motioned to her sister to take Helene's other hand. Gram teleported, confident the captain would talk of the wondrous robot who teleported people about the universe.

Gram gave Helene the chore of introducing the two girls to the rest of the people in the dome. He staggered into his home. Gram threw himself on his bed and flashed a message to Okursis and Ihan to wake him in four hours. His sleep was dreamless. His psyche slowly restored its reserves.

He fought to open his eyes when Okursis called telepathically. Gram wanted to sleep for eight hours more but he commanded his blood sugar level up to normal for full awareness. Then Gram raised the oxygen content in his blood and was awake.

Outside, Mrs. Horvath and Mrs. Roggers had set a table under the trees and were serving trays of hot food. The two Beaulieu girls served Gram his breakfast. They flashed him shy smiles and almost immediately Helene climbed into Gram's lap when she saw the girls being friendly with him.

Gram ate until he thought he would burst. At last, he sat back, enjoying his second cup of a hot drink. The other settlers gathered around waiting for any news he had to offer them. They wanted to know how he had rescued the girls. Then they wanted to know if he had had any contact with their friends who were still out there with the enemy.

This gave Gram an idea. He asked them to concentrate on the people they knew on the various planets. Gram gathered the information from each of them and told them he was planning to use the information to search for their friends.

Reading their thoughts was embarrassing to Gram. He was becoming a legend among them. The people felt nothing could touch them as long as Gram was their protector.

The situation on the various Federation planets was changing, too. Gram and his robot became superheroes, not only to the humans but in the news media. They spread the story of his rescue of the girls and saving the star ship. Anytime Gram appeared on a planet the government was more than happy to see him.

Sometimes the government used the media to advertise to the enemy that the Terran colony on their planet no longer existed after Gram removed them. Most of the governments were happy the Terrans had found a place where they would be safe. All enjoyed the publicity it generated among their own peoples.

After Gram had extricated a hundred or so people, he came upon an intricate plot to kill the Terran colonists in a certain building and him if he attempted to rescue them. Gram probed the building before he made any attempt to rescue the people. The enemy had planned well.

Any additional weight on the floors of the building would detonate explosives. They hid scanners so every millimeter of the building was covered should Gram attempt to remove the people.

Gram chuckled to himself. He had no fear that he would

set off the trap by rescuing the Terrans, but he did want to cause the enemy to relax their terrorist tactics on the other Terrans he had not discovered yet. The enemy must believe they had destroyed the human beings in the building.

He froze time and removed the people to Bonne Amie. Next he moved the citizens of the planet who were in danger to a safe place. He replaced the people and the citizens with protoplasm that resembled the Terrans and the citizens. He returned time to normal and projected protoplasmic images of himself and Robert entering the building. The thoughts of satisfaction that escaped from the enemy brought a smile to Gram.

Something tickled about the edges of Gram's consciousness. He could not quite make out the essence emanating from the enemy; hatred cloaked it too heavily for him. He knew he would recognize it if he could ever penetrate the hatred.

As the building blew skyward in a glut of flame and smoke, Gram tried again to identify the enemy. The wall of hatred, lacking all color and light, was dark beyond all measurement and concealed the enemy. He could not perceive the enemy essence in the wall of hatred. He extended his probe into the dark coiling mass.

It choked him. He gasped and tried to clear himself of it. It clutched and sucked at his very soul. Gram panicked. He screamed for Robert to get him out of the darkness. Robert exerted his full power to return Gram to his body. It fused Robert's circuits and the Llan had to replace them before Robert was functional again.

This worried Okursis and Ihan; what effect did the contact with the enemy have on Gram? As they probed Gram, they discovered there were no new shields erected against the enemy. Gram recognized them checking over his mind and he mumbled sleepily to Ihan and Okursis, then relaxed into a deep sleep.

He had exhausted every erg of energy in his body and he needed to replace it. The Llan soothed him, noting his psyche had grown to the size of a basketball. He was still cloaked in the impenetrable shell.

TWELVE

Gram heard the alarm bells ringing as he ran up great halls toward the sound. He climbed and his head ached. It was a long trip. He leaped into the air and it became water. He swam to the surface.

He awoke. Gram glanced at the time. He had been asleep thirty hours. He moved listlessly into the refresher and saw the reflection of his face. He body looked healthy enough; only his eyes betrayed his exhaustion. The constant use of his talents had drained the well of his psyche and his reserve strength was depleted.

Gram asked Robert to bring him food. Elfrum heard him and flashed, "I'm surprised you're awake. You should rest; Robert and I can tend to your needs while you sleep."

"I was awakened by a call from the outside. There is

danger and I am needed."

"You are overreaching your mental capacity. You are endangering yourself, and you may burn out," said Elfrum.

Ihan and Okursis joined in on the conversation. Okursis's thoughts betrayed her concern. "Gram, using your mental capabilities can be compared to learning endurance running. You don't start running twenty kilometers the first time."

Gram finished his meal but nothing satisfied the inner hunger. "I know what you are saying, Okursis, but there isn't time to build up my strengths. Who else can rescue the Terrans, if I don't? Do you think I should leave them to the enemy while I rest and regain my strength? Who else in the dome is ready? Steve, Randy and Helene are probably the most developed talents, but I can't send babes before the enemy. Sandy McShane is the next most developed talent, thanks to his using his 'hunches.' After him are the Beaulieu girls, Jeanette and Audette. None could face the enemy or protect the Terrans."

Ihan made a sound that whispered through Gram's mind. "You are right, Gram. You must go. Your only hope of relief is that the development of the group's talents goes more swiftly. We Llan must redouble our efforts."

Gram reached out and touched his three friends. "Don't blame yourselves; we Terrans are slow students. I will be all right. Remember, I have Robert to help."

"Yes, and you remember you fused Robert's circuits the last time you had to use him," scolded Okursis.

"Yes, ma'am, I'll be more careful," Gram promised Okursis. "Now I must go, someone is in danger."

With the promise to Okursis, Gram probed into space. It was a subether signal from a far sector of the Federation. The person sending the signal was not a Terran but a commander in the Galactic Federation fleet. His fleet was guarding a planet sheltering over two hundred human beings. The enemy slowly pounded the commander's fleet back toward the planet's surface.

Three juggernauts had burned great holes into the Federation fleet. Gram reached out to them and teleported the enemy fleet into the heart of the star. No ship's screens built could withstand the forces generated in the heart of a stellar furnace.

Gram teleported his body and Robert to the surface where the commander sent the message. The commander's jaw dropped as Gram and Robert appeared. "I've heard your robot possessed great powers, but I didn't think they included going through solid walls!"

"Robert has more spectacular talents than traveling through walls. He destroyed the enemy to save your fleet from destruction," said Gram. "I see you have two hundred six Terran colonists here. I suggest Robert be allowed to take these people to safety before you and I talk about your plan to ensnare the enemy."

If the commander was astonished as Gram appeared before him, it surprised him more to hear Gram knew his plan that he had not voiced previously. He followed Gram into the hall. One of the crowd recognized Robert from pictures and shouted, "It's Robert, the robot, and Gram Ancile, the defender!"

A hush settled over the crowd. Gram moved to center stage where he spoke. "I'm here to take you to a planet where the enemy can't find you. Come up on the stage in groups of fifteen or twenty and Robert will transport you to Bonne Amie, your new home."

The people started shoving and pushing. "Don't crowd the stage! This whole operation won't take more than a few minutes."

He teleported the people almost as fast as they arrived on the stage and formed groups. As they arrived on Bonne Amie, the Llan and the settlers moved them clear of the arrival area.

They stopped crowding Gram and Robert as soon as they realized there was not a waiting time as they reached the stage. The first hundred fifty had been teleported before Gram began to feel completely drained. He drew heavily on Robert's power, but Robert's design would not support the amounts of power required to teleport. Gram drew upon all the energy about him so as not to cause too heavy a drain on Robert. Even the hall became chilly as Gram used the heat energy.

It came down to the last ten people to teleport, including the Federation Commander. Gram had to rest from the task; his energy levels were so low he felt dizzy. It was as though he had lost his sense of balance; he groped for a chair.

A red-headed beauty rushed to his aid, helping him into the chair. Gram felt sparks race up his arm as her hands touched him. He could not explain the strong emotional attraction he felt. In spite of his weariness, Gram gave her his full attention. Gram could not deny the magnetism.

Her dark red hair fluffed about her face, framing it like a valentine. Her eyes were deep blue, which were frank in her admiration of Gram. Gram could smell a hint of fragrance. It was a part of her as much as the color of her unblemished tan. Gram had to be near her.

"My name is Flora Campbell. Have we met before?"

"I don't know.... I...do you sing? I have this feeling you have sung to me. I heard you."

Neither realized they were holding hands. They did not realize the restlessness of the people until the commander spoke. "Young man, this is no time to become a romantic! Have your robot transport the rest of us to Bonne Amie."

Gram sighed; he felt so weak and tired. He flashed a message to Robert. "I'm leaving you here. I don't have the strength to teleport this last group. I'll give you the signal and you'll have to supply the power to do the teleporting. I cannot spare the energy to probe Elfrum, Okursis and Ihan to inform them."

"It is my opinion you should conserve all your energy, do not waste it. I advise you to wait until you have rested to teleport. It would tax me to the utmost to teleport you to Bonne Amie. You use tremendous amounts of quantum energies converted to your sophisticated power to teleport. I doubt I can supply the amount you need," Robert flashed to Gram.

"I have to chance your ability. I can't wait. The enemy will reinforce their position here if any of us remain. I can't stand a powerful onslaught. We must get back to Bonne Amie where I can rest," said Gram.

Robert cleared his circuits, anticipating the shock of the power drain. Neither Gram nor Robert realized how much Gram contributed to the power drain when teleporting. Robert's circuits withstood the drain about half as long as required to complete the trip. There was an internal explosion, then Robert's casing melted.

Gram wrapped himself about the essence of the beings with him. Something was madly wrong—he had to complete the teleport or he and the others were lost. They drifted toward eternity. Gram screamed two words.

"Helene! Okursis!"

* * *

Helene stood up with a start. Gram had called her for help. She had to go to him, where was he? "Gram...Gram!"

Okursis got the message at the same instant; immediately she mind shared with the other Llan and they sought out Helene. As soon as Helene joined the probe, it began to search out the hair-thin threads that joined Gram, Okursis and Helene. It stretched out over the top of the galaxy, then to a point where it disappeared into another dimension.

They probed through the dimensions searching for Gram. Okursis supplied the formula for teleporting she had learned when she and Gram mind shared. The others of the probe followed her commands.

Gram disappeared between dimensions, somewhere out among the different planes he crossed to teleport.

It was something akin to piloting a space craft; if you had plenty of fuel, you punched in the coordinates of your destination, then sat back and relaxed until you arrived. Run out of fuel somewhere along the line, and someone will spend much time looking for you.

In one of the dimensions they searched, thoughts appeared as light. The common mind projected a call for Gram and it scintillated into color flashes. It burst as a brilliant white light and the edges flickered until the center changed to yellow, then to orange, to red, forever deepening in color until all the energy was dissipated. Each new thought brought new flashes until the probe realized what happened and limited its thoughts. Satisfied Gram was not in this plane, the mind moved on.

The most horrifying dimension was the one where they saw time segments splintering from their main destiny, showing possible futures of each of the members of the common mind. In some of the destinies shown, they found Gram down the path of the future, in another they were lost with him, another showed them being too late to rescue Gram.

The third dimension had three planes or sides: height, width and depth. The fourth dimension has four planes or sides: height, width, depth and time. These were simple dimensions that the common mind could cope with. It became confusing when paradox became one of the planes of the dimensions.

It became nearly impossible to maintain what was fact and what only appeared as fact. The common mind did not have enough scope to maintain a sense of balance while traveling in the higher levels of the continuum.

The probe returned to the third dimension and split into its individual beings. Helene protested. "We've got to find Gram. He's lost. He needs us."

Ihan tried to soothe her. "Helene, my dear, we didn't abandon Gram. We're exhausted and must feed to restore ourselves. Tomorrow we'll join the rest of the settlers to our probe so we can start again. Meanwhile, I'll contact them and explain the situation."

The sun had not cleared the horizon the following morning when the settlers' minds linked with Helene, Okursis and the other Llan. Helene, with Okursis's guidance, took over control of the new probe. It was like an ungainly baby attempting its first step. It fell and rolled at first, then it stood wobbling, taking its first step, then another and another. It soared like a graceful bird; its power appeared unlimited.

The new mind probe approached the dimensions as though they were a part of a single fabric in which each thread had to be searched to locate Gram. It was similar to searching for a single speck of lint on a large tapestry. The mind traveled the dimensions swiftly, sorting and sifting the information as it searched.

Beyond the fourth dimension, time was one of the planes forming the higher dimensions. It was frozen relative to the third dimension; but to any level above the fourth dimension, time appeared to pass to the travelers. A person could spend a week in the fifth dimension, only to discover absolutely nothing had changed in the third. When paradox appeared to the probe, it was no longer confusing; it became a new mode of thinking.

The probe traveled to the *N*th dimension and found no Gram. It returned to the third dimension to rest at Ihan's insistence. He did not want the new probe to overtax itself and become lost in the continuum. Helene cried herself to sleep.

A week's time passed in the third dimension and the probe had not located a trace. The settlers were becoming discouraged and were thinking of Gram as lost forever. Helene refused to allow any such thoughts to penetrate her being. When the others began talking to Ihan and Okursis about giving up the search, Helene formed a song to sing to Gram. She claimed he would hear the song and know they were near.

The song smelled of lilacs, it was as bright as sunlight, it scintillated like a rainbow, it sounded of soft music, it tasted of fresh cool water, it felt like a baby's skin and it was filled with love. If Gram could sense it, he would answer as they passed through his level.

Again the mind traveled the continuum from the highest to the lowest. Nothing. The conclusion the probe formed came to the forefront: Gram was incapable of answering. The common mind widened the song so any human hearing the song would know help was nearby. This way, one of Gram's passengers could hear and answer.

* * *

Gram remained unthinking. The tiny reserve left to him concentrated on keeping the atoms of the Terrans together so they would not drift away, lost forever without form. The common mind passed twice without Gram's knowledge. When the bandwidth of the song widened, there was a stirring within Gram's charge.

Flora Campbell recognized the part represented by the Llan. They were the same who had asked her to sing to Gram a long time ago, when Gram first developed the shield to protect his psyche from the enemy.

She had failed to crack open his armor the first time, because she was on the outside trying to enter. This time she would not fail; she was inside. There could be no blocking her out. She burst into song.

The entire dimension radiated her song. She sang of love. She sang of heroes. She sang of her man and their future. She touched him and he responded. The common mind surrounded Gram and his charges.

Gram reached to Flora and his essence glowed. He touched the common mind and tapped the wells of the human psyches to complete his teleport. None of Gram's charges ever realized they had been in trouble, except Flora.

Flora's talent had developed enough that she could mind share as well as being telepathic. Flora recognized Gram as her lifemate and would not leave his side. As soon as Helene saw Flora, she knew she had been fooling herself into believing she would someday marry Gram.

Helene felt sad, but at the same instant as she realized Gram was Flora's mate, she saw and recognized her future mate among the newly arrived boys. The boy would never realize how he managed to attract the love of such a beauty as the future Helene Horvath, although both Helene and Flora knew. The two girls hugged each other and wished each other a happy life.

The newcomers were made welcome and the common mind broke into its component parts. Elfrum carried Gram to his house as Helene and Flora followed. Gram found the strength to undress and climb into bed. He was too weak to use his telepathic abilities so he spoke aloud.

"Helene, I want to thank you for the beautiful song you formed. With Flora's help, I was able to use it to tap the resources of the Terrans. Flora..."

Gram gazed into her eyes, then slipped into unconsciousness.

Flora's mind shared with him as he slipped into a coma-like sleep. She eased the depth to which his mind sank. She caressed him with her thoughts and her love. Slowly, the dangerously low level of his psyche began to fill. Flora formed a permanent link with Gram's psyche; never again would either one be without contact to the other.

It was a common bond. Gram, in his unconscious state, welcomed the link. It was like having another arm. Each person was an individual, entirely complete now.

THIRTEEN

As Gram slept, he dreamed. He was running through fields of uncut grass, dotted with tenacious flowers that the grasses could not crowd. The sky was blue with fluffy white cotton balls of clouds drifting. The yellow sun smiled upon Gram. This was a racial memory of the past. This was Earth and he was home.

At his side was a rainbow image. In this rainbow was Flora's beautiful face, watching and caring for Gram. Everywhere Gram leaped and frolicked, the rainbow of Flora appeared. Gram stopped and touched the rainbow face often, just to make sure it was with him. The rainbow of Flora would respond by pouring forth her love. This filled the well of Gram's psyche.

After a time, Gram came to a lake and he dove in. Flora's

rainbow followed. Gram swam toward the surface; his many friends met him. Helene—whom he hugged and kissed. Ihan, Okursis and Elfrum—he grasped and hugged the three of them. The rest of the Horvath family—George gripped his hand; Mrs. Horvath kissed him on the cheek. The Beaulieu girls—Audette and Jeanette each hugged him. Jack and Phyllis Roggers and their son Tim—Sam and Betty Coulter—Gus and Rose Orosz and their son Aton—Sandy McShane—and the rest of the settlers all greeted Gram. Gram paused to thank each with spirited feelings. These were the people who had rescued him from the depths of the continuum.

Gram awoke to full consciousness. Flora, Helene and a limb of Elfrum were in the bedroom. All the rest waited outside; now they knew of his condition through his contact with them as he approached consciousness.

Helene leaped upon the bed with Gram, smothering him with kisses and hugs. "I'm so happy you're OK. Flora sat and held your hand all the time you were asleep."

Gram squeezed Helene and looked up at Flora's tired face. He requested permission of Flora to probe her body and he explained what he planned. She nodded. Gram purged her body of the toxic poisons in her bloodstream and removed the viruses that were building to a dangerous level, and she felt refreshed as though she had slept for nine hours.

It took so little of Gram's time that he answered Helene almost as fast as she finished speaking. "I recognized Flora's rainbow essence when I was unconscious. And yours, you little pixie, reminds me of a closed flower, not ready to bloom; but it has a pleasant essence!"

"You mean that's what you see of me with your mind?" asked Helene.

"Yes."

"Ha! You look like a giant shield with a shiny light coming from it and you smell of goodness and kindness!" Gram never examined his essence before so he felt embarrassed when Helene explained what she saw.

Flora smiled and touched his hand. "It's a very good

essence, be proud of it. No one wears such a cloak in the universe. You are a very special person to all beings, although few recognize the importance."

"How do you know all this?" quizzed Gram.

"I sense it," she said. "Just as you sense that you and I are very special to each other. There can never be any other person for either of us. Even Helene knows this. She's found the person who'll mean the same to her someday. The boy of her dreams doesn't know his fate yet, but I'm sure Helene will be sure to remind him."

Okursis entered into the telepathic communications. "Are you well enough for this prolonged visit?"

Gram laughed and invited her to probe him. When she had satisfied herself he was healthy, she withdrew her probe but remained in contact. "You have better control of your talents, but we, the humans and the Llan, want you to learn more about them before you meet with the Galactic Federation Commander.

"He is impatient to meet with you, but we keep him shielded from you. The human population agrees with the Llan, you should relax before seeing him. They are keeping him busy elsewhere until we feel you're ready to meet him."

"I know why he wants to speak with me," said Gram. "He has a plan to trap the enemy."

"All the more reason to wait," said Okursis. "We, the Llan, feel you need time to develop your newly found powers. Flora will be the greatest help since she is the most mature in her psi talents. We Llan will help you in any capacity possible."

As all the females withdrew so Gram could use his refresher and dress, Gram flashed a message at Elfrum. "You remind me of a cedar, that essence is like a breath of spring air."

"I'm happy you are pleased with it," said Elfrum. "You remind me of a giant Llan which blocks out several suns. None has such an essence."

He finished dressing and stepped outside. Gram blinked in the bright sunlight. He took Flora's hand and carried Helene in his other arm. All the people shouted their greetings. Since most had not developed their abilities with telepathy, the conversation remained verbal.

Okursis took the commander out on a sand sled so the human population could greet Gram.

The few houses had grown to a small town now and were reminiscent of an Earth village which Robert had shown Gram. It was beautiful and restful—a sleepy little town nestled in the hills away from any bright lights or any hustle and bustle. The humans relaxed for the first time in several centuries.

All wanted to talk to him and show Gram their community. Gram made sure every human got a chance to speak, although Gram kept Flora and Helene close. Each family showed Gram how they had arranged their house differently from their neighbor's house.

What truly amazed Gram was how the houses reflected the essence of each family. Some were very orderly with no decorations, others were ornate, some were messy, some were quiet, and others were loudly decorated. All reflected the essence of the family or of the individual who lived in the house. If a family had children, then their essence reflected in the house.

The greatest pride of the village seemed to be the fields of grain. Gram got the vaguest hint of a shield in all the people's minds, of something deeply hidden in the recesses of the subconscious; Gram did not pry. Humans resented invasion of their privacy. Often they would welcome you into their minds, if you requested permission. They had all learned this much about their talents.

Later in the day, Gram, Helene and Flora swam with the children. The Llan had enlarged the swimming area to accommodate the entire community. Madeah sprouted many pseudopod limbs for everyone to use as diving boards. The physical contact with Madeah was helping the children develop their talents. None was aware of this except Flora and Gram.

Gram would dive and chase Flora as she swam away from him. She would call upon Helene to help her escape Gram.

Flora knew every one of his strategies to get her in his arms but the only time he could catch her was when she willed it to happen.

The three of them played until Mrs. Horvath called Helene to supper. She offered to set places for Gram and Flora, but Flora begged off, saying she planned to cook for Gram. Flora surprised Gram by cleaning and preparing the food herself. It was the first home-cooked meal Gram had eaten in his home. Somehow it tasted better than the prepared food in Gram's kitchen, which only required popping into the warmer. Gram enjoyed the small talk after dinner as he finished his second cup of hot drink.

Later in the evening, they walked near the water's edge. The telepathic members of the community realized where Flora and Gram were and warned the other people not to visit the water, so the two lovers could have a certain measure of privacy. The Llan pulled their contact with the pair so it was as private as could be among telepaths. A certain awareness of each other existed no matter how they attempted to isolate themselves.

They watched the stars together while Gram had his arm about Flora's slender waist. They were mind sharing and for the first time could maintain control of their bodies while they were probing elsewhere. They walked about the small lake while they probed Haven's planets. Gram wanted Flora to see and know everything he had found in this system.

After they visited the birthplace of the Llan, Gram escorted Flora to her new home. He kissed her good night and returned home. He debated whether he should cleanse the poisons from his system and refresh his body so he would not require sleep, or whether to sleep for the night and restore his body with the old-fashioned method. He decided a good night's sleep suited him best.

The morning sparkled when Gram felt the nudge of Flora's mind probe. She prepared his breakfast and waited for him. She used her probe to tickle him, forcing him to jump out of bed. It became a game they played; neither had to be forced to join the other.

Gram wasted five minutes with his refresher before he teleported to Flora's kitchen. The warm kitchen air assaulted Gram's nostrils with mouth-watering smells he had never sampled. Flora used information she learned of Earth to conjure up eggs and bacon with jellied toast for breakfast. The food tasted better than the synthetics of Bonne Amie; its taste differed from foods of other planets.

By the time they had finished their leisurely breakfast, Okursis announced her presence. Gram told her how great it was to be alive, then challenged her to a sled race. Okursis accepted the challenge, then offered to modify Gram's sled so the weight of Flora would balance the sled in the place of Robert.

Gram and Flora ran to the airlock hand in hand. Gram helped Flora suit up. Within minutes, they were racing before the wind.

It frightened Flora, but then she mind shared with Gram and tasted the thrill of tearing across the sand. She relaxed and enjoyed the half-sailing, half-flying ride at breakneck speeds. She probed with Gram as he searched out the screaming gale for the sudden cross current that could flip the sled.

They listened to the screech of the runners against the sand. They heard the snap of the sail as the wind tore at it, and the sound of the wind as it whistled over the crest of the dunes. It tore at them as though to remove them from the planet's face.

The three of them stopped at the birthplace of the Llan. Here, while probing the crystalline forms, Flora developed the talent of psychometry. She taught it to Okursis and Gram. By touching the forms in the former sea, they witnessed history before the Llan formed. They saw how the first Llan left the soup of their birth and how they discovered each other. The history of the Llan was as the Llan knew it.

Finished with examining the birthplace of the Llan, they sailed over to a field of large rocks. They found one to shelter them from the wind and the glare of the sun.

Okursis broke into their reverie by communicating to them. "Gram, you appear fully recuperated from your recent experience."

"I feel fully restored," said Gram. "I believe most of the credit is due to this young lady."

"I am happy to hear it," said Okursis. "It is time you test your ability to handle the psi powers before you meet the Galactic Federation Commander. Practice using your powers every day and we Llan will check each evening to see how low your powers drain. It means the rebirth of man or his demise."

"Do you want me to practice by myself or can Flora join me?"

"You just try putting me on a shelf, Gram Ancile."

"I think she settled the question for you," said Okursis. "I cannot think of any reason why Flora shouldn't practice. Two psi talents, finely honed, are more valuable than you alone in the coming battles."

"I was hoping you'd say that. I like the idea of mind sharing with her."

"Well, you're not going to flirt with me when we are trying to improve our skills."

"OK, you two, I'm not impressed by the show you try to use on me," said Okursis. "A good place for you two to practice would be the outward planet from Bonne Amie. There you'll have the privacy and the room you'll need to practice. "We Llan believe it is essential you learn to restore your reservoir when it is drained. Now let's race back to the settlement."

Gram missed Robert for the first time when he and Flora boarded the *Lares Compitales*. His empty niche stood out like an open sore. Gram teleported the burned-out hulk to the ship. He willed Robert back to his former condition with improvements.

One of the improvements guaranteed Robert would never burn out his circuitry again. If the power drain became too great, he could tap the raw energy of a sun rather than exhaust his own resources. Robert became invincible; no juggernaut had the reserves now built into him.

Gram patted Robert's steel shoulder. "Welcome back, old friend. You'll pilot our ship while we practice for complete control of our powers. By the time we finish, we should be ready for the adventure of a lifetime.... To put mankind's enemy on the run."

"I'm sorry, Gram," said Okursis. "We Llan think Robert should remain here on Bonne Amie while you practice."

Gram purged his body of the poisons requiring Earthmen to rest about eight of every twenty-four-hour period. Flora-Gram mind shared and teleported the ship away from Bonne Amie while everybody slept.

The first test of their combined strength was a permanent change in the controls of the *Lares Compitales*. She created a machine to reproduce the galaxy as it existed for a hundred light years around. The ship represented the exact center of this reproduction and as the ship moved forward and new stars appeared, they would leap into view in front of the ship and drop off those beyond a hundred light years behind the ship.

Flora-Gram teleported the ship a hundred light years forward and watched the configuration of stars change. The star map worked as planned. She could see the galaxy as it appeared outside the ship.

Back at the planet beyond Bonne Amie, Flora-Gram seized an asteroid and built up its speed and placed it an orbit about the planet. She maneuvered the ship in an orbit about the asteroid, then she reached out with the probe and slammed the asteroid to a complete halt while maintaining the orbit of the *Lares Compitales* about the asteroid.

The ship nearly slammed into the asteroid. When the danger was over, Gram laughed. "Well, honey, I think we've chosen a task to keep us busy until we learn to do two things at once. Then we'll graduate to controlling more objects."

Flora-Gram went back to speeding the asteroid about the planet, then orbiting the *Lares Compitales* about it. One time the ship and asteroid slammed into the planet and she had to abandon the asteroid and ship to protect her and Gram's bodies from annihilation. The asteroid and ship hit with such force that the planet's surface, the asteroid and ship turned to magma.

With the two bodies safe, she studied the best way to rescue the ship from the molten surface. She slipped into the fourth dimension to study the problem. The image of the ship had already combined with the surface and the asteroid. She traveled to the more complex dimensions.

About the fiftieth dimension she found the ship still intact. She tried to will the ship back to the third dimension; it nearly tore the dimension asunder. She returned to the third dimension and to Bonne Amie.

It alarmed Okursis and Ihan. Ihan probed them and saw how low their reserve strength had been depleted. "Why did you try to remove a frozen image of the ship from the fiftieth dimension to the third? You know it can't be done. It's contradiction of the two dimensions. It still exists frozen in the fiftieth and it has been destroyed in the third. You can't steal from one dimension and teleport the object to another dimension."

"We wanted to see if it could be done," said Flora-Gram. "We didn't want to lose a good ship."

As they conversed, Okursis noted something startling. "A moment ago, your reserves were nearly gone, now they are almost normal. How did you do it?"

"I have no idea," said Flora-Gram. "Gram and I were giving each other a little hug and kiss but I didn't notice anything."

"You have filled the wells of your talent, not consciously knowing how you do it. Go back to the planet and practice, then try filling your wells knowing you are doing it," said Okursis.

Flora-Gram returned to the planet and stretched their capabilities to the maximum. When they returned to Bonne Amie, they brought the *Lares Compitales* with them when they teleported.

"How did you manage to bring the *Lares Compitales*?"

"Easy," said Flora-Gram. "It was impossible to bring the *Lares Compitales* from the fiftieth dimension so I used it as a model and recreated it. How are my reserves now?"

"They are full," said Okursis. "Did you learn how you restore them?"

Gram and Flora returned to their respective bodies and

Flora squeezed Gram as she answered. "We learned our love for each other tended to restore the level of our psyches. With a little intuitive probing we found an easier way to do it. The same thought which binds the universe loves all its creatures, and this is the source of the power in the well of the id. We simply reach out and draw this power to us. It exists all around us."

"This is the edge you need against your enemy. It is time to meet with the commander," said Okursis.

"Wait, Okursis," said Gram. "We can restore our bodily needs without eating or sleeping, but we enjoy the habit of eating and the commander isn't able to do without it. To make up for not seeing him immediately, we'd like to throw him a dinner party. So give us an hour or so to get ready."

"Come on, Gram," said Flora. "With our talent, we can be ready in five minutes. Bring him to my home now. We'll be prepared."

The table was a surprise even to Gram. It consisted of all the commander's favorite foods from his home planet, served in the exact style the commander would have chosen. When he sat down, the commander could not hide his delight.

"I never thought the Llan could produce such delicacies as this. It is marvelous!"

"Would it disturb you to discover the Llan never produced this food? As you started for my house, you were thinking how wonderful it would be if the food was from your home planet. You dismissed the idea because you thought it was impossible; I made the impossible happen," said Flora. "The food and wine I teleported from your favorite restaurant, including the grauta for dessert."

"Then it isn't your robot who performs the acts of magic. It is you and Gram Ancile," said the commander. "I'm beginning to understand why the enemy wants Earthmen dead."

"Commander, do you fear us?" asked Gram.

The commander glanced from Gram to Flora, then back to Gram. "Fear you? No, I don't fear and I don't hate you. I believe I'm more in awe of you than fearful. I believe we are fortunate you are a part of our galaxy."

Gram squeezed Flora's hand. Serving the commander's favorite foods was a touch Gram had not thought of doing. He flashed to her how thoughtful it had been of her.

After the meal they were relaxing in Flora's comfort room when the commander remarked, "On my planet, if someone serves you your favorite foods, it signifies great kindness and respect for the person being so honored."

Flora and Gram bowed in the custom of his planet and uttered the words that signified the kindness and respect of which the commander spoke. "Grutt Ver Cann, be honored at our house." Commander Ver Cann nearly spilled his wine. Off-world persons never offered these niceties. It was new and a great honor to the commander to be the first to receive this special praise.

It pleased Ver Cann to be considered worthy of such an honor in Flora's home. This forswore Ver Cann as a lifelong friend of Flora and Gram. He sipped his second glass of wine very slowly, remarking upon its distinctive bouquet.

Etiquette demanded he pay honor to his hosts by complimenting them on their choice of a fine wine. Of course, the commander did not have to pretend. He had never tasted such a fine wine. Normally, the ultrarich reserved this wine for themselves. A mere commander would have to save his salary for an entire year just for one glass of the wine.

Ultimately, Commander Ver Cann approached the subject that the Galactic Federation had commissioned him to discuss. He set his glass down and sighed. He could still taste the meal and hated to bring up business.

"It amazes me that two of you possess your unique powers."

"Eventually, all humans will possess our talents," said Gram.

"Will this be beneficial to us?"

Flora smiled. "If we used these talents as I did to prepare a banquet, would you consider them to be harmful?"

"No, I would not," said Ver Cann. He paused for a

moment, then plunged into his task. "Now, I must attend to Federation business. The Federation want you to help us capture your enemy. This enemy has wreaked havoc on hundreds of worlds in their attempt to wipe out all human life. The Council of the Federation has commissioned me to set a trap to end this wanton killing.

"I have full power to devise the method to accomplish this end. No one except you and I shall know how the trap is baited. My idea is to go back to my base wildly proclaiming humans are absolutely protected by your powers from the enemy and you that you plan to return to the solar system to restore your planet, Earth.

"What I won't say is, the space navy will be hidden from view but will be able to provide you with protection. We will surround the enemy when he attempts to attack. When we know who he is, we'll quarantine him to his home planet. We will deprive him of the ability to leave his planet. No other races shall be allowed to visit him."

"Your plan sounds great," said Gram. "If I may, I would like to make some alterations in the story you spread about us. Don't mention that the psi powers belong to me and Flora. Tell everyone I have a wonderful mechanical robot which performs our miracles. I believe the enemy will be more prone to attack us if he thinks of our miracles as weapons of a mechanical robot."

Ver Cann scratched his chin. "Yes, I see what you mean."

Flora raised her hands in protest. "Wait, you two! What you are planning involves all the settlers. I think they should be asked if they are willing to risk everything."

Gram grimaced. "I forgot. Commander, I can't commit these people to something as risky as this without their blessing. I'll have to ask them."

"I'm sorry," said Ver Cann. "I have been a fool. I know they must be consulted."

The people gathered the following morning to listen to Gram, Flora and Ver Cann explain the commander's plan. One of them called to Gram.

"You mention the plan calls for telling everyone we are

going back to rebuild Earth. Gram, could you use the common mind of the people and actually rebuild Earth?"

Gram's jaw hung agape. This was the first time he had given serious thought to rebuilding Earth. "Maybe we could...yes! Yes, we can do it. I know we can!"

George Horvath, Jack Roggers, Sam Coulter and Sandy McShane looked at the other human beings gathered about. The crowd nodded consent to the four men and Sandy McShane spoke. "Take us out to the grain fields."

Gram teleported the four men plus the commander out to the fields. Jack Roggers asked, "Can you shield our minds so no one can read our thoughts?"

"It is done. Why all the secrecy?" asked Gram.

George Horvath replied, "Well, it's the Llan...we ...ah...well..."

"Tell 'im!" stormed Sandy. "Don't beat around the bush! Tell 'im!"

"Well, we figured...that is...It wasn't my idea, mind you, but..."

Sandy grabbed a handful of wheat stalks and waved them under Gram's nose. "Great orbiting ships! What's so hard to tell 'im? I'll bet he knows as well as we do this grain is phony! The grain on these stalks is nourishing but it is synthetic like everything else! No one has said anything because we didn't want to hurt the Llan's feelings. We're sick to death of cultivating these fields of phony grain. We know the Llan come in here at night and make daily changes in the grain to make us think it's alive and growing.

"No Earthman can be fooled by synthetic plants for long. Great orbiting ships, Earthmen have spent their entire history growing plants—even the old city dwellers knew how to raise grass and flowers!"

"The Llan have been very kind to us," interposed George. "We wouldn't hurt their feelings for all the world. But it is boring not having any constructive work to do. The grain would be provided whether we work ourselves silly in these fields or not.

"We all agree. We cannot remain on Bonne Amie because of the boredom. We have been trying to find a way to tell you we wish to leave. The thought of reconstructing Earth was beyond our fondest hopes."

Gram laughed and removed the barrier. The Llan would understand the concern of hurting their feelings. They would prefer knowing why the Earthmen had to leave their planet. They would grieve the departure but they would not impose their will upon the Earthmen. Gram marveled at the manner in which they had managed to keep the secret from him.

Planning for the elaborate trap to catch the enemy occupied most of the night. Everyone offered suggestions for capturing the enemy. Even the Llan offered their help. Most of all, the Earthmen wanted reassurances from Gram it was possible to reconstruct Earth.

They decided Gram and Flora would teleport Commander Ver Cann to his home base. He was to spread the story that the Earthmen would use a powerful planet-building ship in conjunction with Robert to reconstruct Earth. The Federation would build the planet-building ship and give it to the Earthmen.

No mention would be made of the human psychic powers, in hope that the enemy would take the bait.

The Llan would construct a ship that looked like a battered old freighter to carry all the humans to the commander's base. At the base they would pick up the planet-building ship. Gram, Flora and Robert would pilot the *Lares Compitales*. It would cloak the Terrans' ability to teleport.

FOURTEEN

Flora and Gram mind shared while teleporting Commander Ver Cann. She moved them backward over the fabric of time as they teleported. They arrived twenty minutes after Gram had tried to teleport the last group of humans to Bonne Amie. Flora-Gram spoke to the commander.

"We teleported backward through time to twenty minutes after Gram teleported you to Bonne Amie. One reason is so you could direct the mop-up operation. The second reason is to cover up the fact you have been on Bonne Amie with us planning our latest strategy. We want to keep the enemy off guard.

"You enjoyed the wine at my home and I wonder if you would accept these two bottles of wine as a gift from me and Gram."

The gift impressed the commander; he did something none of his race would think of doing. He kissed Flora's hand. "I wish Gram was here too. I'd like to invite you both to a meal."

Gram did not have the heart to tell the commander he resided in Flora's mind. It would offend the commander's sense of propriety. "Gram and I will be here in a few months. Let's set a dinner date for when we arrive, Commander."

"Yes, it is an excellent idea. So we have a dinner date when we meet again," said the commander.

Flora-Gram teleported back to Bonne Amie after they heard the first broadcast in which the commander expounded on the plans of the Earthmen. It would be a matter of a few days before the whole Federation knew the Earthmen were planning to rebuild Earth. The plan called for the enemy believing the Earthmen were gathering in one place. They certainly would try to stop the Terrans at the meeting place with Ver Cann and if they failed there, they would war on them in the solar system.

The old-looking new freighter was ready for the Terrans soon after Flora-Gram returned to Bonne Amie. The next morning Flora-Gram went in person to say good-bye. As they mind shared with the Llan, Flora-Gram felt the sadness of the entire race. The Llan did not want the Terrans to leave. They wanted to be with their friends.

The Flora part of the probe pleaded with Gram to do something. The Gram entity had an idea and Flora-Gram presented it.

"Would you leave your planet and come with us if it were possible?"

The entire group of Llan spoke through Okursis. "We have decided to go with you even if it means our death due to oxygen poisoning. We feel it is better to die in your company than to return to the lonely life we led prior to your arrival. We are building a ship to accommodate all of us and we will follow you."

Flora-Gram enlarged the probe so they could hug all the

Llan. "My friend, it isn't necessary for you to make the supreme sacrifice. I have a plan where I will alter your bodies so you can live in an oxygen atmosphere. I'll alter your gene pattern, so when you reproduce, your off-spring will automatically be able to adapt to an oxygen or carbon dioxide atmosphere. Now when you 'sweat' crystals they will be gemstones which will make you rich."

The Llan showered their gratitude upon Flora-Gram and within an instant they could breathe either their own atmosphere or the same as the Terrans. Flora-Gram made one more adjustment to the Llan; she reduced them to the height of seven feet so they could fit into the same freighter with the Terrans.

The children cheered when Flora-Gram teleported the Llan aboard the freighter. But it annoyed the children that they could no longer swing on their limbs. Flora-Gram explained the height reduction was only temporary until they all could live on the new Terra.

Okursis decided she wanted to travel on the *Lares Compitales* with Gram and Flora. Flora-Gram teleported herself and Okursis to the *Lares Compitales*. Gram's body sat in the pilot's lounge; Flora's body sat in the lounge next to Gram. Flora-Gram spoke to Okursis. "I have designed a lounge especially for you here with us. Perhaps you would rather retire to your cabin during blast-off."

Okursis examined Flora, Gram and Flora-Gram. "I see you have mastered the problem of controlling both your bodies and your probe. I think I'll remain on the bridge for the time being."

Gram grinned at Okursis. "It's fun probing with Flora but I think it impresses the rest if I use my own form to lead this expedition. It exercises my and Flora's minds if we probe at the same time."

He flipped on the communicator and Sandy McShane's face popped onto the screens. He was the pilot of the freighter. "I'll blast off first, Sandy, and meet you in orbit."

"Stop talking so much and let's go! The enemy'll get tired and leave if you continue to gab," thundered Sandy.

The warp drive seemed slow and time-consuming to Gram. It would take months to reach the commander's base by warp drive. Gram could have teleported the entire group there in an instant. It chafed him to travel this slowly.

But it was necessary; the commander needed time to build the planet-making ship. It also gave the commander the needed time to maneuver units of the Galactic Federation fleet to the vicinity of the solar system and to reinforce the fleet located near his home base.

The commander took a ship or two from one squadron and some from another squadron and kept shifting them back and forth. Steadily, individual ships received special orders and soon they formed two of the largest fleets ever assembled in two parts of the galaxy. None of the units knew where they were reassigned and none could communicate with each other except by dispatching a messenger from one ship to another.

Another reason for allowing so much time to pass was to give the enemy time to dispatch its fleet to the solar system. Ver Cann wanted the enemy to attack the Terran's three ships near Saturn or Jupiter. Then he would surround the enemy and give them a chance to surrender or be destroyed.

Gram knew the odds of the commander's plan succeeding were marginal. The enemy had never been repulsed. Gram had no delusions about Commander Ver Cann's fleet being able to protect Earthmen.

The enemy had outwitted every attempt to learn its identity; the enemy had outwitted every government's plans to protect Terrans. If a government made it too difficult to reach the Terrans, the enemy did not worry about destroying half a planet to achieve its goal.

If the Earthmen were to continue on after this total war, it would be Gram, Flora, the Llan and the rest of the human beings who would have to bear the brunt of the attack. Everyone on the freighter knew the risk facing them. They knew and refused to leave the freighter.

Knowing it frightened the Terrans made Gram resolve that not one human being would die as long as he drew a breath.

He, Flora and Okursis probed deep into space, practicing their talents, trying to find cracks in each other's armor. Okursis made evaluations to locate the weak points, and Gram and Flora would make adaptations in their strategies.

There were times when they did not tell the other of their stratagems. Gram showed signs of being too confident of his control and it displeased Flora and Okursis. Flora devised a plan to outsmart Gram.

Flora probed out about a light year from Gram and Okursis. She announced she was going to penetrate Gram's defenses before he realized what was going on. A person could not hide his essence from a mind probe, so Gram watched Flora's rainbow as it drifted lazily.

It puzzled Gram that she drifted without doing anything. He started to challenge her when everything went blank. Flora had control of his body and cut him off from his subconscious mind. He could not do a thing until Flora released him.

It angered him; then as he had time to think about it, it frightened him. Suppose the enemy was capable of such trickery. Mankind depended upon his leadership and if they could knock him out, then mankind did not stand much of a chance. Suppose the enemy developed a strategy that penetrated his defenses. It frightened him and he listened to Flora and Okursis.

Gram knew what strategy Flora used almost as soon as it happened to him. She'd formed a single particle of anti-thought, enclosing a part of her essence. She teleported it behind Gram and pushed it toward him. Anti-thought absorbs rather than radiates energy waves, so when she reached his shields she passed through them without effort. The sensors he had placed in his shields did not report anything. They did not detect Flora. She slipped inside his mind before he could react.

Having been shown this weakness, Gram became easier to work with on new stratagems. It made him more wary of traps. Flora was unable to slip by his guard, except the one time he trapped her by letting her think she had managed a second time to slip by his sensors.

Gram found Flora could be a raging tigress when teased while trapped. It took several days before Okursis could intercede for Gram and rid Flora of her pout. Even so, Flora remained cool toward Gram. Gram thought there were flaws in a woman's thinking he would never understand even when mind sharing.

When the freighter and the *Lares Compitales* approached Nashar, Okursis suggested Flora, Gram and she mind share to see if they could discover the enemy's identity. Gram-Okursis-Flora visited the asteroid Gram had crashed into the enemy ships. The asteroid had cooled to a glassy slag but his probe could learn nothing.

Even the talent of psychometry yielded nothing. They watched the two ships explode and the coil of hatred die with it, but there was no hint of the enemy's identity.

The explosions scrubbed the area clean of identifiable clues. Gram-Flora-Okursis lacked the training to rebuild the clues. Someday Gram and the others would do it as easily as Gram could scratch his nose.

In the Nashar system, he explored the asteroid where his father and he had made their home. All identifiable traces of his father had vanished; nothing seemed to linger here either. Yet something in the Nashar system haunted him. It was like a clue but he could not place it nor could he trace it. It slipped through his fingers like water.

Gram-Okursis-Flora went over the system asteroid by asteroid but he could not trace anything concrete. There was an aura too elusive to probe. Finally, in anger, he broke free of the mind sharing and focused all his talent into one mighty thrust. All the asteroids broke free of their orbit and began crashing into each other. When the holocaust was complete there were three planets orbiting Nashar.

Flora-Okursis watched Gram vent his anger before they contacted him. "You've sped up nature here. It would have taken thousands of years before enough of the rocks collided to begin the process of building a planet. Now let's mind share and see if we can cool one of the planets enough to start the formation of the crust plates."

Gram rejoined the mind sharing; the idea of molding a planet enticed him. It was the opportunity to see if Earth could be rebuilt. He dissipated the surplus heat from the molten surface. After the plates formed, he quick-chilled the hot gasses, causing it to rain. The carbon dioxide would never absorb enough heat to make the planet a hothouse as had happened to Venus. Gram-Okursis-Flora had created an E-type planet, which oxygen breathing beings would someday occupy.

The three practiced many different exercises to increase their powers. Gram was usually the first to discover new secrets about the talents and he could exert approximately twice the amount of energy into a given project as the other two. It baffled Flora and Okursis how Gram could concentrate his power so perfectly.

His concentration was like a large laser beam compared to a broad-beam portable light. Flora and Okursis would mind share with him to watch how he projected, but there seemed to be no secret to share. The power he projected was the same at a hundred light years as it was at ten meters.

Flora could teleport fifty light years without difficulty. Any farther and her power diffused, so she could not teleport beyond this limit. Gram had not found any such limit to his powers. Flora could shift the orbit of a planet. Gram could shift the direction of a star.

The three of them, mind sharing, could effectively shield a star, causing all radiation to be reflected back into the sun. They were able to do this for five minutes before Flora and Gram found that their psyches drained at a rate faster than they could replace their energies.

One rest period, Okursis asked Gram and Flora to consider practicing control with all the human beings. "You and Flora act pretty much as a team and I don't think there is much more to be gained by the three of us practicing alone. Perhaps when one of the three of us develops a new talent, then we can practice alone until we have the talent under control."

Flora slipped her hand into Gram's and said, "I agree with Okursis. It is most important that we get the rest of the human beings and Llan trained to operate as a single mind probe. This should help the rest of the people to develop their psyches."

"That's a great idea," said Gram. "I don't think it'll take over two or three practice sessions before all of us operate as a team."

"I don't think the children should be exposed to the malignancy of the enemy's hatred," said Flora. "I don't think their parents would agree to let them participate."

"That is true," said Okursis. "Although I believe the Beaulieu sisters, Audette and Jeanette, should be allowed to join us if they are willing. They are among the best of the psychics of the Terran group."

"If you think it's best," said Gram. "It's too bad Helene Horvath isn't older. She is the best, outside of me and Flora."

"Oh, no," said Flora. "You can't be serious, Gram. To subject a sweet baby like Helene to an all-out war could stunt her development for all time."

"Don't worry, I don't plan to let Helene anywhere near the battlefield," said Gram. "But it is too bad because she'd be a valuable asset."

At the evening meal, Gram contacted all the people and Llan to explain Okursis's plan. It excited everyone and they could hardly wait for the following wake period to begin their training session.

The children nagged their parents to let them help. They pouted because the parents said no. Not Helene—she walked up to Gram and demanded, "I want to go with you to help!"

"Now, honey," said Gram, "I can't take you along, you might get hurt. Then what would your mother and father say to me? Maybe—"

Gram never got a chance to finish, Helene kicked him in the shins so hard the force sent her sprawling. Gram reached down to help her to her feet. She pulled away from him and marched toward the Horvath compartment. Tears of pain came to Gram's eyes and he blocked the throbbing shin bone.

He stared at Helene's disappearing form as she stormed from the dining area.

In the morning, all the people and the Llan assembled in the dining area. They waited for Gram to start their probing lesson. The probe reminded Gram of a giant soap bubble that bounced and bobbled in all directions with a whim of its own. He could not get the people to concentrate on the same subject at one time. Their private thoughts got in the way of the common effort.

Finally, after several hours of practice, Gram released the people. He was unable to control so many minds. He wondered how Okursis and Helene had ever managed to get the people pointed in one direction when he had become lost between the dimensions. He probed Okursis and posed the question.

"How did you and Helene manage to control all the people at one time? I couldn't get the people to think one thought at the same time. There was no focus today. I couldn't beam a simple thought two meters."

"Well, everyone had the same worry in your case," said Okursis. "You were lost and in danger of never returning. Today each one had their own particular problem which was more important to them. What you need is a secondary. Helene got them to think a single thought by vocalizing the thought she and I wanted them to focus on. Even then, it took us several attempts before we were effective. Why don't you practice with some of the more developed talents among the humans before attempting the entire group?"

Gram called a meeting with George Horvath, Jack Roggers, Sam Coulter, Sandy McShane and the two Beaulieu sisters. "I called you here because you are the most developed talents among the humans with the exception of some of the children. I tried to control all the humans and the Llan. It didn't work because most of the Terrans haven't learned how to control their thoughts. We must learn how to work together if we plan to rebuild Earth and defeat the enemy. Okursis believes the nine of us should learn to work together before bringing the rest."

Sandy McShane found it the easiest of the four men to join the common mind; Jeanette was the first of the two girls. Gram-Okursis-Flora taught those two to function in the group before the others joined. Jeanette proved to be a little ahead of Sandy in her development of mental abilities. Audette and the others fit into place and by the end of the work day the team functioned as a unit. Gram acted as its focusing force.

Their practice continued until the ships reached the planetary system of the commander's base. Gram-Okursis-Flora-Sandy-George-Jack-Sam-Audette probed a light year around the galactic base for telltale signs of the enemy's hatred but found none. There was the telltale aura of the hatred lingering about the planet at the base but the enemy had vanished. This made the common mind suspicious of why the enemy had left before the arrival of the Terrans.

Although Gram could not control the total Llan and Terran population in a common mind, he was certain the nine of them could protect the two ships against any devilment the enemy might spring. The enemy had been here and gone.

Why?

When the ships landed, Gram, Okursis and Flora greeted Commander Ver Cann. The commander's work in spreading the story of the Terrans rebuilding Earth had spread to the farthest reaches of the Federation. The scanner services from all over the Federation were present.

The news media wanted to know about Gram's rescue of the human population. Gram claimed a good share of the credit belonged to his robot, Robert. Then they asked if it would be possible to gather all the people and Llan in one place for a news shot. Gram scanned their equipment and took them aboard the freighter.

The shabby-looking interior of the freighter caught the media's attention. They wondered how these pioneers could brave the rigors of space in such a wreck of a ship. Silently, Gram congratulated the Llan for such a masterful disguise. No one suspected the freighter was more spaceworthy than most space ships.

Eventually, the questioning became more personal after the media discovered Flora and Gram were sweethearts. They wanted to know if the two pledged to marry. Gram looked at Flora without mind contact with her and answered yes.

Gram could feel Flora cuddle closer both physically and mentally. Her joy was almost overpowering. In this moment, Gram knew he had to carve a future for himself and Flora as well as the balance of the human race.

Okursis caught the media's eye. Okursis grew a pseudopod voice box and answered their questions herself. She created quite a stir among the reporters when they discovered she was a sentient being. After what seemed hours to Gram, Commander Ver Cann rescued them.

The commander invited them to sup with him and it perplexed him to discover Okursis did not eat food but got her nourishment from the ground. Okursis soothed his conscience by requesting she be allowed to tap the nutrients from his garden soil. She explained this was much preferable to the minerals aboard ship.

The meal served by Commander Ver Cann was one Flora and Gram would remember for years. It started with raw vegetables diced and served in a spicy sauce. It progressed through eleven more courses. By the time the commander brought out a bottle of the rare wine Flora had given him, both Gram and Flora felt as though they had consumed a rock.

They spent the entire evening eating and talking.

Okursis joined them and the commander displayed his collection of rare gems. Flora was the most impressed by the beautiful stones, causing the commander to become more enchanted with her. Okursis became a close friend when she offered him a new jewel for his collection. It was a clear blue stone without a flaw and about the size of Gram's thumb.

After the good-byes, Okursis, Flora, and Gram rode back to the space port. They were in mental contact. Their discussion covered the possibility of sabotage of the planet-building ship. Gram thought this was the reason the enemy had left the planet. They had completed their dirty work. Flora suggested they get Jeanette to help them and search the ship before the first passenger boarded.

Flora chose the front or nose section, Gram chose the holds, Jeanette chose the passenger section, and Okursis ended up with the engine rooms and the tail section. Gram had started the second hold when Okursis called him.

"Gram, there's something wrong with this tail section,"

Gram teleported outside the ship just behind Okursis. Okursis sprouted two pseudopods and drew Gram tight to her body. Her grasp of Gram was so violent Gram was knocked unconscious by her crystal-hard body.

When he recovered, Flora was kneeling next to him sobbing. Something was horribly wrong; Flora was not crying for Gram. Gram quested. "Okursis?...OKURSIS!"

There was nothing. It was like shouting into an empty room. The call echoed and reechoed without any presence answering. She was dead. Gram screamed her name in agony and every telepath in the galaxy felt the magnitude of his grief. She was as important to him as...as a mother would be to anyone else.

Flora nodded at him through her tears. "Jeanette's dead. The enemy killed her, too!"

At that moment, Gram would have caused the enemy's planet to crash into its primary, if he only knew who it was.

FIFTEEN

Gram teleported the Terrans and the Llan back to Bonne Amie for Jeanette Beaulieu and Okursis's funerals. The Llan held Okursis's funeral first. The was the first funeral ever for a Llan and since they did not have a ceremony of their own they adopted one from Earthmen. Gram willed a crystal spire at the head of her grave. During the day, it reflected a blue light about the grave and at night it shed a blue light. The color was the same as the gems she manufactured as a result of breathing an oxygen atmosphere.

They buried Jeanette above ground. Gram created a clear crystal coffin and placed it on a marble bier. The ceremony for her was led by Sandy McShane and when he finished her eulogy all the humans sang a song. Gram teleported the entire group back to the commander's headquarters. He gave Jeanette and Okursis a final salute, then followed the others.

Immediately, the tri-dee screens were alive with the news events that caused Jeanette's and Okursis's deaths. The bombs were devices set within the skin of the ship and the bulkheads. The bombs were human-sensitive. When a human came within range, the bomb exploded, hurling gallons of highly corrosive liquid. Okursis had sensed this as Gram materialized and she shielded his body at the cost of her life.

Jeanette was not as fortunate as Gram. When she reached the human-sensitive panel, it exploded, burning her to death. Okursis's death warned Flora and she stopped searching immediately. The panel in her section never exploded.

Gram probed every millimeter of the ship and located the other human sensitive bombs in the metal walls. There were two human-sensitive, time-delayed, corrosive bombs in the control room. Flora had activated them by her presence. They would destroy the control room a week after she triggered the time device. They would trigger hundreds of corrosive bombs.

Mentally, Gram kicked himself for a fool. It was not necessary to explore the ship in person. It could have been probed first to expose the danger.

It had been a big show for the media, to lull the enemy into believing the Terrans had only ordinary means to examine the ship. It had gotten out of hand. There was no excuse for his carelessness; two beings were dead because of him. Ihan cut into his reverie.

"Don't throw away Okursis's and Jeanette's deaths for nothing. Let the enemy think we believe those are the only bombs."

"We can't use the ship—it's a deathtrap. If a human being steps aboard it, they'll trigger hundreds of bombs," said Gram.

"I agree we can't use this ship," said Flora. "Let's mind share with those we've practiced with and teleport this ship into the system's primary. We'll create another almost exact copy."

"I would like to probe with you in Okursis's place," said Ihan.

The newscasters with their cameras never suspected that they had substituted another ship for the original planet-builder ship. They made the replica complete down to the last detail except for the bombs.

All this took place while Gram was speaking to the newscasters. "The bomb exploded while we were examining the ship. I've decided no one will go aboard the ship until after my robot has had an opportunity to examine the ship for more traps. I can't risk any more lives to the enemy. So if you'll excuse me until Robert completes his examination, I'll give you the complete news story then."

As soon as the reporters gathered up their camera people and left the area, Flora and Gram mind shared. Immediately, they sensed the loss of the glowing thread linking them to Okursis's psyche. The only psyche link of the original group was Helene, and in the excitement they had forgotten her. Flora-Gram teleported to her.

Helene was petting the doll Gram had given her. She joined them as soon as she sensed their presence. She touched Gram's essence and poured her love into the ache in his soul. It startled Gram; a baby girl comforted him.

Helene reached into her pocket and brought out a clear blue gem with a three-dimensional picture or flaw in its center. Gram recognized it immediately as one of Okursis's gems. The flaw was an exact reproduction of Okursis.

"I mind shared with Okursis as she lay dying and she gave me this stone to give to you. She wanted you to have it because she said it will be the key to a secret you'll unlock. She wanted you to wear it in memory of her, Gram."

Gram's mind reeled. "Your mind shared with Okursis when she died?"

"No," said Helene. "She chased me out a second before she died. She said the feeling you and she shared wouldn't die as long as you wear the stone."

He created a platinum chain for the gem and placed it around his neck. The gemstone flashed and glowed with a light of its own. Gram removed the stone and the light died; he shrugged and replaced it around his neck. A dampening of his grief for Okursis occurred once the gem rested around his neck.

Gram probed the stone, checking for the essence of Okursis, but he found nothing. Flora touched the stone with her mind. "It's as though something of Okursis has been locked in the gem. Do you suppose she locked her essence inside?"

"I probed it," said Gram. "There is nothing there I can find. When I put the jewel about my neck, I feel her death less acutely.... She was the only mother I ever knew."

"She knew how you felt about her, Gram," said Helene. "She said you weren't to grieve her death or to let it make you bitter and seek revenge. She told me to tell you she locked her love for you in the stone."

Gram sighed and rubbed the stone. The stone soothed his loss, but what about Audette? She was an orphan without a single relative to share her grief. Gram touched Flora and Helene. "I think we should go to Audette Beaulieu; she has no one in the group. Helene, how would you like to go with Flora and me?"

"Yes. Audette is my friend," said Helene.

The three of them teleported to Audette's compartment. The room was like the void as Audette radiated her grief; Helene, Flora and Gram mind shared and touched Audette. Audette's sorrow spilled over them like water over a broken dam as the tears streamed from her eyes. They cradled her until there were no tears left. A fury built up in Audette, wiping out all traces of her sorrow. The enemy was responsible for Jeanette's death and it would pay.

Audette's anger was a seething almost as dark as the hatred the enemy felt. It forced Gram-Helene-Flora from her mind. Gram blocked her feeling from the rest of Terran group.

"Audette," he said. "Please, stop this hatred. If you continue to let it build, we will be forced to leave you here at the commander's base. We cannot stand your hatred any more than we can tolerate the enemy's. You are driving us away."

She stood with her eyes blazing, and as she realized what they were telling her, she clenched her fists. Gradually, the anger died from her face and Gram-Helene-Flora rejoined her in mind sharing. "For the sake of mind sharing with the entire group in our final battle, I've buried my hatred. I must be there."

Helene stirred in the common mind. "I want to fight the enemy!"

"No, you are too young," said Gram. Their common mind felt the shock of the withdrawal of Helene's probe. She kicked Gram in the shins mentally and teleported to her own room. Gram teleported his body to her room but Helene repulsed him by erecting a shield. He turned to Flora-Audette.

"We agree she is too young!"

Gram did not rejoin Flora-Audette in probing together. Instead he teleported to the commander's office, determined to get the Terrans away from the danger. The commander turned with a start as Gram materialized.

"Your method of entry is rather sudden, to say the least!"

"Sorry, Commander, but I don't have time to waste," said Gram. "We discovered the ship you had built for us was loaded with enemy traps. We teleported it into the primary of this system and created another ship. I have created a panel with one of their bombs in this new ship which I want you to remove. I cannot come near it because it is human-sensitive.

"You arrange tri-dee coverage and we'll explode it before the galactic networks. Perhaps the enemy will see the telecast or at least hear it. I am going to issue an ultimatum."

The commander rubbed his chin. "Are you sure it is wise?"

"I don't plan to let the them know I possess psi powers," said Gram. "I'll convince them Robert is the source of my mechanical powers."

"I'm not sure I understand your plan completely but I'm willing to see it unfold," said the commander.

"As soon as your people remove the bomb, replace the sections which blew when Okursis and Jeanette were killed," said Gram. "I don't believe we should remain here after I issue the ultimatum. The enemy may decide to attack while we are still here rather than waiting for us to reach the solar system."

The commander nodded pensively. He realized that Gram had suffered a great loss and worked under a tremendous strain. Almost as quickly as Gram finished talking, the commander issued orders to carry out Gram's plan. His outer offices became a beehive of activity.

Robert guided the bomb removal crews to the human-sensitive bomb. As soon as the crew cut the section free, Robert sealed it inside a force field. A tri-dee camera fitted on Robert's head broadcast the scene. The media asked hundreds of questions of Gram as Robert and the bomb removal crew appeared with the bomb.

"How is it you located the bomb if the other two exploded when they were approached?"

"I'll let Robert explain it to you," said Gram.

"The other bombs exploded when Gram and Jeanette approached," said Robert. "The device has a human-sensitive triggering mechanism, so I had to probe for its location. Then I used a nonhuman crew to remove it."

"You say you probed for it—what exactly do you mean?"

"I have X-ray vision as well as normal vision." What Robert said was true; the bomb was probed for and he did have X-ray vision. He simply let the newscasters draw their own conclusions by not going into detail.

Gram turned to Robert as the workers placed the section in the test area. "Enlarge the force field to include the dummy of a human we placed in the test area."

A humming sound rose from within Robert. A barely visible beam of light issued from Robert's body as the field shifted to include the dummy. Gram began to walk toward the metal plate containing the bomb. Flora flashed Gram a message.

"You and Robert are two of the worst ham actors I have ever seen! When you will the bomb to explode, why don't you throw up your arms as if to shield yourself from the explosion?"

"Thanks for the tip, I'll do it."

Gram could hear the peals of laughter from the telepathic members of the Terran group. Gram's display amused the Llan, too. Flora snorted her disdain to Gram but secretly it pleased her how well Gram carried off the show.

As the section exploded, Gram threw up his arms and stumbled backward as if to escape injury. His reactions convinced the commander Gram's reactions were normal.

Robert released the field to allow the televising of the corrosive's effects. Gram added a bit more smoke to the scene than was created by the corrosive. It highlighted the danger to the humans. One of the reporters approached and asked more questions.

"Sir, in light of what has happened here, how can you be absolutely sure there are no more bombs aboard the ship?"

"As Robert has said, the ship has been probed. I believe it to be safe after Robert checked it. It isn't likely the enemy succeeded in changing more than the three panels. Commander Ver Cann's security system would have prevented it from happening," said Gram.

"Do you believe the planet-building ship can succeed in pushing the broken parts of Earth about to form a new planet?"

"The tractor and pulsar beams are the most powerful known," said Gram. "Robert has smaller versions of the beams we plan to use. I'll have Robert demonstrate how his beams work, then you draw your own conclusions as to how successful we'll be. Of course, we realize it'll be centuries before we can return to live on Earth, but it will be there and it will be ours."

"Where will you live until Earth cools?"

"We plan to build a base on Luna and live there until we can inhabit Earth," said Gram. "Robert is ready for the demonstration."

Robert repeated the trick with the boulder he had done after the Llan added the pulsar and tractor beams to his ability to protect Gram. He held it above the heads of the reporters with a pulsar beam; Robert pulverized the rock to dust with a combination of the pulsar and tractor beams. He lowered the dust to the ground so the reporters could examine it. After they had poked in the dust, Robert seized the powder and lifted it above their heads again. He flashed another beam on the powder, causing it to become molten. The heat drove the reporters back.

At this point, Gram used his talents to drain off the heat and to shape the mass as Robert displayed phony beams of light over the rock. When the display of lights finished, there spun the globe Earth. The crowd gasped; the display impressed the Terrans and Llan. Everyone felt they had witnessed a little bit of magic.

"What you have seen here can be duplicated by the ship," said Gram. "I want to give our enemy a word of advice. Back in the solar system, we won't be vulnerable individuals on a planet. We'll be on a ship capable of being used as a warship. If you choose mayhem, be warned. We'll grind your fleets to dust. Robert and this new ship are all we need to stop your war."

The miniature Earth spinning lazily above Gram's and Robert's heads was awe inspiring, but coupled with Gram's words became quite chilling. If the enemy heard this broadcast, they would know to shift their war to the offensive. It would have to be an all-out effort to finish the Earthmen.

Gram predicted the Earthmen had a half-year before the enemy could gather its forces at the solar system.

Newscasters had a field day analyzing Gram's actions and his "throwing the gauntlet of challenge in the face of the enemy." Some predicted Earthmen would not survive a full-scale war.

They directed the team of reporters and cameramen to board the planet-building ship. The Terran leader used the freighter to carry supplies for the Terrans. This would suffice until they could restore an old dome on Luna as a place to live and grow food.

Flashing red lights drove back the remaining reporters from the launch area. The broadcasting continued aboard the planet-building ship. Just before the ships winked into hyper space, the newscasters aboard the ship signed off.

Immediately after the ships went into hyper space, Gram teleported Commander Grutt Ver Cann aboard his fleet command ship located near the solar system. This fleet was to remain hidden beyond the solar system until Gram and the Terrans teleported it to the battle zone.

It would be a little over a month before the three ships of the Earthmen would approach the solar system. Until then, Gram and Flora would concentrate on the control of the common probe with the Earthmen and Llan participating.

SIXTEEN

Before Gram could relax enough to attempt to control the common mind probe, he and Flora had to check out the solar system. It would be a little over a month in hyper space before the three Terran ships would reach the outer limits of the system. Flora-Gram probed every planet, satellite, asteroid and comet that orbited through the solar system. They found no trace of the enemy.

Flora-Gram materialized dozens of small satellites that would sense the hatred of the enemy and relay the information to Robert. They placed them in strategic locations about the solar system. It would be impossible for the enemy to sneak into the solar system.

Now Gram could relax without worry. It was time to master the control of the common mind.

Ihan replaced Okursis in the probe alongside Flora. Within minutes he was handling his part in the probe almost in the same manner as had Okursis. Along with Flora, he fed the energy of the others to Gram. Audette and Jeanette had served as partners directly under Flora and Okursis. With Jeanette dead, Audette attempted to supply all the energy the two had supplied.

Gram felt the probe falter as Audette depleted her strength. He and Flora showed the others the secret of replenishing the well of their strength. Even so, Audette eventually depleted her strength again. Gram reorganized the internal structure.

He brought Sandy up from his position with Jack, George, Sam and Gus and placed him with Audette. Gradually, Sandy learned to cooperate with Audette and the power of the common mind grew. Within days, the probe felt as normal to Gram as his own hand.

The first attempt to use all the Terrans and Llan in the common mind was disastrous. It ended with Gram and the others pulling the untrained minds along. It cut down the total power of the group.

"I say we should drop them," said Sandy. "They aren't of any help to the unit."

"No, I disagree," said Ihan. "Every iota of strength will be needed. Even the Llan must help. Everyone worked well together when we all thought Gram was lost forever between the dimensions. They must learn to work as a team again."

"I agree with Ihan," said Flora. "We cannot afford the luxury of not training everyone. It was done once and we must do it again."

"Maybe it's me," said Gram. "Maybe I'm so used to working by myself or in small groups that I'm a hindrance to the entire group."

"It's not you, Gram," said Sandy. "I'm impatient with the new members. I get the feeling they aren't trying to work."

"Why don't we pick out eighteen of the best psi talents, each of us take two, and work with them until they learn teamwork?" questioned Audette.

Gram agreed with Audette's suggestion and they selected new members. This time most of the newcomers were Llan. Once the new group became linked with the original common mind, the probe's power doubled. Within an hour, the unit operated as a single mind.

Sandy was certain the common mind, with its present members, was sufficient to handle any problem the enemy could deal out to the Terrans. He wanted to leave the balance of the group out of the coming combat. Jack Roggers agreed with Sandy.

Ihan, Flora and Gram disagreed. Their argument centered on the hatred of the enemy. It was the enemy's most powerful weapon, more powerful than the fleet they would assemble. Sandy and Jack scoffed at the idea. They were certain the members of the probe could handle anything.

Gram asked Audette to dwell upon her hatred of the enemy until it was a raging sickness. Sandy was to lead the group and penetrate her hatred.

After a few moments, Gram rescued the unfortunate team. Flora, Ihan and Gram worked several minutes with Audette before her hatred abated. No one argued after that experience. Gram chose another fifty-four Terrans and Llan to work with the probe.

It took weeks to assimilate all the Terrans and Llan. The strength of the common mind did not improve much. Those with the least psi powers had little to contribute to the strength of the probe. Gram felt its strength would increase with training.

As the three ships approached the solar system, Gram grew tense. He drove the common mind to exhaustion, then released it with the greatest reluctance. He paced the control room of the *Lares Compitales,* driving Flora to distraction.

She ordered him to stop worrying and sit down. He sat for a few minutes until he thought he would explode. He left the ship on the pretext of needing to check the ships. He teleported to the bridge of the freighter and ran head on into Sandy.

"Well, what is it this time? A complete inspection of the

ship again? You are becoming a real pain, sonny," Sandy growled.

"No, I know the ship's OK. It's just..."

"Look," said Sandy. "The human race will make out OK, if you let us carry our share of the worries. Most humans are sturdy stock, even if they don't control all those fanciful powers of yours."

"Maybe we should have waited," said Gram. "If we'd developed the common mind on Bonne Amie, maybe Okursis and Jeanette would—"

"Great blazing comets, man! You still think you are solely to blame for their deaths? Let me tell you something—I'm to blame, the Llan are to blame, all the Terrans are to blame, and Jeanette and Okursis must take part of the blame, too," said Sandy.

Gram started to protest and Sandy held up his hand, signaling he had the floor.

"Let me finish. You are acting as though you are some super type who shouldn't make mistakes. I said Okursis and Jeanette were to blame. I meant every word I said. They should have been probing their sections rather than walking and making visual inspections. They knew the enemy had been at the construction. They should have suspected something devious."

Sandy took a deep breath and continued. "The Llan should have counseled you about the possibility of a trap based on what they knew about the enemy. This was their mistake.

"The human group and I have let you take the brunt of the action and planning. We said, 'Let's go back to the solar system,' then sat back and depended on you to plan our moves. The Terrans have a terrific amount of first-hand knowledge of the enemy, but they have never pooled it. So it is also their fault the deaths occurred.

"You may have superior talents compared to the rest of us but you are a Terran and Terrans make mistakes. You are as mortal as the rest. Your not recognizing this fact is your fault and your part of the blame in the deaths."

"I agree with Sandy McShane," said Ihan. He had teleported to the bridge. "We are as much to blame for the deaths as you. We must share it equally. It doesn't help us to have you attempt to shoulder the blame. We must mind share as a group and bring Robert into the group, too. He can record all the information on the enemy, then summarize it. Then we should be able to plan some action against the enemy and have the advantage over them."

Gram submitted to Ihan's request and contacted the Llan, Terrans and Robert. Gram remained on the bridge during the mind sharing. Everyone contributed what they knew of the enemy. When they finished, Robert summarized for them.

"The enemy is most successful whenever mankind is careless and repeats himself in the form of a pattern. The enemy uses any repeated pattern to arrange an accident. They are very persistent. It is known that they have made attempts against some Terrans as many as a dozen times to kill them. They have always succeeded. Most human beings are creatures of habit and it has been used against them. The Terrans with some level of psi powers have succeeded in evading them.

"The enemy doesn't worry about the consequences of destroying half a world to get one human being. They are so intense in their destruction, no planet is safe harboring a Terran.

"Gram almost read the enemies' thoughts once. He couldn't do a complete scan of their thoughts because of the intense wall of hatred they feel. The human mind goes insane if exposed to such hatred for more than a few minutes. Gram is troubled by his partial contact with the enemy. He knows he has met the enemy prior to his becoming sensitive.

"Two strong conclusions can be drawn from the knowledge I have gathered. One: The enemy fleet is very large. I reached this conclusion from the number of ships they place along an escape route when a Terran is driven to flight. I believe their fleet is larger than the Galactic Federation's.

"Two: The enemy knows some Terrans have either developed or are about to develop extrasensory perception. It is not certain they believe I am the source of your power. It is reasonable to believe they are fearful of Terrans developing the psi talents. I conclude this is the reason they are murdering every human they find."

The common mind digested all the information, then drew some conclusions. The enemy would launch an all-out war upon the human community in the solar system. The attack would take place within five months. It would take them this long to marshal their fleet.

The fleet of Commander Grutt Ver Cann must not participate in the war. He had only a partial fleet. This fact chilled the hearts of the human community.

Gram would be the main target of the enemy because they had reason to suspect that he had partially developed his psi powers. Robert would also be a main target. He had demonstrated some amazing mechanical powers at the commander's home base before tri-dee. The rest of the Terrans would be next on their list, followed closely by the Llan who had befriended mankind.

The one fact weighing heavily for the Terrans was their ability to control many of the psi powers. The enemy did not realize the extent of control Gram had developed. It would be their greatest weapon against the enemy.

Knowing they considered Gram the most dangerous Terran, Gram would have to draw the enemy into battle. He would lead and direct the battle. Flora and Ihan must feed the common mind's power for Gram to direct, followed by Audette and Sandy.

While the common mind developed its strategy, the news crew accompanying the Terrans had no idea anything was happening. The Terrans and Llan were careful not to divulge the fact that they possessed psi powers. They were not afraid to let the galaxy know they were gifted. They were afraid the enemy would change their tactics if they were certain the Terrans had developed the talents.

So the newspeople planned how they would occupy their newscasts once they reached the solar system. They knew their audience would not tolerate the same old trivia day after day until the battle began. They knew Gram would not allow an interview daily.

Somehow they would have to examine the solar system and set the stage for the audience for the upcoming battle. Perhaps they could persuade the Terrans and the Llan to let them use a shuttle craft occasionally to examine the planets as they approached Luna.

The common mind was aware of the newscasters' plans. The mind felt it was necessary for the news media to be given a shuttle craft to advertise the presence of the Terrans in the solar system.

After the meeting ended, all the Terrans and Llan returned to their own bodies. Gram and Flora were about to probe back to the *Lares Compitales* when George Horvath contacted them. He wanted them to talk with Helene.

They teleported their bodies aboard the freighter and left Robert to pilot the *Lares Compitales*. They followed George to his apartment. Before they could enter, Helene opened the door. The boys, Steve and Randy, pestered their father to help them with a puzzle. He promised, then turned to Flora and Gram.

"Helene claims you won't win the fight with the enemy if she's not allowed to help," said George. "My wife and I...well, we thought the two of you could handle the problem better than we can. She'll listen to you."

Flora and Gram sat down on the sofa, one on each side of Helene. Gram asked, "Why must you help me and Flora, Helene?"

"Because."

"Because why?"

"Because you can't beat the 'Reans without me. I got to show you how."

"Do you know how to beat the 'Reans, Helene?"

"Not exactly, but you can't do it without me."

"Who are the 'Reans?"

"The 'Reans are the enemy."

"Yes, but where do they come from?"

"I don't know."

"Can I mind share with you, Helene?"

As soon as Helene nodded her consent, Gram entered her mind. The stark simplicity of her thoughts always startled Gram when he mind shared with Helene. Mentally she patted him on the cheek and welcomed Gram to examine her thoughts. Gram saw the world as a six-year-old.

He did not understand how she arrived at some of her thoughts. There were no shadings of meaning in her thoughts. If her parents told her something was true, there was no room for doubt. If her brothers told her something, there was room for doubt.

They could be telling the truth, or they could be teasing; they could be lying because they wanted to be mean, or they could be lying because they did not know the truth. In any event, most things the boys told her must be checked out by asking an adult. Sometimes it was months before Helene knew the truth about statements made by the boys.

Gram saw how Helene had changed her mind about marrying him when Flora mind shared with her and taught her how to identify the correct life string that tied two psyches together. Gram knew now that no woman would ever marry the wrong man in the future.

He saw the plans Helene was making for her future husband and he felt sorry for the boy. She had already introduced herself to him with several kicks to the shins and he retaliated by tying knots in her hair. The boyfriend should not have done that trick. Helene planned to make him pay for it many times.

Gram was not Helene's boyfriend anymore; instead he was her warrior who was the smartest person in the whole universe, excepting her mother and father. There was nothing he could not do. No one could be hurt as long as Gram protected them. Gram even had Okursis safe.

He puzzled over the thought and he tried to correct Helene. Helene was very stubborn and erased any attempts by Gram to change the thought. Finally, Gram gave up, but he did manage to have her accept his version of how Okursis had died as an afterthought. Someday she would have to sort out the truth from what she believed.

The thought of Helene's 'Reans intrigued Gram. There was the smell and flavor of the thought Gram had captured of the enemy when he rescued the people from the mined building. In Helene's thought there was the hint of knowing the enemy without being able to recognize who they were. Gram examined the thought from every angle. He tried to locate the source of Helene's name for the enemy.

Her knowledge of how she knew was more vague than Gram's feeling that he knew the identity of the enemy. Gram could not locate the source of her knowledge. It was like a pool without a rivulet entering or leaving the pool. The thought existed without reaching the conclusion from knowledge. Gram recognized the name as being the truth without being able to identify it.

Helene believed with the same positive knowledge that she would be instrumental in concluding the war. Gram could judge the thought about the 'Reans because he had experienced something similar. Helene's thought that she would play a major role in the war had no basis on which Gram could judge.

Gram asked Helene if Flora could join him in tracing the facts of Helene's thoughts. Helene held out her arms to Flora. Flora-Gram tore her thoughts on the 'Reans and the war to shreds, tasted it and smelled it, then looked at each segment from every possible view, and when they finished they returned each segment to its proper slot in the thought. The probe used Flora's talent to probe the past.

It found nothing. At one point, the thoughts did not exist; then in the next instant they were there. It had popped into her mind.

The probe pondered. It began to examine the fabric of time for future events in Helene's life. The mind saw Helene remained by herself, nursing her anger and hurt by Gram without any knowledge of what happened outside her room.

Helene forced Flora and Gram from her mind with a shock

neither had experienced before. It was a cold fury, and a complete rejection of the two. She kicked Gram in the shins, then ran to her room, slamming the door. Gram tried to reach Helene with a mind probe but bounced off a shield Helene had erected. He thought of penetrating the shield. Flora warned him against it and asked that Helene be given time to herself.

Gram rubbed his shins ruefully and explained to George and Mrs. Horvath what had taken place. George wanted to force Helene to listen to Gram—make her accept Gram's explanation of why she must not enter the war.

Mrs. Horvath and Flora both protested. If George tried to force Helene to accept Gram's explanation, it might result in Helene never forgiving Gram. Both thought it was better Gram didn't try to see Helene before the battle. Let her learn the facts for herself.

Once Helene realized she did not participate in the fight, she would no longer blame Flora and Gram for doubting her. Gram was not so sure Flora's and Mrs. Horvath's philosophy had merit. He could not picture Helene forgiving them because Flora and Gram withheld her from participating. It was more likely she would blame them for keeping her from her destiny.

George and Mrs. Horvath invited Flora and Gram to remain and dine with the family. The boys played games and soon they talked Gram into playing with them.

It was a circular board with three equal sections. The object was to get your pieces through one opponent's section, then on to the third player's section to win. Until you reached the second player's section of the board and had your pieces crowned in his back row, you could only move directly ahead, one square at a time until the piece became crowned.

Once crowned, you could change direction and move into the third player's section. Once the piece was into the third player's section, it was possible to move as many spaces as necessary to capture either of the other two players' pieces.

As soon as the first aggressor moved into another's territory, the other players became partners and both had to remove the aggressor's pieces from the board before they could battle each other for the championship.

This was the strategy Steve and Randy used on Gram. They let him become the aggressor and eliminated him from the board, then they battled it out until one of them won. Randy won the first game and Steve won the second game after long seesaw battles.

The third game Gram lost his first piece to Steve when he heard a mental snicker from Randy, his thought uncovered for an instant, then Randy never slipped again. It was enough to put Gram on his guard. He probed so gently, the boys never suspected he was on guard.

Gram found the boys were mind sharing. He saw nothing wrong with this; it helped improve their psyche development. He would have to play more strategically to whip two agile minds, but there had been Randy's snicker.

He lost another piece.

There was nothing to indicate Gram's thoughts were probed. The common mind of Steve-Randy rested near the boys and there was no indication they were probing and analyzing Gram's thoughts.

Steve-Randy captured another of Gram's pieces.

Somehow the boys were reading Gram's thoughts. Gram planned his next move as he watched both his and the boys' psyches. There was a slight movement to his psyche when he planned his next move. Steve-Randy responded one hundred eighty degrees out of phase with the movement of Gram's psyche.

Gram slipped a screen between his psyche and the boys' common mind.

The screen was only one electron thick and would not shield any thought. It was there to detect any energy flow between Gram and the boys. There was a flow of energy anytime Gram had a thought. It radiated in much the same manner as magnetic flux does from an electrical wire.

He used his probe like a skilled surgeon, carefully, so as not to arouse any alarm in the boys as to what Gram was doing.

What he found stunned him; immediately Gram mind shared with Flora, George and Mrs. Horvath to show them this extraordinary talent these boys had developed.

The equal but opposite vibration reaching Steve-Randy from Gram's thought was held before a mental mirror where the vibration became a readable thought again. Flora-George-Mrs. Horvath-Gram smiled.

These two would be the trickiest to watch in a school exam; they would read the answers directly from the instructor's mind without probing the instructor. The new Earth would struggle to stay ahead of cheating. Flora-George-Mrs. Horvath-Gram alerted the entire adult population to the new talent.

Gram separated from mind sharing and planned his next move as he smiled. It startled the boys when Gram wiped out Randy's pieces, then went after Steve's with a vengeance. It bewildered them. They read the vibrations from Gram's thoughts in their mental mirror only to discover the thoughts had no connection with moves Gram made on the board.

"Well, you won." Steve stood up and put his hands in his pockets.

"Want to play another?"

"Nah, I'm getting tired anyhow," said Steve.

Steve put his arm around Randy as they left to discuss what had gone wrong with their game. They would not understand until they were adults what had gone wrong. It was a secret adults kept from children until they had children.

Now George and his wife understood how the boys had been able to counter every argument with their parents. They knew their thoughts as soon as they formed.

SEVENTEEN

The three Terran ships returned to normal space about a billion and half kilometers out from Sol, somewhere between the orbit of Uranus and Saturn. Robert gave the Terrans, Llan and the news team a view of the most famous sight of the solar system. He had turned the scanners to Saturn, a mere hundred eighty-four million kilometers away. Saturn—in its golden glory, crown of ice rings, and attendant satellites—made an excellent place to begin advertising to the enemy that the Terrans were home.

Gram told the reporters that he planned to search Iapetus, Rhea, and Titan, the three largest moons of Saturn, for evidence of an enemy base. He invited them to come with him.

The Terrans and the reporters were hungry for information and the sights of the solar system. Gram ordered Robert to focus the scanners on Saturn and to recite all the information he had on Saturn, its moons and the Cassini division of the rings.

The ships passed within a few kilometers of the outer ring and he took the reporters aboard a shuttle craft. Gram explained that he planned to investigate Rhea first, which was the smallest of the three largest moons and the closest to Saturn. From there he planned to visit Titan, then Iapetus.

Gram adjusted the scanners of the shuttle to let the newsmen view the rings. The particles of ice ranged in size from a centimeter to several centimeters. They sparkled like so many jewels in Saturn's reflected light.

When they had taped their story of the rings and Saturn, Gram moved on toward Rhea, passing near Mamas to give the reporters a chance to film it. Gram crossed the orbits of Enceladus, Tethys, and Dione.

Rhea—named for the daughter of Uranus and Gaea, and the wife of Cronus and the mother of Zeus—was much too small to sustain an atmosphere. It was only fifteen hundred seventy-seven kilometers in diameter and deeply pocked from collisions of planetesimals. It delighted the newsmen when Gram gave his audience a running commentary on how many objects located in the solar systems were named after Greek and Roman mythical characters.

Gram made a big show of using energy detection equipment to locate any foreign activity on the moon. The reporters duly noted on their tapes that there was not an enemy base on the small moon. Gram moved on to Titan.

Titan, as Gram described it to the reporters, had one quarter of the mass of the former Earth, and had an atmospheric pressure almost equal to the former Earth. Reddish-brown clouds obscured the surface. Gram took much longer to search out signs of the enemy because the moon was almost the size of Mars.

Volcanic action caused the energy detection equipment to gyrate wildly. Gram acted as though he believed it was an enemy base. He switched to infrared scanners showing the lava flow from a twelve-and-a-half kilometer volcano. The reporters settled back with a sigh when they realized it was a volcano.

Iapetus received the same careful examination as Titan. When it was completed, Gram joined the three Terran ships out beyond the orbit of Phoebe, the tenth moon of Saturn.

Flora joined Gram and the reporters aboard the planet-building ship. She welcomed them and offered the reporters twelve-year-old bourbon and water. One of the reporters asked where she got the bourbon since no one had seen bourbon in the galaxy since shortly after the destruction of Earth.

"Oh, there are a few of us who can still make good bourbon," said Gram. "We weren't all in Kentucky when Earth blew."

"You made this bourbon? It's excellent," said the reporter. "You could sell the formula and make a fortune."

"Go ahead, tell him how you make the whiskey!" Flora beamed at Gram as she poured the reporters another round. "Tell them you're teleporting these ships to Jupiter's orbit too! You'll make a big hit with them."

Gram gave a slight bow to the reporter who asked him to sell the formula and spoke aloud. "Thank you, sir, for the kind words, but I think I'll keep my secret."

Gram preferred a hot drink to alcohol and he stopped to sip the hot liquid. It was still too hot to drink so he continued talking.

"While we were examining the moons, our people planted warning devices to indicate the presence of any ships entering the solar system. This early warning system will prevent us from being surprised.

"Our next stop will be Jupiter after a short hop via warp drive. We'll continue our search for enemy bases on all the moons of Jupiter. You'll get a real break there. Flora plans to guide you. You won't have to put up with my running commentary.

"She'll show you Ganymede and Callisto, while I examine the three inner moons, Amalthea, Io and Europa. Other members of our group will search the rest of the moons."

"Thanks for nothing, Gram! I'm not interested in being a tour guide!" Flora signaled.

"Sorry, honey, it's part of the plan," flashed Gram. "I have to be on Amalthea when your ship develops trouble. How are we going to convince the enemy we haven't developed extraordinary talents? I know the plan is dangerous, and I wish it was possible to send someone other than you."

"Don't you dare replace me," she signaled. "I wish we could be together on this plan."

Flora smiled at the reporters. "I was beginning to think he wasn't going to share you people. He's such a ham he'd keep you to himself just to be on camera."

Gram gave her a hug, then laughed. "You don't suppose she's jealous of all the coverage you fellows have been giving me?"

What appeared to be almost an hour to the reporters' minds on a warp drive hop was in reality less than a second as Gram teleported them and the ships.

Ihan and Sandy took one of the freighter's shuttle craft. George and Madeah went in another, and Elfrum and Flora went with the reporters in another shuttle. Gram signaled Robert to put the launch in an orbit with Amalthea. The Earth committee had agreed that using shuttle craft in as close as Amalthea was to Jupiter would be entirely too dangerous. Gram and Robert used the launch. As they neared Amalthea, Gram flipped on the recording scanners.

Amalthea had no outstanding features. Its hundred-fifty-kilometer diameter made it smaller than the asteroid Psyche, but a giant when compared to Jupiter's retrograde moon.

Gram felt no interest in Amalthea but the violent storms of Jupiter did attract him. He shivered a little as he probed Jupiter. Had they made a mistake planning their charade so close to the surface? He was sorry he had agreed not to use his psi powers.

The storms in the upper atmospheric layer of Jupiter were the worst he had probed. The wild fury in which he had sailed his sand sled on Bonne Amie seemed like a calm sea cove compared to those of Jupiter. The hydrogen winds raged about him as he probed deeper, down into the crystallized ammonia layer, then into the ammonium hydrosulfide layer. He probed deeper, to a layer of ice crystals, then to liquid water; finally he stopped when he reached the layer of liquid metallic hydrogen. The tortured state of the atoms in this layer screamed at and oppressed his psyche.

Gram returned to his body and waited until it was time to start for Io. Gram circled Amalthea several times, then called the freighter to report that he had not found a trace of the enemy at Amalthea and he was on his way to Io. Io was the amplifier of Jupiter's radio noise.

This was Flora's clue to cut in on Gram's static-ridden broadcast. "Gram! I think the enemy sabotaged this shuttle craft! We've lost all power to our drive, we're dead!"

"Flora, put the craft into a shallow glide about Jupiter! I'm on my way to pick you up!"

"I can't, the craft is in a power dive and headed straight for Jupiter!" she said.

"Have you use of the lateral rockets?" questioned Gram.

"No, the ship's completely dead," said Flora. "I'm broadcasting on emergency power."

"OK, I'll contact the planet builder, they should be able to use a tractor beam to change your course," said Gram as he signaled Jack Rogger, the pilot aboard the planet builder.

"I can get enough of a grip on her to put her in a glide path about Jupiter. I advise you put the launch at full power. She's disappearing behind the planet from me and the magnetosphere is warping the tractor beam," said Jack. "By the time I can change orbit, she'll be lost. She'll begin dropping toward Jupiter at a terrific rate."

The *Lares Compitales* entered a particularly strong field of Jupiter's magnetosphere. Robert began a wild wind-milling motion with his arms and he ran to one side as if to regain his balance. The magnetosphere affected Robert's delicate brain. Gram pulled his emergency cutoff switch; there was no reason to allow Robert to destroy himself.

Gram switched the controls of the launch to manual. As Gram passed through the worst of the storm it affected his vision. Everything seemed to melt and flow before his eyes as he fought to keep his composure, then he was through the storm.

As Gram rounded the bulk of Jupiter, he saw the shuttle. The picture on the screens faded in and out. The dead craft was already inside the orbit of Amalthea and fast approaching the outer limits of Jupiter's atmosphere. Gram called Flora and repeated the message several times to make sure she got the message.

"Flora, I see your craft now and I'm coming in under full power! Suit up and stand by the escape hatch, I'm going to pick you up!"

"Don't try it, Gram! We're too close to the planet. You'll be killed, too. Good-bye, my darling, I love you!"

"Stop talking and suit up. I'll get you out of this if I have to chase you all the way to the planet's core," said Gram. "Don't let me hear any more talk of dying."

Gram's hands danced across the keyboard as he locked Flora's craft with a tractor beam. His ship groaned with the effort. The beam slowed her descent but her ship was still falling at a faster rate than Gram. The tractor beam stretched like a rubber band. Gram flipped more switches and two more beams leaped to touch Flora's shuttle craft. He heaved a sigh when the beams held. Slowly, he brought the two crafts together.

The ships sank into the upper reaches of the planet's atmosphere and tumbled about as corks. Sweat beaded on Gram's face and arms as he fought to join the two ships. Pressures outside were building dangerously high. Flora's ship was not built to withstand the atmospheric pressures.

Gram had the ships within millimeters of locking when a powerful updraft tore the two ships apart. Gram snapped on another beam and brought them to the locked-ports position. His launch creaked and groaned under the stresses as he reversed the direction and headed out-planet. He was bathed in sweat. Water dripped onto the deck from his tunic.

Opening the airlock, the reporters and Flora stumbled aboard, followed by Elfrum. The launch gave a nasty lurch as Gram cut the power to the beams and the shuttle was cast loose. All the reporters and Flora were bleeding from numerous cuts and bruises.

The shuttle craft imploded as it sank in the Jovian atmosphere and disappeared from the *Lares Compitales* screens. Gram gave the ship full throttle and it bucked and thundered as it pulled away.

"I can't spare the time to look after your wounds until we get free of the magnetosphere's worst effects. I had to shut Robert down. As soon as it is safe I'll switch him on and he can handle this ship while I dress your wounds," said Gram. "At full power, this should be the peri-Jovian of our orbit."

The ship circled Jupiter as it rocketed further and further out. Approaching maximum thrust of the launch, Gram flipped all tractor beams on Io as it appeared over the horizon. He switched on the pulsar beams and aimed them at Jupiter. Even at full power and with the help of the beams, it was not enough to keep them from plunging back into the Jovian atmosphere. The hull became cherry red and the scream of air over the hull penetrated the ship like a banshee wail.

Gram kept it at full throttle. The ship bounced back into space with a bone-crunching lurch as it spiraled outward from the planet. Their velocity remained great enough to escape the gravitational pull.

"Well, the worst is over. Robert should be able to take over now. Let me check your wounds."

Flora flew to Gram's arms and sobbed. "It was horrible! I thought we were dead."

Gram patted her on the back gently and spoke softly to soothe her. "There, there, it's all over. You're safe."

Flora drew back from Gram and rubbed her palms on her hips. "You are soaking wet, as though you were in a shower!"

"I admit I had a scary moment or two," said Gram. "Let me give you some first-aid treatment for those cuts and bruises."

Gram applied a liquid with a swab on the cuts and applied an ointment for the bruises. As he applied the medication he used his talents to remove the hurt and heal the injured flesh.

Finishing with Flora, he turned his attention to the reporters. One remarked how completely the medication removed the sting. Gram gave the Llan the credit for developing the medication. As he finished with the last reporter, Gram turned his attention to Elfrum. It was the first time he had seen an injury to a Llan.

"I had to make it look good," came her mental voice.

Gram laughed with her, then smeared another liquid on Elfrum's gashed trunk. He healed the wound and replaced it with an artificial one. By now, Robert had matched orbits with the freighter.

As the reporters left the launch, they requested permission from Gram to use the scanner tapes from Gram's ship for their broadcast. It just so happened Gram had left the control room scanner running. He gave them this tape to use along with their tapes.

After the evening meal, Gram, Ihan, Flora, Sandy McShane, George Horvath, Madeah and Elfrum were in the temporary council chambers watching the telecast. Flora snuggled close to Gram on a couch. Sandy and George sipped bourbon drinks they had made. Sandy did not go through the pretense of pouring it from a bottle. He willed his drinks into existence in his glass. He was proud of his ability.

"Boy, I think I'm getting better at this bourbon manufacturing. It tastes better with every glass I create," said Sandy as he watched the rescue. "Flora, you'd make a good actress. It was a top-notch performance where you were slammed about as the two ships made contact."

"Who was acting? I simply didn't use any of my talents to protect myself," she said. "What about Gram, he had the hardest job trying to keep the ships together."

"Yeah, I liked the touch of allowing the two ships to spring apart just as you started to transfer to the *Lares Compitales*," said Sandy.

"That wasn't premeditated," said Gram. "Those shear winds yanked us apart. I'd never do it again just to fool the enemy. It was too dangerous without using our talents."

"Then our big show wasn't faked," said George Horvath. "I never liked the idea of using the Federation peoples in a hoax."

"Great blazing comets," growled Sandy. "We didn't do it to fool the Federation peoples, we did it to throw the enemy off. We don't want them to know we've developed our talents. I think those tapes will make them think our talents are minimal."

"I know, but—"

"But nothing, George! It is an all-out war; we have to use every advantage we can conjure up," said Sandy. "The more confident the enemy feels about being able to defeat us the easier we'll have it. If you feel strongly about deceiving the Federation, draft a resolution to the council, asking that they apologize to the Federation after the war. I'll sign it."

"I admit you are right, Sandy. I just think we shouldn't make a practice of this type of diplomacy," said George.

"You'd have been a big hit in the olden days of the individual Earth governments. They lied to each other all the time," laughed Sandy.

Gram held his peace. He was thankful the Terrans had chosen a council to represent them, and that George and Sandy were two of its leaders. This allowed him to plan the upcoming battle, of which he was the chosen leader.

EIGHTEEN

The three ships chose a parallel orbit to Phobos as they surveyed Mars for signs of the enemy. They chose the orbit so Phobos would pass within a hundred meters. This gave the Terrans and reporters a close look at the satellite of Mars while Sandy McShane checked the surface.

Gram could see Olympus Mons near the horizon, even from this height. The volcano was over five hundred ninety-eight kilometers high and twenty-four kilometers wide. Numerous vents on the slopes showed molten rock had poured forth during its long history. Several vents had traces of gas.

The deserts attracted Gram's attention. It reminded Gram of Bonne Amie. There were vast differences in temperature, but the winds tearing at the sands reminded him of Bonne Amie's deserts where he had so much fun. Gram probed closer.

Yes, it was down-right freezing, and the atmosphere was very thin compared to Bonne Amie, but the hundred-sixty-kilometer winds would make a very interesting sand sled race. All he had to do was teleport the sleds to Mars and get Okursis....

He had forgotten. Gram withdrew his probe to the freighter. He could not visit Mars now; it created too many sad memories. Gram showed no interest in the satellite, Phobos, as it passed. Flora attempted to mind share with Gram when she saw the sadness.

Gram had planned to narrate the story of Mars and its satellites for the newscasters. Sensing his sorrow, Flora took over the telecast for Gram.

The next stop was the moon of the former Earth, Luna. Its features appeared different from the way Earthmen recorded its surface. There were great craters where particles of the exploding Earth had ripped mammoth holes. The satellite had a great fracture where the moon almost split in two from the bombardment.

There were the lava plains; created by the explosive force that obliterated the more familiar scenes. No one who lived on the moon when Earth exploded survived the upheaval.

Flora-Gram mind shared to explore one of the moon bases. The broken bodies of Earthmen lay as they had when the air vanished. She could sense the haunting echoes of the dead Terran thoughts. There were dreams: dreams of wealth, dreams of a girlfriend and a future family, dreams of power, dreams of returning to Earth and owning a piece of land, dreams of visiting new worlds and dreams of good times with friends.

They all existed here, like so many dead flowers, never to be fulfilled.

Flora-Gram located several artifacts among the ruins and teleported them back to the *Lares Compitales*. Someday, they would build a museum of human history where the era of the catastrophe would occupy one small corner.

Activities aboard the three vessels increased. The majority

of the people transferred from the freighter to the planet-building ship. They would perform the tasks of rebuilding.

The council agreed upon a small group taking the freighter and the *Lares Compitales* to explore the inner planets for traces of the enemy. They elected George Horvath to lead the search of Venus and Mercury.

While George was doing this, Sandy McShane captained the planet builder into Earth's former orbit. He mapped all the particles of Earth that must be brought together for the planet-building process. The council rechristened the planet builder the *Phoenix*. Sandy, Sam, or Jack would control the planetoid sections of Earth as they were rejoined.

The scanners fed directly to the computer banks of the *Phoenix*, recording the location and mass of each fragment. The highest concentrations of component pieces were recorded at the point where Earth should have been spinning in orbit. As the ship progressed farther away from Luna on the Earth's former orbit, fewer planetesimals were found.

George Horvath and the other Terrans who scouted the inner planets returned to the *Phoenix*. They organized a meeting to discuss rebuilding Earth. Sandy chaired the meeting and stood before a large read-out screen.

"As you can see, we've mapped everything in the Earth orbit and there isn't enough material to rebuild Earth to its former size. We miss the mass by several hundred million tons. Over half of the atmosphere and water are missing. Some of the material we've mapped isn't part of the original Earth, such as this asteroid labeled 'Fast-moving Object Helin.'"

"Is there anything which says we must use only the material from the original Earth?" asked Jack Roggers. "I'm for using anything which helps make up the loss of material. I don't see why we need a big meeting about it. We want Earth—what difference does it make where we get the needed material? The asteroids will probably crash into the new Earth someday anyhow."

"What I'm saying is, one of the main things missing is the

atmosphere to create the proper density," said Sandy. "Just gathering rocks won't replace the missing air. Isn't that right, Gram?"

"Why bring me into this, Sandy? You're the one who suggested we capture some of the Venusian atmosphere to replace the missing volume," said Gram.

"Great blazing comets! Of course I suggested it, but you are the one who said it could be done," said Sandy. "It was you who suggested we take it before the council so there would be no bloody screaming about our choices afterward! That's why I brought you into it."

"Now, now, Sandy," said George Horvath. "We have an elected governing body and we should bring any important matter before it. I'm in agreement about bringing some of the Venusian atmosphere to replace the missing air."

"I think the council should appoint Sandy, Gram and myself as a committee to make all necessary decisions in building the new Earth," said Flora.

"Hold it," said Jack. "How about including myself, Sam Coulter and Gus Orosz on the committee? And another thing, the Venusian atmosphere contains mostly carbon dioxide and sulfuric acid. We don't want to create a hothouse effect like on Venus."

The council called Robert to the floor to give a report on the Venusian atmosphere. The robot reported some replacement air could be taken from the Venusian atmosphere but oxygen must come from elsewhere.

A discussion developed on the necessity of obtaining extra hydrogen and oxygen to create water. Gram point out enough water could be obtained directly from the Jovian atmosphere. Another council member wanted to know if it was feasible to bring it from Jupiter. Robert discussed all the problems of retrieving moisture from the Jovian atmosphere.

"Enough!" shouted Sandy. "Elect any common, ordinary John Doe Citizen to office and right away he takes on the airs of a politician. All government seems to do is hold discussions and make reports. Why not do the blasted job and forget the talking and the reports? Who's going to read the blasted reports anyhow?"

"I disagree, Sandy," said George. "All this must be recorded and our government must put on its stamp of approval. It is possible some citizen may disapprove of our actions and sue us individually. The government is our only protection in this matter."

"Hah! What can they do about something we've already done?" asked Sandy. "As far as suing me, they can't get something I haven't got. I've never had any money and don't expect I'll ever have any. I say Gram is our natural leader and he should be the one to make all the decisions."

"I feel the same way, but Gram doesn't want it," said George. "The next best thing we could decide on was this council."

"My job of war chief in the upcoming battle with the enemy will occupy my time," said Gram. "I don't have time to worry about the details of running a government."

"Hey," said Jack Roggers. "How about putting Sam and Gus on the committee to make the necessary decisions on how to build the planet?"

"It wasn't in the form of a motion," said George.

"OK, wise guy, I make a motion that all Terrans and Llan vote on forming a committee consisting of Sandy McShane, Gram Ancile, George Horvath, Sam Coulter and Gus Orosz, to make all the decisions in building the new Earth," said Jack.

"How about putting some women and Llan on the committee too?" someone from the floor shouted.

"Sorry, all motions must come from the council," said George.

"Well, how about my motion?" asked Jack.

"Nobody seconded it," said George.

Sam Coulter spoke for the first time. "This meeting is getting out of hand. I make a motion we adjourn."

"A motion has been made to adjourn," said Sandy. "Since the council agreed to adjourn after one hour's debate, such a motion is in order. Does anyone second the motion?"

"Second," said Gus Orosz.

Sandy slammed his gavel on the table, drowning out Jack's protest. "So be it! The meeting is adjourned!" Jack cornered Sandy and Sam and began his argument again with the news crew still broadcasting the scene. The reporters commented on the arguments between council members as being riddled with the same flaws as the former Earth's governments, three steps ahead and two-and-a-half backward. The commentators were wondering if the Terrans and the Llan stood any chance against the enemy.

The Terrans and the Llan sauntered off in groups of twos, threes and fours. All were discussing the merits of having Llan and women on the committee. After the news team left the council meeting, Gram and Flora headed for Sandy McShane's cabin. The other council members were already there.

"Well, the reporters swallowed our act," said George. "This ought to convince the enemy we haven't changed since the explosion. We still fight battles with reams of red tape before making the simplest decisions."

"Let's hope the enemy believes we are that way," said Flora. "I don't want to become complacent in my attitude toward them. We haven't won any major battles against the enemy yet."

"I agree with Flora; we can lose this battle if we become overconfident," said Ihan.

"Ihan, we know our chances are slim and Gram is our ace in the hole," Sandy flashed testily.

"Gram is mortal. He can die as quickly as did Okursis. A simple knife could do the trick if he is caught unaware. Flora has her skills perfected second to Gram. I don't think she could withstand the full might of the enemy's hatred," said Ihan. "Audette and you, Sandy, are the next strongest psi talents. I know you two cannot withstand the enemy's hatred. Your greatest chance of success lies in your continuous practice with extrasensory perception."

"Great blazing comets! I practice E.S.P. all the time," said Sandy. "Why do you think I make so much bourbon all the time? For practice, I drink it, then change it to water in my stomach. But with all my concentration I cannot move a single grain of sand a micromillimeter."

Gram grinned at Sandy. "I know you practice trying to move objects and I know why you try. If we win, you want to use the talent to mine the asteroid belt. I know you are worried about the coming battle. This is why you are so sensitive about the progress you make."

"Are you reading my mind, sonny?"

"You know better than to ask such a question," said Gram. "As for the talent of psychokinesis, your approach is wrong. At our next council meeting I want you to introduce a motion to form a committee to be in charge of terraforming consisting of two men, two Llan and Flora. Flora and I will mind share with you to show you how to move objects. Be warned: although you will know how it is done, it doesn't mean you'll be capable of performing the act."

"Because of my age?"

"Yes."

"I don't think Sandy will be limited," said Ihan. "He has been practicing with his talent for years, much longer than you, Gram. He called them 'hunches' or 'lady luck' when he rolled three dozen sevens in a crap game."

"Thanks for the morale boost, Ihan," said Sandy. "It's like Gram said, I'm testy because of lack of talent for the coming battle. I know what the Llan stand to lose if we don't put more effort into the common mind. I apologize."

"I'm changing the subject before Sandy starts kissing everyone," teased George. "I wonder if the enemy is listening to the broadcast. If they believe them, they may send more troops and ships than we can effectively handle with the common mind."

"Maybe we should start building our new planet to give the common mind more practice," said Jack Roggers. "I would hate to think we should have spent our time more profitably with practice."

"My biggest fear is that they will be suspicious of our

talents because the *Phoenix* never destroyed itself," said Flora.

"Honey, I am hoping my plan for the *Phoenix* will satisfy their curiosity," said Gram. "If I fail in the coming battle, I want you to lead the rest of the Terrans and the Llan to safety."

"No, I am not leaving your side in the battle!"

"I don't think they will succeed, but if they do defeat me, well…"

"Gram! I am not listening to you!"

"Come on, you two!" roared Sandy. "We have as much say as you in this coming battle! We voted. We fight to the death, if need be, but we don't run."

"Amen to that," said George.

"All the Llan agree," said Ihan.

NINETEEN

Gram was the last to arrive at the council meeting. The council argued although the meeting had not been called to order. The camera crews were broadcasting every word. They commented that the Terrans and the Llan lacked the organization they demonstrated when they chose the news crew traveling with them.

A hush fell on the crowd as Gram stood before the council. "Mr. Chairman, fellow council members and friends. Yesterday, a council member made a motion..."

Sandy rapped for attention. "I haven't called this session to order yet, and I haven't announced the agenda."

"Sorry," said Gram.

"I call this meeting in session," said Sandy. "The subject of today's agenda is the selection of a committee to make all decisions on what materials shall be used in the rebuilding of the planet Earth. OK, Gram, the chair recognizes you."

"Thank you, Mr. Chairman. Yesterday, one of the council members made a motion to include me as one of the committee to make the decisions in rebuilding Earth. I wish to withdraw my name because it places too many of the decisions in my hands. I am in charge of the fighting forces of Earth and I shouldn't be involved in the civilian branch of the government," said Gram.

"Mr. Chairman!"

"The chair recognizes Jack Roggers."

"Thank you, Mr. Chairman. I disagree with Gram. This isn't a formal governing body and I see no reason why he shouldn't be included in the decisions committee. I make a motion Gram Ancile's name be placed in consideration for the decisions committee."

Gus Orosz seconded the motion and the debate began. An hour passed before the council voted to turn down Jack's motion. The choosing of the committee's composition followed. Some of the chosen withdrew their names. When the group chose the decisions committee, it consisted of Sam Coulter, Sandy McShane, Flora Campbell, Helen Horvath, Ihan, Madeah and Elfrum.

The council agreed to accept the names in nomination. George brought forward another motion to make the selection representative and legal by letting all the people and the Llan vote.

After George made the motion, Gus seconded it. They all agreed that voting for the committee would take place at four o'clock. The meeting adjourned and Sandy joined Gram and Flora to learn the secret of psychokinesis.

"Well, if all that speechifying didn't convince the enemy Earthmen haven't changed, then nothing will," said Sandy. "Now, how about teaching me the secret of moving rocks with my brain power?"

Gram-Flora slipped into Sandy's mind. Sandy quipped. "Hey, you lovers! I can't stand all the love and mush."

"Don't you want us to show you the secret of psychokinesis?"

"Yes, but I feel like I intruded on something sacred to two people in love," said Sandy.

"Don't feel that way; we want you to share our feeling for each other. We want the whole universe to know exactly how we feel. Now, can we mind share?"

It embarrassed Sandy to invade their intimacy and he squirmed a little before admitting them. It was new and sweet to him. He had never been in love and the pleasure belonged to him.

Flora-Gram showed Sandy the secret of being in control of his body while he probed. He still piloted the freighter while he probed space. Sandy-Flora-Gram enjoyed the feel of space about him. The duro-steel walls of the ship no longer inhibited him. Sandy-Flora-Gram could see the tumbling asteroids as they winked in the sunlight.

He could hear the vibrations transmitted upon the ether, the roar of the ship's engines, the hissing roar of raw energy released from the sun, and the whispering echo of the energy waves reflected off Luna. He heard the screeching sound of the ship's metal hull as the ship turned, exposing frigid metal to the hot energy of the sun.

It reminded Sandy-Flora-Gram of a world where he had stood on a cliff. He was one with the sights and sounds of an ocean pounding against the rocks below, and the wind blew through his hair.

Space was alive with sounds and sights; he could see it in the full spectrum of color and hear it with all the frequencies of sound. Never would he be alone in space—he would enjoy it to the fullest—it was his ocean.

The Flora-Gram part was stirred by the emotion Sandy transmitted. To them, space had always been something that was there and had to be crossed to reach some interesting world. They never considered space as an ocean with sights and sounds.

Flora-Gram thanked Sandy for opening their mental eyes

to the beauties of space. Sandy shrugged and reminded them they had shared their love with an old bachelor.

Sandy-Flora-Gram reached out to a particle the size of a pea to study the forces that caused the piece to follow its orbit. Grasping the interacting forces in his mind that acted upon the pea-sized grain, he reached out and concentrated the energy particles from the sun on one side. On the other side, he drained the forces holding the asteroid in orbit. The particle shifted orbits.

He concentrated more energy from the sun to the stone to give it impetus. As it built up speed, Sandy-Flora-Gram directed it toward the core of the former planet. It hit the core with such an impact it nearly passed through the dense material. The force heated the core, causing it to scream and groan from the temperature change.

Sandy-Flora-Gram seized another asteroid and slammed it into the core. He wanted to do it again but the Gram part of the probe called a halt. He told Sandy the *Phoenix* recorded the temperature changes. Gram had to change all the records to show the core had always been at this temperature. Any more temperature increases before the election of the committee to guide the rebuilding might get back to the enemy, making them suspicious of the Terrans. Sandy agreed as they returned to their bodies.

Sandy flashed a thought to Gram and Flora. "You know, psychokinesis is the same as kicking a man, then creating a hole for him to fall into!"

"You've got the idea, Sandy. Tomorrow, after your stint on the bridge with the pulsar and tractor beams pushing and shoving the pieces of Earth back together, you, Flora and I will join to practice again," Gram thought to Sandy and Flora.

A short meeting elected the rebuilding committee. The group chose Sandy for the honor of using the *Phoenix* to start the rebuilding. His chest popped out so far it was a wonder the buttons did not pop off like bullets propelled from a machine gun.

Gram stood behind Sandy on the bridge observing the

reporters warming up their Federation audience. Sandy locked a tractor beam on the sun and another on Jupiter. He explained his actions to the reporters.

"I have locked a tractor beam on the sun and another on Jupiter. This will hold the *Phoenix* steady while I use a pulsar beam to push a sliver of rock into the Earth's core."

The *Phoenix* spun like a top. It startled Gram until he realized what had happened. He flashed his congratulations to Sandy. "Hey, that was a masterpiece of ingenuity. The enemy will think you're a clumsy oaf not remembering to anchor the *Phoenix* on a tripod of beams. Congratulations, Sandy!"

Sandy growled his thoughts back at Gram. "Who was thinking? I did forget!"

"Oh."

The reporters had a field day reporting what happened. Sandy was so angry with himself he refused to comment on the actions. The news crew tried to get Gram to narrate, but he refused. He had embarrassed himself by his remarks to Sandy.

Gram looked at Sandy and the mirth bubbled to the surface. They both laughed. It must have been a sight to see the *Phoenix* spinning tail over bow.

Sandy locked a third tractor beam on Venus, then nudged the planetoid into the core of Earth. The planetoid shattered into the core, throwing it out of orbit. After the dust settled, Sandy moved the core back on course.

The next asteroid he slowed in orbit until the core struck it a glancing blow, causing the core to spin at a much faster rate. Sandy maneuvered the asteroid again. He moved it out from the orbit of the core and built up its speed, then slammed it back. This time the core glowed a cherry red and a plume of lava bounced outward from where the asteroid struck.

One of the rock fragments had an eccentric wobble and when Sandy touched it with the pulsar, a small piece splintered off. This gave the main particle a terrific spin. Sandy's angry thoughts touched Gram. "Great blazing comets, now I have to stop the spin."

"You are doing OK, Sandy. Leave the spin or increase the

spin, then slam the rock into the core. The core is plastic now and the frictional heat as the asteroid hits will turn the core molten," said Gram.

"Is this the way we'll build the entire planet?" asked Sandy.

"No, this method is too slow, but it will disguise our slamming particles by psychokinesis," said Gram.

"I was wondering whether you planned to change the council's original plan," said Sandy.

"Why did you ask?"

"Don't get mad, Gram. I only meant that I'm sure if you did want to build the entire planet with the *Phoenix*, the council wouldn't object."

"Nothing has changed. If I wanted to change the plan, I'd discuss it with the council first," said Gram. "I hope this makes it clear to all of you I don't consider the job of running the government of the Terran and Llan mine. I am the war chief because I have the greatest talent and you all insist I do it."

"I suppose you have reasons for not wanting to lead our new government," said Sandy.

"Yes, I do. There are hundreds of things out there I want to explore and study. I don't want the responsibility of making the decisions," said Gram. "I'll return when you are off duty and we can practice your psychokinesis."

Sandy shrugged. Gram was becoming more touchy. Sandy was glad he did not have Gram's responsibility as leader in the coming war. Gram was not sure he could handle the job either.

When Gram returned with Flora, he had forgotten his worries. He joked with Sandy as they set out to improve Sandy's abilities. Flora brought along the filming crew which was going with Gram, Sandy and her in a shuttle to film the collisions of the particles into the core from a close vantage point.

As their bodies piloted the shuttle and gave a running commentary on the action, their minds formed a probe. Sandy-Flora-Gram reached out many times, taking large boulders to heave at new Earth.

Sandy improved as he spun the asteroids to the shattering point, then slammed them into Earth so hard they almost penetrated the planet. The magma would leap high into the gassy and ash-filled atmosphere, then crash to the surface with reverberating detonations.

All at once, Sandy-Flora-Gram realized they had cleared the space about Earth of debris. They had been out for hours, helping the *Phoenix* in its job of Earth-building. The reporters on the shuttle became tired and wanted to return to the ship. Flora and Gram suggested to Sandy that they quit for the day.

Sandy wanted to continue. Gram suggested they return to the *Phoenix* and gather up all the Llan and Terrans and form a common mind for more practice. The common mind under Gram's leadership probed out to the Trojan Asteroids.

They gathered a group of the asteroids to hurl them toward the planet Earth. When Gram was certain this would make up most of the missing mass of the planet, he gave them the boost toward Earth.

Gram suggested that the common mind gather up water from the Jovian atmosphere. Flora poured the energy from the common mind into Gram. He focused the power to induce the water droplets to cohere into a solid layer. It became the stickiest water ever known.

The stormy winds taxed the strength of the common mind to hold the water layer in place. Gram formed it into a ball to allow the ammonium hydrosulfide crystals and ammonia crystals to drift lower. He inserted a ball of hydrogen into the center of the water ball, then froze the water ball around the hydrogen.

He teleported it into space and sent it toward Earth.

By now Sandy and the rest of the group felt the drain on their psyches. Neither Flora nor Gram made the effort to restore the common mind's energy level because Sandy would have insisted on continuing to build the Earth when they wanted some time to be by themselves.

Several days of practicing with the common mind had passed. Very little of the debris from the exploding Earth remained in free orbit. The Terrans and the Llan had slammed it all back into one planet, and included any other material roaming nearby.

Jack Roggers was at the controls of the *Phoenix* explaining to the reporters what the committee planned for his watch. "As soon as the decisions committee decided to use material from the Trojan Asteroids and Jupiter, we began bringing the needed volume to Earth. You will see the arrival of the first of this material within twenty minutes."

This set up a clamoring among the reporters to use a shuttle to film the arrival. The decisions committee authorized Flora to pilot a craft for them. She had become a big hit as a narrator among the reporters.

At the same time, Gram took the common mind out to slam the asteroids into the planet. He maneuvered one the asteroids into position, then drove it deep into the planet. Magma leaped hundreds of miles into the gassy atmosphere and the reporters' ship approached closely. Gram chided Flora.

"Hey, beautiful lady, don't get so close to the magma!"

"There's no danger," she answered. "I reached out and touched the planet and I foresaw exactly how high the particles were going to be thrown out. I stayed outside the maximum distance."

"Hey, that means you were performing three tasks at once!" said Gram. "You are piloting the shuttle, directing the power of the common mind to me and probing the planet."

"I'm funneling the power to you but it doesn't require all of my attention," she said. "It is similar to singing, dancing and thinking at one time."

"I notice the common mind is working much more effectively, too. It is like having a lightning bolt poised and waiting for someone to give it direction. A few more days' practice and I think we'll be ready for the enemy," said Gram. "We may be able to crack through their hatred with the power the mind puts at my control."

"I wouldn't become too confident, Gram," said Ihan, entering into the conversation. "Remember what the enemy's hatred does to your mind. If you just thrust into the enemy's hatred without checking the effect on the common mind, you could drive the entire common mind insane."

"I didn't plan to dive in without checking first," said Gram. "It does seem it should be possible to construct a shield to protect ourselves."

"You more than likely could, if you could lower the shields protecting your own mind," answered Ihan.

The conversations between the individuals of the common mind continued until all the asteroids slammed into Earth. By then several hours had passed and it was time for Sandy to replace Jack Roggers at the controls of the planet builder.

Although the common mind was doing the actual work of rebuilding, the operation of the ship's beams needed manning to give any enemy watching the impression the Terrans and Llan possessed no extrasensory powers.

Sandy reached for the controls and it appeared he directed the ice-ball from the Jovian system into Earth. The ice-ball entered the upper reaches of the atmosphere. Sandy switched to sophisticated sensing devices to check the condition of the ice-ball. Boiling cloud layers issued from and about the super-cooled ball.

When the ball reached the lower atmosphere, some of the outer layer began to melt. It fell to Earth as rain, superheated by the atmosphere, then rose again as steam. Approaching the ice-ball it cooled to rain and returned toward Earth.

The sight on the scanners before Sandy was awesome. Clouds rose to the very upper limits of the atmosphere, boiling and raging. Great shafts of lightning leaped from cloud to cloud and earthward. Slowly the storm spread outward from the ice-ball. As greater amounts of ice melted, the clouds became lactescent rather than their normal raw sienna from the metallic gasses. The metals condensed out of the atmosphere and fell to the planet. A giant hurricane formed before them on the screens.

The ice-ball melted through the bottom first. The escaping hydrogen shot a stream of liquid gas to the surface. The molten rock turned black as the common mind cooled it. The planet now had a floating crust that extended several hundred miles across. It was not permanent because of the extremely hot temperatures of the molten planet.

Rain struck the surface for the first time, sending off screeching, rending sounds the common mind heard through the probe guided by Gram. The rain flashed to steam, converted to snow by the hydrogen stream and stormed to the surface again as white fury.

The uneven cooling of the rock caused great fissures to appear. The molten rock and boiling gases from below oozed up through the crack, forming the first volcano.

The camera team with Flora on the shuttle craft returned to the *Phoenix*. The cloud layer was much too thick to see anything. The crew in the control room transmitted much better pictures of the storm. The ship's sensors supplied a good picture of what was happening to the ice-ball and the planet.

At the end of Sandy's shift George took over the controls. Gram and the common mind let the ice-ball bounce around to give the impression George was not as adept as Sandy at the controls. This, too, was a part of the scheme to deceive the enemy. Gram was careful not to make it appear all the human operators were equally skilled.

When Gram and Flora stopped to eat, most of the other people aboard the ship had finished with their meal. The dining salon was nearly empty, giving Gram and Flora the privacy they desired. Although they were working with the common mind, they blocked their private thoughts as they ate in the dining area.

Gram and Flora were with George Horvath on the bridge when he began his spiel with the reporters of the night shift. "As you can see, the atmosphere is about six hundred forty kilometers thick. This isn't as much as the old Earth had, so we are stealing from the atmosphere of Venus to make up the difference. If you will watch the scanners, you'll see me remove a section with the tractor beams, and I will keep it in a compact ball by spinning it with the pulsar beams."

The beams from the *Phoenix* lashed out at the planet Venus. The common mind's probe waited at the planet for the arrival of the beams. It appeared George reached into the atmosphere with the beams as Gram directed the probe to lift out a section of the atmosphere.

George continued to talk to the reporters. "Now I'll compress the gas and remove the heat from the ball. By the time it reaches Earth it will be dry ice and I'll feed it to Earth's atmosphere directly opposite where we fed the ice-ball from Jupiter. This will help to balance the temperature differences of the two hemispheres.

"It won't be enough to cool the surface to a temperature where the rock will remain solid, but it will be a start. It may be centuries before the planet has a permanent solid surface."

Jack Roggers relieved George before the dry ice reached Earth. He made a big show of maneuvering the ball into the atmosphere as Gram used the common mind to shift the ball.

The ball trembled as the hot gasses ate into the ice. It boiled away in great white clouds as it settled over the magma. The lava changed from white hot to a dull red as it quick-chilled. Rain began to fall as the air cooled to the dew point and thunder rumbled as lightning lashed out from the clouds.

Gram used the combined talent until the ball disappeared. The common mind had been working for forty hours without rest. He checked each individual and discovered they were nearly as fresh as when they started. He restored their vitality to normal, then released everyone.

Jack told the reporters the planet building was complete until they could assess the reactions to the cooling process. Everyone left the bridge except Jack, Flora and Gram.

They sat watching the planet on the screens and Gram dozed off with his head resting on Flora's shoulder. Gram's next conscious thought was Flora screaming in his ear. Her fear touched him with its knife edge.

"Gram! Gram! The deep space detection system failed! The enemy has just tripped the warning system we planted within Saturn's orbit. The enemy is almost to Earth!"

Gram stood up and stared at the scanner. In the center of the screen was a strange ship. Gram was terror-stricken. The enemy had outwitted him. They had slipped by his early warning system.

He could not focus his mind; Gram was unable to use his powers!

TWENTY

Jack Roggers screamed at Gram to answer the alarm as he grabbed the intercom. Ihan tried to contact Gram. Gram was in total shock—he had allowed his fear of the enemy to override his thoughts.

Flora organized the common mind and with Ihan's help she slammed the probe into Gram's mind, seizing the paralyzed center. After she kneaded out the knots of terror, Gram took control. He instantly understood the situation. Somehow the enemy had slipped past the early warning system without tripping it.

Gram hurled a probe toward the strange ship. He ordered Robert to bring the launch alongside the *Phoenix*. He directed the freighter to orbit between Earth and the *Phoenix*. The *Phoenix* would provide protection for the freighter and the people aboard while Gram took the launch to investigate the ship.

The reporters clamored to send a news crew along in the *Lares Compitales*. Gram consented to allowing one crew to go. While he talked to the camera crew, the common mind probe examined the strange ship.

The first thing Gram noticed was that the familiar, nameless, writhing hatred boiling forth from the enemy ships was absent. Gram sent in the probe to the ship.

There were seventeen humans aboard. They had heard of the plan to rebuild the planet Earth and the people's stand to fight a final battle with the enemy. These people on the ship had sickened of running away from the enemy. They wanted to join the rest of mankind in the coming battle.

A few moments later, Gram materialized the *Lares Compitales* near the invading ship. Gram called on the radio. "Attention, you on the space ship! You are in Earth Territorial Space. Identify, or be blasted from space!"

"Greetings! This is David Selner, a fellow Terran. There are five Earthmen, nine Earthwomen, and three children aboard. Are we glad to see you—our power failed and we're on emergency power; another hour and we would be without lights."

Gram examined the ship with the probe and wondered how they had managed to get this far. Gram did not dare to let on he knew its condition.

"Robert, I'm boarding the ship. If anything goes wrong, blast it from space. The rest of you remain here on the *Lares Compitales*."

As the two locks lined up, Gram went aboard the other ship. David Selner greeted him. His jaw dropped as he saw Gram with a drawn handgun.

"We are expecting the enemy any time now, so if you don't mind I would like to examine every compartment."

David gave Gram a tour through the entire ship and when he finished, he called Robert to allow the reporters to come. The news crew could not believe the condition of the ship and the people. No one who remained sane would attempt a trip in the shabby ship. These people had suffered the hardships of deep space to reach Earth.

Seventeen refugees crowded aboard the *Lares Compitales* with the crew Gram had brought. One of the children tugged at his mother's skirt, saying, "Momma, when can we eat? I'm hungry."

Gram sensed the adults had not eaten in several days because they were saving the food for the children. The children had not eaten in the past twenty-four hours. Gram ordered Robert to prepare a meal. He answered the little boy for his mother.

"Right now is when you can eat, fella. My robot's preparing the meal now. How about the rest of you? There is plenty to go around."

"Thank you, we would appreciate it," answered David. "We ran out of food."

"Where do you people hail from?" Gram quizzed, although he already knew the answer. He had to keep up appearances.

"We are from the colony of Selene. We sold everything we had to buy our ship. It isn't much of a ship, but it got us here. We would have had enough food if the hyper drive hadn't broken down out near Pluto. We got to where you found us on atomic engines. We thought we were finished until you found us. How did you know we were out here near Saturn?"

"We have warning satellites in Saturn's orbit about the sun. Your ship tripped the sensors," said Gram. "I must say, you gave us quite a thrill when we saw your ship on the scanners. We thought you were the enemy!"

"I take it you are expecting them soon?" said David.

"Almost any day now. You didn't pick the best time to return to Earth," said Gram.

"Oh yes we did! We are tired of running from the enemy! We feel there's no better place to have the final showdown with the enemy than Earth itself."

By the time the *Lares Compitales* reached the *Phoenix* and the freighter, the new arrivals had finished their lunch. Gram hurried them aboard the freighter. He signaled Ihan.

"Will they be any help to the common mind?"

"Elfrum, Madeah and I have checked them both physically and mentally. They may be able to supply some strength to the common mind if the war with the enemy lasts for any length of time. None of them have developed a talent yet; we Llan will start working with them immediately."

Gram's head tilted to one side. The common mind formed immediately without Gram's urging. The devices, from deep space outside the solar system, broadcasted an alarm all talented Terrans and Llan heard. The enemy had just tripped the devices Gram has placed to warn the Earthmen. This was not a false alarm. He contacted Sandy.

"It's time to start the final phase of our plan. Sandy, you take all the reporters out to view the planet Earth below the cloud layer. I want all the reporters off the *Phoenix* immediately!"

As soon as Sandy had the reporters within the Earth's atmosphere, Gram teleported all human beings and the Llan off the *Phoenix*. He replaced them with protoplasmic replicas complete with blood and bones. Gram materialized the corrosive bombs the enemy had planted on the original planet builder, and he exploded them.

Screams filled the radio waves. Sam Coulter, who piloted the freighter, yelled to Gram aboard the *Lares Compitales*. "Gram! The *Phoenix* has just exploded! It looks like some of those bombs that killed Okursis have destroyed the *Phoenix*!"

Gram called Sandy on the shuttle craft; it so happened the craft's loudspeaker system remained on. "Sandy, take the reporters back to the freighter, then come over to the *Phoenix* to give me a hand with the casualties. It looks bad from what I can see of the ship. There may not be survivors."

Sandy whipped the shuttle craft over to the *Phoenix* instead of taking the reporters to the freighter. "Gram, I can take a load of wounded back now and save time. The reporters will give us a hand until the shuttle craft from the freighter arrives."

One of the reporters brought a camera and broadcasted the scene live. Gram asked him to put down the camera and help with the wounded personnel. The news man positioned the camera so it had a good view of the bridge, then helped check the bodies. The camera continued to broadcast the scene.

The ship was a total calamity. Bulkheads, decks and overheads had burned away; the reporters helping had to be careful where they walked. After several trips, all the bodies were transferred to the freighter. Gram thanked the media people.

"It's a dirty trick we have played on them, letting them think those bodies are real human and Llan bodies," thought Sandy. "Will we ever tell them the truth?"

"It will be up to the Federation government," flashed Gram. "They approved of our plan to deceive the enemy, so if the rest of the galaxy finds out it will be up to their governing body. I suppose it will depend on how detrimental the government feels it will be to our relations with the rest of the galaxy."

All other activities ceased as the Terrans and the Llan prepared to bury their dead comrades. They decided to eject the bodies into space. The *Lares Compitales* would guide them into Earth's atmosphere with its pulsar and tractor beams.

Robert guided the bodies until the gravitational pull took over. The media people were overcome with emotion as they described the final rites.

The Terrans and the Llan attempted the repairs to the *Phoenix*. They scoured the burned metal and welded new plates over the missing areas. After weeks of work, they made the bridge of the *Phoenix* airtight and then they set to work on the ruined control system. Weeks stretched out and still the control system did not function. The council met and after hours of bitter fighting, they voted to abandon work. It could not be repaired.

A pall hung over the remaining people; no one wanted to admit the loss of the *Phoenix*. On the day Robert used the *Lares Compitales*'s beams to send the *Phoenix* crashing into new Earth, the dreaded alarm from the satellites sounded again.

This time there was no mistake. The scanners showed wave after wave of ships passing through the orbit of Saturn. Gram had never seen such a fleet. A quick probe proved there were over a billion ships in the fleet. Gram felt the prick of fear.

The warm touch of the probe bathed Gram, cheering him with the determination it showed. The scanners of the satellites showed the fleet passing through Saturn's orbit, causing the reporters to buzz about the size of the enemy fleet. For the sake of the reporters, Gram asked Robert aloud about a plan he had.

"Can you project a fifty-kilometer-high image of myself in front of the enemy ships and renew the projection from microsecond to microsecond? This body should be solid and capable of delivering injuries. I want the image of me to be dressed as an ancient Spartan soldier with sword and shield. The body is to glow with a light of its own so as to attract the enemy."

"Yes, Gram, I will do as you say. I will alter the circuits of the tri-dee star map so the image will appear there with the enemy ships. You will be able to direct the action of the image from the control room of the *Lares Compitales*."

Within minutes, the image projected in space near the front wave of the enemy fleet. The fleet slowed its forward motion and sent a small contingent of ships to destroy the image.

Gram broadcast on all frequencies, making it appear that the message came from the fifty-kilometer-high image. "To our enemy! I'm here to stop your invasion. You have harassed us for the last time. We didn't start this war but I shall finish it here between Saturn and Jupiter."

As this message was being beamed on all frequencies, Robert beamed a narrow, tight-beamed message to Grutt Ver Cann, commander of the Federation fleet.

Commander Ver Cann
Special Services Force to Earth
Galactic Federation
Commander:

The enemy has struck the solar system. I believe it may be possible to fight a holding action between the orbits of Saturn and Jupiter. They have a fleet over one billion strong of every type. Should the enemy overpower me, the rest of the human race and the Llan will be under whatever protection my robot can provide. Hoping I'm still around when you engage the enemy.

Gram Ancile

Gram probed out to the image. It stood glowing in a light of its own, like a great bronze warrior in Spartan battle dress. The image became Gram as he entered the apparition.

He gripped the short sword, which was over thirteen kilometers long, and smacked the broad side against the shield. Gram threw back his head and laughed. The sound transmitted through the subether to vibrate against the hulls of the ships and then reconverted to sound inside the atmosphere of the enemy ships. Gram felt the untold power of the common mind.

The common mind, being channeled through Flora and Ihan, waited for Gram to draw upon its strength, plus he had the power of an indestructible body.

He raced toward the first enemy ship—a juggernaut pouring out so much fire power it would destroy a fleet of ordinary fighting ships. He lashed out with his short sword and severed the engine room from the ship.

It drifted, powerless. Gram threw a screen about the ship that dampened communications between the juggernaut and the fleet. He threw out a hypnotic blanket causing the crew to believe they were in battle.

The next group he attacked almost proved to be his undoing. They were single-seat attack fighters barely forty meters long and his sword was useless. They were like gnats buzzing about his head. They aimed at his eyes with their laser beams, temporarily blinding him.

Robert restored his vision each microsecond but he had a hard time seeing. He irritably brushed them aside with his shield arm by the hundreds. Small atomic explosions marked the location of each ship crushed by the shield.

Gram felt remorse for all the lives lost by the reflex motion of his shield arm. It was his intention to immobilize the enemy, not to kill them. He caused giant ropes of lightning to leap from his sword to each of the fighters, fusing the tail sections, making the ships powerless.

Gram dampened all communication on the wrecks, then threw a hypnotic trance on the crews, making them believe they still fought. If the fighter pilots realized their plight, they would destroy their ships rather than be captured or recognized.

Only the ships still in the battle knew the ships were powerless. It became necessary for Gram to defend the powerless ships from their kill-crazy brothers. The enemy did not want anyone to identify them or their home planet.

The battle intensified. Hundreds of battle cruisers bore down on Gram and the disabled ships. Gram slashed ship after ship with his short sword as he roared at the incoming enemy. The sound of his voice reverberated throughout the ships.

Some of the ships managed to slip past Gram's guard and blast the helpless ships. In exasperation, Gram cast the wrecks into another dimension where the enemy could not harm them. After slicing the power plants free from the ships, Gram created an atomic explosion after he teleported each derelict to safety. This way the enemy would think their ships were destroyed after they became disabled.

Gram hacked and slashed until he lost all track of time; still the ships came. Finally, the ships broke off the actions against Gram's image and headed for Earth. He shook his sword in rage and raced toward the nearest juggernaut and sliced off the tail section. Gram knelt beside the ship as though he was about to peel it open.

The enemy reconverged upon him, but some of the ships did not return. Those were destroyed with the pulsar beams Robert sent out from the *Lares Compitales*. No one lived through slamming head-on into the beams when the ships were traveling thousands of kilometers per hour and the beams were moving faster than the speed of light in the opposite direction. It converted the ships to raw energy.

Gram stood up and rubbed the knuckles of his sword hand against his forehead. He had a blinding headache. Gram could not stand being deep in the pall of the smoky hatred of the enemy. He withdrew, leaving Robert in charge of the fifty-kilometer-high image.

He reported to the battle council room of Terrans and Llan. Before he released the common mind he removed all traces of the headache. He noticed all the Terrans and Llan appeared tired. They had been supplying energy for the battle for well over thirty hours. Gram and Flora restored the well of every psyche before they withdrew to their own bodies.

"Ihan, I cannot remain near the enemy over prolonged periods of time," said Gram. "I find their hatred overpowering. I cannot describe the fear it generates within my subconscious mind. Perhaps someone else should lead the attack. If it hadn't been for the encouraging thoughts from the common mind, I would not have lasted five minutes near the mammoth fleet."

"We know of your fear, but changing leadership is out of the question. The others can't stand the raw hatred without your shielding them from the brunt of the force. We will have to explore other avenues of assault; we must find a way to bypass this fear they generate."

"I hope there is another method. We are fast arriving at a stalemate," said Gram. "I can't stay in the vicinity of the enemy after thirty hours, I get an ungodly headache."

TWENTY-ONE

Gram ate, rested, then went to the bridge. He wanted the reporters to see him. He also wanted to know how Robert handled the image and the *Lares Compitales*. Robert's prime directive was to protect the *Lares Compitales*, the freighter and their passengers.

When Robert felt the three were threatened, he chose the simplest solution—eliminate the enemy. Gram could not spare the time right now to reprogram Robert to teach him the finer techniques of protecting the passengers and allowing the enemy to survive. Gram simply shook his head and left the bridge.

Ihan contacted Gram in the hall near the battle council room. "Gram, please come to the council room. We believe we may have a method by which you can penetrate the hatred of the enemy without danger."

Gram teleported. "What's your idea?"

"Can you teleport Robert into the enemy ships? Their hatred does not effect Robert. He could notify us of their identity, then we can bring Ver Cann and his fleet to finish the job."

"I like the idea of using Robert to identify the enemy, but I refuse to bring Ver Cann's fleet in against them. When Ver Cann formed his fleet, none of us expected the enemy fleet would be anywhere near this large. It would be suicide to expose Ver Cann's small fleet," said Gram.

"We understand," said Ihan. "Will Robert be able to operate and maintain the image while he's aboard the enemy ship? Sandy can take over the controls of the *Lares Compitales* while he is gone."

"There is no reason to believe Robert cannot handle the image and the ship while he is spying, but I don't want to chance it," said Gram. "The enemy might get in a lucky shot at Robert or something and leave us without any protection for a few minutes. That is all the enemy would need to get a few ships into our perimeter."

Sandy took over the controls of the *Lares Compitales* and Gram commanded the image. He formed the common mind to teleport Robert aboard an enemy ship.

When Gram teleported anything from one part of the galaxy to another, part of him went with the teleported item. He had never analyzed how he did it.

As Robert reached his destination, Gram smothered. He was unable to free himself. The feeling was the same as being trapped in a bin filled with flour. It choked him mentally. He formed the pattern for teleporting in his mind and ordered Robert to free them.

Robert tapped into the ship's power and teleported back to liberty. Everyone knew something was wrong; the lights failed aboard the *Lares Compitales*.

Gram was unconscious.

The image of fifty-kilometer-high Gram wavered, then

held. Robert stabilized the image from his own power reserves.

The enemy, sensing something had happened, redoubled their effort to destroy the giant. They swarmed over the image and some slipped past the image. They pushed toward Earth and the lifeless *Lares Compitales*.

Flora and the common mind were in a helpless situation. They could not withstand the onslaught of the enemy's hatred and had to flee.

Gram's safety was Robert's first priority as he probed along the thread Gram had attached to Robert's mind from Gram's id. Robert found Gram's consciousness curled up in the fetal position. He probed Gram awake.

Drawing upon Robert's reserves, Gram restored his well of strength. He became aware that Robert fed the image from his own power source. Gram tapped the sun to rebuild the ship's power plant.

With the power restored, Robert took over command of the ship from Sandy. He demolished the ships that had broken free of the image and rocketed toward Earth.

The common mind did not supply one hundred per cent of their effort battling the enemy ships. Ihan and the council members were busy trying to devise a way for Gram to penetrate the enemy's hatred. Only Gram and Flora concentrated their total energies on the battle.

Robert had been teleported onto a vacant part of the enemy ship and was unable to identify the enemy. Ihan and the others examined Robert's memory banks for the faintest shred of a clue to help them, but to no avail. There was not any useful information in Robert's memory banks.

The enemy changed its tactics. They realized whatever had gone wrong with the image had rectified itself. A small segment of the fleet continued battle with the image while the main body of the enemy fleet went into hyper space.

Gram sent a probe with the main fleet as he fought with the rear guard. He watched the main fleet until he realized what they were planning.

They planned to attack the *Lares Compitales* and the freighter. Gram became alarmed and contacted Flora. How could he teleport the enemy ships back without encountering the enemy's hatred?

Flora wasted no time. She asked, "Can you curve space without coming directly in contact with them?"

I'm not sure. What's your plan, honey?"

"Try curving space in front of their ships, if it doesn't effect you, curve it enough to bring the ships back to their starting point. When they come out of hyper space, they'll be at the same place they started," said Flora. "Just in case you can't do it without coming in direct contact with their hatred, I'll have the common mind stand by to jerk you free."

Cautiously Gram curved a section of space, ready to abandon the project if the enemy's hatred felt like it overpowered him. The ships entered the curved space and Gram felt a tremendous surge in pressure against his being. It was not similar to when he was in direct contact. It was similar to what he felt through the sword Robert created for the image.

He curved the space back to the ship's starting point.

Emerging into normal space, the fifty-kilometer-high Gram Ancile stood before them. Gram glowed as the lightning played over his body and the jewel around his neck gleamed with a blue light, causing Gram's face to appear ghoulish. He tilted his head back and laughed.

"Were you going somewhere, my friends? I want to play, so Robert brought you back to me."

Gram gave them something else to think about. He piped sounds of the highland bagpipes at ear-splitting volumes into the ether from Robert's memory banks. The sound transmitted into the ships. There were such tunes as "Donald Blue," "Highland Cradle Song," "Skye Boat Song" and "Scotland the Brave."

The enemy attacked with renewed fury. Wave after wave dove on Gram, firing at his head. The explosions and force beams were so heavy Gram could not see. He withdrew from the image so he was clear of the bombardment. As they concentrated on the head, they launched explosive missiles at his knees.

Gram allowed the explosions to buckle the image's knees. The enemy brought every ship that could find room to fire on the image. Gram caused the sword to rise. Thousands of bolts of lightning raged from edges of the sword. Disabling the attacking ships, Gram teleported them out of the area.

To the enemy, it appeared that the bolts of lightning had blown the ships apart.

The enemy withdrew to regroup. They had lost fifty per cent of their fleet. Gram withdrew the probe to the council room, taking advantage of the lull. He restored the energy levels of the Terrans and the Llan. The common mind separated to their individual bodies, relaxing a few minutes from the tensions of battle.

Gram paced the room. He could not penetrate the hatred of the enemy to learn their identity. Flora offered him a hot drink and he downed it without tasting it.

"Blast the enemy and their hatred! It is a more effective shield than anything else they could devise. I'm beginning to think we'll have to destroy them. I had hoped to end this mad, insane war against mankind. I don't want to destroy the fleet only to have their home planet build another and begin anew."

"Maybe we could scare them into fleeing to their home world," said Sam Coulter. "We could probe back with them and learn who our enemy is."

"Sorry, Sam," said Gram. "I hate to throw water on your idea but they'd commit suicide before they would reveal their home planet. I would say, judging from the size of their fleet, that most of those on the ships were born in space and have never seen the home planet."

Gram sat next to Flora and she began kneading his neck muscles. Some of the tension flowed out of Gram's body. He flashed another thought at no one in particular. "Lord, aren't we ever going to be able to penetrate their hatred?"

"Perhaps I can help."

Everyone turned to the body that materialized. Slightly behind Gram stood one of the most beautiful girls Gram had seen, excluding Flora. She was barely one hundred fifty-seven centimeters tall and had a shape to make beauty contests look tame. Her dark hair hung in natural waves to her shoulders. The cream color of the skin highlighted the natural blush of her cheeks. Gram raised his gaze to her eyes; he was sure any young man could easily become lost if he gazed into their dark brown beauty very long.

She was a stranger. Gram tried to probe her. It was like jamming his forefinger into a marble wall. There was absolutely no give. She mystified Gram.

Flora put her arm around Gram and asked, "Don't I know you? I feel I should know you."

"Yes, Flora, and I'm piqued because Gram didn't ask me to help."

Gram stuttered. "You weren't invited?"

"That's correct."

"Everyone aboard these two ships is helping," protested Gram.

"Not me!"

"Who are you?" demanded Gram.

The young lady grinned impishly and sent an energy bolt slamming into Gram. He had the distinct feeling a certain six-year-old girl had kicked him in the shins. He hopped over to the young lady as he rubbed his shin bone. He threw his arms about her as he swept her into the air. He gave her a kiss.

Turning to Flora, he said, "It's Helene! I don't know how she did this, but it is Helene!"

"I told you I hadn't been asked to help," she laughed. "I did tell you, you couldn't win this war without me!"

Gram held her at arm's length and grinned. "Wow, are you some beauty! How did you manage this? Your talents are so far advanced, I feel like a babe compared to you."

Helene's voice tinkled like a silver bell as she laughed. "I've learned to teleport to the past. In my time, I'm nineteen and I've just completed my tutelage under Ihan's watchful eye. It pleases me to be better than you, Gram—the talent master of all time."

Flora gave Helene a hug and kiss, then asked, "What do you mean by master?"

"Well, maybe my choice of words isn't perfect. I mean Gram is the most powerful psi power. Of course, your talent is nearly as good as Gram's, Flora. Sandy's isn't far behind the two of you either."

"Helene!" George Horvath held out his arms to his daughter. She ran to him for a hug and kisses, then kissed her mother.

Ihan entered the conversation. "I assume we won the war or you wouldn't be here."

Helene skipped over to Ihan. She touched him as she looked him up and down. "Ihan, my beautiful Llan! I think I like you twenty-five meters tall. I still have fond memories of climbing among your many limbs."

Ihan's limbs quivered slightly. "You know man's enemy?"

"I know those of whom you speak," came her answer.

Gram interrupted. "Well, what's our enemy's name?"

"To which period of history are you referring?"

"The present!" shouted Gram.

"Easy, Gram," soothed Ihan. "Evidently, there is a block preventing her telling us the answers."

"Is this true?" asked Gram. "Can't you answer my questions?"

"You set the block in my mind yourself, before I came back to this time period," answered Helene. "I'm here for a reason much different than what you believe."

"You mean you aren't here to help us?" asked Gram.

"Oh, I can help," said Helene. "I can do anything as long as it doesn't effect a change in the natural course of history for this period."

"Well, that's better," said Gram. "Let's mind share and finish off the enemy!"

Gram was a little nervous as they all joined in the common mind until Helene joined, too. He thought there might be some kind of block preventing her from helping directly. He flashed her a message.

"Well, lead off, Helene Horvath of the future. You can control the group better than I."

"No, I can't," she said. "I can help and you can use my energies in the battle, but I cannot lead. I cannot do anything which would change the future."

TWENTY-TWO

Mind sharing with this nineteen-year-old Helene proved a new experience for Gram. He had never mind shared with a superior human talent. It was like being given a new toy you knew had magical powers without having the faintest clue as to how to tap them. She could help supply the energy and do it more efficiently than the others, but she could not show him any powers he did not possess.

Out of pure frustration, Gram tried to pierce the barrier the future Gram had set. Helene's silver laughter tinkled in his mind. Flora waited as Gram tried to break through the barrier. After a time Flora ordered him to stop.

"Come on, Gram, stop acting like a little boy and settle down to the business."

Gram chose to reenter the image to continue the battle with

the enemy as they attacked He laughed exuberantly as hundreds of bolts ripped through the attacking fleet. Helene's addition to the common mind was a catalyst. She refined the energy from the group like a finely tuned atomic engine—it responded easier and much more swiftly.

There was no need to withdraw from the battle zone to recuperate; all he had to do was construct a shield between the enemy and the common mind. He had all the power he needed.

Something nagged at his subconscious level. He called himself all kinds of a fool. He realized he had the answer to the enemy's hatred.

All he had to do was construct the same shield he used to protect himself when he teleported the enemy ships. He had the answer all the time and had not thought to use it.

First, he tested his theory on the command flagship situated near the center. He eased the shield through the hull of the ship and tested for effects of the hatred.

Nothing.

So far so good. Gram brought his probe in the hull and looked at the enemy through the shield. The entire common mind shuddered.

Here was the enemy! The one race thought to be the true friend of mankind. They had sought and received favored trade agreements with the former Earth. Both had waxed fat on those agreements.

After the explosion of Earth, the enemy had been the first to offer shelter. They had destroyed their own cities with their fleet in the pretense of protecting mankind.

Terrans trusted them even after they fled the so-called friend's planet because the Terrans thought they were the ones bringing destruction to the enemy's planet.

Often as not, one of the enemy that helped died when the Terran in their protection died. All Terrans were taught to seek the protection of the enemy.

Gram probed the bridge. The commander of the enemy fleet was the same being Gram recognized from a picture. Steve had shown a picture of him to Gram. He was the one

Steve Ancile had asked to protect Gram's mother when Gram was born.

If the common mind had not supplied Gram with the strength, Gram would have gone into a total state of shock, unable to function.

The shield did not permit Gram to listen to what they said aboard the ship. He altered the shield like the membrane he had used when he checked on Steve and Randy Horvath. The shield could vibrate with the sound of talking and Gram translated this into speech.

"Bring in squadrons L-6-MN-3852 and L-6-MN-3853 to attack the giant figure of Gram Ancile. While they occupy the image created by his robot, have squadrons Q-8RR6-LMN-4 and Q-8RR6-LMN-5 ease back from the main fleet. When they have drifted back a good distance from the fleet, they are to go to hyper space for at least a parsec, then attack from the opposite side of this system.

"We must get the two squadrons through to knock out Gram Ancile's launch. Once the robot is finished, it shouldn't take us long to finish the Terran race," ordered the fleet commander.

Gram watched and listened until the units ordered by the commander began to move back. Gram caused them to be disabled by bolts of lightning. The commander watched the two squadrons of ships disappear from his screens. He shouted orders.

"The Terrans are not using the robot to project the image. They have developed their psi powers. Send the destruct order to the fleet!"

Gram projected a bolt at the command ship before they acted upon the commander's order. As the bolt struck, Gram directed it to fuse every electronic and manual control aboard the ship.

He teleported the ship to the other dimension with the crippled ships. Gram cast a telepathic blanket on the crew so they thought they still battled. Gram withdrew from the battle while the enemy fleet was in a state of confusion.

He withdrew from the common mind and stood with no shields to protect his mind from the common mind. He directed his thoughts to Helene. "Take command of the common mind and blast asunder the shield I've built to protect my subconscious mind."

The bolt struck true; Gram shivered. He felt naked without the shield, but he used his conscious mind to prevent another shield from being formed. He increased the ties between his conscious mind and subconscious; his power increased tenfold.

Sure of himself now, Gram created a new shield about his mind. He could probe through it as though it was nonexistent, but nothing could penetrate inward unless he willed it.

Helene made contact with Gram. "I have done the job I was sent here to do. You are free of the barrier that hampered your growth."

"Yes, the seal upon your mind is no longer necessary. I command it to be lifted," ordered Gram.

After the seal evaporated, Gram took command of the common mind again. He drew vast quantities of energy from the sun. For an instant the sun winked out as Gram focused all the power into the sword of the image.

It vibrated with a life of its own, and when satisfied it had enough power to do the job, Gram commanded the great bolt of lightning toward the enemy fleet. As it neared the ships, the bolt divided and redivided until there was a separate bolt for each ship. The heavens of the area became as bright as the sun as seen from Mercury and the enemy fleet disappeared.

Next Gram teleported Ver Cann's fleet to the dimension with the enemy fleet. Ver Cann ordered his fleet to surround them. He contacted Gram. Gram could feel the icy thoughts as he teleported aboard Ver Cann's flagship.

"The plan was my fleet would subdue the enemy!"

"I am sorry it appears to you we sought glory by reducing the enemy. The fact is, we were afraid your fleet would be destroyed in attacking a superior number. The enemy is suicidal. If they thought we knew who they were, they had orders to self-destruct to protect the identity of their home world.

"As it is, we disabled the fleet without a single casualty to our side. Most of the deaths to the enemy were caused by their own ships. We kept it to a minimum."

"You captured the entire fleet without losing a single Terran or Llan life?" asked Commander Ver Cann.

"Thanks to the help Helene Horvath gave us," said Gram.

"Helene? I don't think I have had the pleasure of meeting this young lady," said the commander.

Flora introduced Helene. "This is a very dear friend. Commander, meet Helene Horvath. She was instrumental in our identification of the enemy."

"Helene Horvath—I should recall the face but I don't recall meeting you," said the commander.

Helene's laughter tinkled melodiously as she answered the commander. "Don't be fretful, Commander. You know me as a mischievous six-year-old. I've teleported from the future to help Gram with his problem."

"You are from the future?" he asked. "You Terrans have developed the most marvelous talents."

I think it is time we took you aboard the enemy commander's flagship," said Gram.

"Then you know who they are," said Ver Cann. "What do you plan to do with them?"

"We wish to make them forget their technology until we can convince them we don't mean to take over the universe as its masters," said Gram.

"That sounds like a reasonable request," said the Commander. "I'm authorized to help you impose any reasonable penalty. Since you don't wish them any physical harm, I consider your proposal reasonable."

When Gram teleported Commander Grutt Ver Cann, Helene, Flora, Ihan and the news crews aboard the enemy flagship, Ver Cann's jaw dropped as he recognized the enemy.

"The Alnairians! Commander Ahunah, the most brilliant

tactician of the galaxy, the leader of these outlaws!"

Commander Ahunah ignored Commander Ver Cann and glared at the Terrans. "So...I was right, you found us out. It proves we were right about you. You are the most dangerous species in the universe. You have developed your psi talents in spite of our attempts to rid the universe of you."

"You developed the talents for us, Ahunah," said Gram.

"We?" thundered Ahunah. "We!"

"Yes, if you hadn't driven me to the Llan, we might have been another century before we developed the talent," answered Gram.

When they told Ahunah the penalty they imposed, he protested. "There are sixty billion of us in the fleet. If you send all of us back to Alnair, it will be murder! Our planet cannot support so many extra mouths."

"We realize the problem this number will create on your home planet. We will supply the extra food and supplies you will require," said Gram.

"Why would you do this for us?" demanded Ahunah. "I'm the one who killed your mother and father."

"For two reasons," said Gram. "It'll help us forget the crimes you've committed, and it'll give us the chance to prove we aren't the ogres you believe us to be. As soon as your realize this, your status as a member of the Federation will be restored."

Later, aboard the *Lares Compitales*, Helene took Flora's and Gram's hands into hers and kissed them both on the cheek. "It is time for me to return to the future. I cannot tarry any longer."

"What's your hurry?" protested Gram. "We thought you'd stay long enough to see us make Earth habitable. Then we'll throw a party for you."

"Ah, yes, help build Earth, then a party, then something else. It would be all too easy to stay here with you," said Helene. "I shall miss you and Flora."

"Don't we associate with you in the future?" asked Flora.

"Yes, but it is different here," said Helene. "Here, we are

the same age, and I feel like an equal. Really, I must go or lose my future."

Finishing her statement, she vanished before Gram or Flora could disapprove. Gram and Flora stared at the spot where Helene had been standing the moment before. Finally Gram spoke. "I think I owe one six-year-old an apology. We did need her as she said we would."